Rommel's Peace

Rommel's Peace

by

Lawrence Wells

SANCTUARY
Oxford, Mississippi

Published by Sanctuary
A division of Yoknapatawpha Press
P.O. Box 248, Oxford, MS 38655

ISBN 0916242-72-2

Printed in the United States of America

Cover and book design by Chad Murchison.

When the government of a nation is leading it to its doom, rebellion is not only the right but the duty of every citizen.... Human laws supersede the laws of the state.

Mein Kampf

I

The Desert Fox slipped behind a sand dune. He stopped and listened. For the moment he had eluded a Propaganda Ministry film crew. Goebbel's filmmakers had to understand that inspections came first. The assignment was a nightmare: Take hundreds of kilometers of exposed beaches and divide it by the 15th Army and 7th Army. Never in history had so much coastline been guarded by so few. For the first time in the war the Luftwaffe formed no part of the equation. It was a paper air force that existed for the distraction of the Führer. Air Marshal Hermann Göring was hoarding his few remaining fighters for emergency use.

Field Marshal Erwin Rommel went down to the beach and passed between signs which read "*HALT - EINGANG VERBOTEN - GEFAHR*!" and proceeded to examine artificial reefs tipped with mines and steel blades. He had given orders to install two hundred million mines and construct thousands of concrete bunkers and artillery emplacements. It was low tide on May 21, 1944. He expected the Allied invasion within days if not hours.

This thirty-mile stretch of the Calvados coast between the Vire and Orne Rivers was especially vulnerable. Naval Command had classified the rocky beaches as unsuitable for invasion but Rommel knew better. Everywhere were gaps and scant materiel or manpower with which to fill them. Eisenhower and Montgomery would attack at the point of least resistance. The Pas de Calais was a short dash from the English coast, a tempting target for Patton.

Instead of an impregnable fortress, he was forced to make do with a chronic deficiency of mines and artillery, a scarcity of petrol, roads and bridges destroyed daily by bombings. To bolster the thin line of concrete bunkers and machinegun emplacements he had quietly brought up a battalion of infantry without notifying *Oberkommando Wehrmacht*. Field Marshal Jodl, head of OKW, had a habit of vetoing his suggestions.

The film crew was two hundred meters away, milling around like sand pipers. They had not spotted him. *Sehr gut.* At low tide the sandy flats reached out toward the ocean for nearly a kilometer, windswept and bare. Breakers spat and hissed in the distance. Low clouds swept overhead like squadrons of enemy bombers–*unopposed,* he noted ironically. He threaded his way among rows of anti-boat obstacles standing like orderly driftwood. Each "nutcracker" mine consisted of a stake set in a concrete housing containing an artillery round. When a landing craft struck the stake, it would press against the detonator and set off a blast. The ammunition was recycled French artillery rounds. Rommel had devised this homemade mine. Some called it ingenuity. He called it stop-gap.

The sand was dry enough to support his weight without sinking. Would it support an American infantryman in full combat kit with extra ammunition? At low tide, the invaders would simply sprint past the obstacles. He turned to the dunes to judge the field of fire from the machinegun nests and found himself looking into a movie camera. The three-man film crew had caught up with him.

The director-Sergeant of Film, Commissar of Nonsense-turned his head, demonstrating the desired effect. "Give us your best side, Herr Generalfeldmarschall!"

MOVIETONE NEWS EXTRA: FIELD MARSHAL ERWIN ROMMEL, SEEN INSPECTING HIS COASTAL DEFENSES, HAS BEEN PUT IN CHARGE OF HITLER'S ATLANTIC WALL. THE DESERT FOX DARES EISENHOWER TO DO HIS DAMNEDEST!

To a propagandist, everything was grist for the mill. Goebbels had plastered his picture on every bulletin board, theatre entrance and news kiosk. He told the director that it was hard enough to do his job without these distractions. Would the filmmakers be on the beach dodging bullets when the Americans and British came? Would they "make hay" out of thousands of dead soldiers of both armies? Perhaps he should point out the machinegun nests so the camera bugs would not get caught in the crossfire-then again, perhaps not.

"Another hundred frames!" the director shrilled.

"I have no time," he snapped.

"*Bitte, mein Generalfeldmarschall*!"

He put his hands behind his back and began to walk slowly

up the beach. "*Ach, gut*!" the director cried ecstatically.

He was hoping the enemy would land at high tide to get close to the beaches. The mines were designed for high tide, hidden beneath the surface. Still, what if the enemy came at low tide?

"Keep going, just a little farther!" the director called.

Who did they think he was, Marlene Dietrich?

The majority of the troops defending the coast were infantry. Due to shortages of trucks and heavy weapons they lacked mobility and firepower. This beach area was guarded by a battalion made up of Russian prisoners of war. In addition many divisions were forced to use captured enemy equipment with a resulting lack of uniformity in weapons and ammunition. One unit was armed with 98 different types of weapons.

"Please pause to inspect those mines, just *there*!" the director called.

"I have inspected them!" He walked on.

The once-proud Wehrmacht had been reduced to public relations. This was what it came down to: pretending the Atlantic Wall was invulnerable and buying time through news features distributed to theatres at home and abroad. The Führer's miracle weapons were deception and false information.

"Slowly turn to your left, please!" the director cajoled.

There was no question the Allies would successfully land troops. The solution was to position panzer divisions near the beaches to counterattack. An invading force was vulnerable in the first twenty-four hours. Land forces held an advantage in logistics and ammunition supply. If enemy aircraft did not cut off reinforcements, the Wehrmacht could bring superior firepower to bear at any given point.

"Look to sea as if watching for the enemy!"

The enemy will be here soon enough.

Swift retaliation was the only hope. He had repeatedly asked Hitler to give him personal command over panzer reserves. The Führer refused to relinquish control.

When he stated his opinion that the war was lost, the Führer ordered him to leave the room-but he was no longer in the minority. Many generals believed that the only course remaining was to achieve stalemate leading to a truce. If they could pin the invading forces down, *that* was the moment to go to Eisenhower and Montgomery and say, "Let us end the fighting." And yet to halt the invasion on the beach would be an achievement surpassing the blitzkrieg of 1940 in which his Spook Division overran France in 19 days.

ROMMEL LOOKS OUT OVER THE BRITISH CHANNEL WONDERING IF THE ALLIES WILL ACCEPT HIS OFFER OF PEACE.

He glanced around self-consciously as if the cinematographer could read his thoughts. He went to inspect a bomb crater next to a concrete gun emplacement. The film crew scurried up the dune after him. Although an explosion had left a hole five feet deep and ten feet in diameter, the bunker walls remained intact. It was amazing how much punishment steel-reinforced concrete could take. He patted the bunker.

"*Ach, wunderbar!*" squealed the director. "Touch it once more."

If the construction corps, the Todt Organization, supplied more concrete, he could create covered staging areas on all access roads to the coast. This would protect the panzer reserves from air attack. Given Hitler's distorted chain of command, however, he could not requisition the Todt directly. He had to go through channels like any company commander.

Surreptitious movement caught his attention. A clothesline was being pulled off a cannon barrel. Unseen hands hauled in the line. The laundry disappeared into the bunker. These Russian troops lived like gypsies. They had volunteered to fight Stalin and found themselves in France. He would have reprimanded the battery commander if he knew the Russian word for *underwear*. The Slavs barely understood simple commands in German. How did one explain that gunners did not hang their wash on their *gun*?

ROMMEL MAKES PERSONAL INSPECTION OF RUSSIAN LAUNDRY. CRACK COSSACK BATTERY RECEIVES HIGH MARKS FOR MAKING A HOME OF THEIR BUNKER.

"Say something inspiring to them, Herr General!" the director whispered.

"*Nein.*"

His Chief of Staff, General Dr. Hans Speidel, had convinced him to go along with the propagandists. Publicity was useful to the resistance movement in Berlin, reassuring the German people that when the time came they could count on Rommel to help rebuild Germany. Before that could happen, however, he had to stop Patton and Montgomery.

Fighting a defensive war was not his style. The French underground was waiting for the allied attack to begin so they could cut communications, blow up railroad tracks and bridges. A recent *Kriegsspiel*, or map exercise, revealed the confusion among German generals. SS panzer divisions were too far inland for rapid counterstrik. Logistics were stretched to the breaking point. The Wehrmacht was, as the Americans put it, sitting ducks.

"Could the Herr General smile, *bitte*?"

"*Nein*."

There was a commotion on the beach. A military patrol had arrested a couple of French girls. He wanted to see how the patrol handled themselves. The soldiers were amused by the girls' angry gestures. He had a standing policy for humane treatment of civilians. The girls could be resistance fighters but they probably were what they seemed, schoolgirls walking on the beach Why shouldn't they? It was *their* beach! The soldiers snapped to attention when they saw him coming. The girls waited, curious and respectful. The film crew raced into position. Nothing was too insignificant, no gesture or word wasted.

THE DESERT FOX GRACIOUSLY ALLOWS FRENCH GIRLS TO WALK ON THE BEACH, THEIR SECURITY AND SAFETY ASSURED BY VIGILANT COASTAL DEFENDERS!

"Nice day for a walk," he said. The girls smiled.

"Terrific, great stuff!" said the director, showing off his American slang.

Next stop, Hollywood.

"If we let these civilians onto the beach, Herr Generalfeldmarschall," a sergeant complained, standing stiffly at attention, "others will come. It is a matter of security." He lowered his voice. "They could be spying."

Rommel ordered the sergeant to button his tunic. The military policemen had been flirting with the girls until Goebbel's parasites arrived.

"Let them go," he ordered.

"Might I be allowed to check their papers, Herr Generalfeldmarschall?"

He shrugged.

The sergeant demanded identification, which the girls provided. While they admired Rommel's full-length leather coat, he was wondering why civilians would visit a beach tainted and corrupted, one might say, by war. Perhaps they saw it as it was, or as it would be again. The French spirit never ceased to amaze him. The director tried to make the girls pose beside the field marshal. They were confused-quite reasonably, Rommel thought-and when the director tried to separate them, placing one on either side of him, they began to cry.

"Stupid peasants!" the director shouted.

"You frighten them."

"They must do as they are told."

"Enough," he said. "I must get back to work."

"*Arbeit*! That's our motif," the director cried. "*Arbeit macht frei*!"

He ordered the director to cease and desist, and returned to his inspections. The sea was grey and noncommital. The bleak horizon, enigmatic and profound, reminded him of the Sahara. Somewhere the British and Americans were loading troops and guns onto ships. He envied their sense of purpose, not to mention their petrol, ammunition and air power.

In 1940 when he spearheaded the invasion of France his advance had been so rapid he had outstripped his supply train. He marked his route with "DG-7" signs nailed to trees or barns: "*Durchgangsstrasse 7*, Throughway, 7th Division." During those intoxicating two and half weeks he forgot about logistics. If the men gave out, they scavenged. Half the petrol came from other Wehrmacht units. His rule of thumb was, "If you cannot keep up, get out of the way." The Ghost Division blasted through field and village until it reached the sea. The Channel had stopped them. Why could it not stop the enemy?

On the way back to headquarters, he stopped to inspect an anti-aircraft battery, a FLAK battalion which he had moved to the coast. The gunners stood at attention in knee-high grass swarming with gnats and mosquitoes. Goebbels' moviemakers, disobeying orders, got out and began filming. Rommel inspected the gunners. They were reservists and militiamen gray at the temples. Their average age-he asked and was told-was thirty-seven. Some had previously been assigned civil guard duty after being wounded. Others had received a temporary deferment because their jobs were deemed useful to the war effort. Some had seen limited action defending the cities, shooting .88s at Allied bombers too high to see. Now they were in this forest, waiting.

It was hard to look them in the face. These amateur soldiers had no idea what was about to happen. Thousands of planes making low-level strafing runs, thundering over the trees. Enemy paratroopers and marines fifteen years younger, in top physical condition, superbly armed and equipped. Bullets and flying shrapnel, the brains of their best friend splattered on their shirts. Going seventy-two hours without sleep, fighting to survive, making life and death decisions in an instant. They looked like soldiers, they lived a soldier's life, they slept out-of-doors and scrounged cigarettes and turned out for mail call and complained about short rations, but in a real fight they would not be of much use.

Surrender was all they talked about. He could see it in their eyes, the apologetic, darting glances. They would fight if they had to, but they hungered for peace. They practiced their English. *I surrender, yes?* It fell to him, at least that was how Speidel characterized it, to rescue these smiling, sleepy, soft bellied reservists and send them home to their wives.

The FLAK unit began queuing for *Mittagessen*. "Would the Herr Generalfeldmarschall join them?" the director suggested. During inspection tours he made a point of sharing the troops' rations. The camera man quickly set up his tripod. The gunners were flattered to have a field marshal in their midst. The cook found a link or two of sausage and some more or less fresh bread. Instead of coffee, they were served tea. The Luftwaffe major in command of the battery joked, "We will become quite *britisch* if we don't get coffee soon."

"I will see that you get some." Rommel then asked about the men, where they were from. The streams on the Cotentin peninsula were full of sea-running trout. Had the gunners brought fishing tackle? For a moment he forgot about the motion picture camera. Gunshots startled him. *Ack-ack*? He could not immediately identify the noise. The major grinned sheepishly. "It was a shotgun, Herr Generalfeldmarschal."

A motorcycle courier armed with a double-barrel shotgun had killed a carrier pigeon. The French resistance used the birds to send messages across the Channel. The courier brought the message tube to Rommel. The cameraman moved in for a close-up. He pocketed the message without reading it.

FIELD MARSHAL ERWIN ROMMEL UP TO HIS TRICKS. INTERCEPTS CODED MESSAGE FROM FRENCH UNDER-

GROUND. CUTS OFF VITAL INFORMATION BEFORE IT REACHES BRITISH AUTHORITIES.

"I'll see that Military Intelligence gets this," he told the unlikely bird hunter.

The troops were shooting down carrier pigeons. How much longer? Naval Command had predicted that the attack would be May 18. All the divisions had been put on alert for forty-eight hours. That was three days ago.The gunners were joking that the Allies were losing their nerve, that they would not come before autumn.

He was 56. If these graying gunners were his sons, he would have fathered them at 16. They were teachers, scholars, mechanics, factory workers, clerks–men with little inclination for war, accustomed to warm beds, beer in their lunch pails. Here on the eve of battle, in the lush *bocage* country of stone farmhouses and pastures rimmed by hedgerows, these old boys swatting at mosquitoes had no idea of the hell coming their way.

He knew how it would happen as surely as if he had attended Eisenhower's briefings. Heavy naval and air bombardment would clear a landing zone. Boats would land marines and light armored vehicles. Airborne troops would be dropped ten or fifteen miles inside the coastline to protect the beachhead and capture vital roadways and bridges.

If only he could meet Patton, face to face, and ask why they would waste the lives of their men when they had a common enemy. Patton had been quoted in the press as not trusting Stalin. Surely he could be made to see that they had a job to do, together, that all good Germans–millions of them waiting to rise up under new leadership–wanted to make amends. Patton was a soldier. If only they could talk on the phone. "Please continue talking," called the director. "Act as if you are having a conversation with the major."

They sat in stony silence while the camera rolled. Neither could think of anything to say. Then the major self-consciously straightened his cap and winked at the camera. The director gave him an ecstatic thumbs-up.

MOVIETONE NEWS PRESENTS FIELD MARSHAL ROMMEL OF DESERT FOX FAME. EATING WITH HIS TROOPS ON THE FRONT LINES OF FORTRESS EUROPE. LUNCH WAS A SAUSAGE ROLL AND A HOT CUP OF JAVA!

II

Officers and enlisted men were to be at their tables no later than 1800 hours. The ranking officers waited until all were present. Though many field marshals had private chefs, Rommel dined with his staff. The men were drifting into the banquet hall thirty minutes ahead of schedule. Rommel asked why. Speidel shrugged. Special menu: dumplings and cabbage rolls.

Chateau La Roche Guyon, situated on the Seine, forty miles west of Paris, had been commandeered as Army Group B headquarters. The labyrinthine cellars doubled as bomb shelters. The banquet hall seating 200 had been converted into a mess hall. The men had grown accustomed to the palatial wall hangings, stags heads, crossed swords and portraits of a long line of dukes including the Marshal de la Rochefoucauld, author of the celebrated *Maxims*.

Rommel extended a standing dinner invitation to the duke and duchess, though they had not accepted and rarely emerged from their quarters. He took pains to keep them informed of repairs or alterations and urged them to safeguard their tapestries, paintings and silver. He ordered his staff to watch for pilferage. He reminded his troops that they were guests. Military occupation, a centuries-old European tradition, had its protocol. The duke stiffly acknowledged these and other courtesies.

Vice-Admiral Ruge, the naval adviser, was late as usual, a source of irritation for the punctual Rommel. "Ah, here comes Ruge! Shall we go in, *meine Herren*?" He led his staff members to the head table. Immediately all took their places. Cabbage rolls were served to boisterous applause. Red-faced cooks wiping hands on aprons emerged from the kitchen and bowed. To the democratic Rommel, it was both fitting and desirable for enlisted men to dine with officers. Exchange of ideas lifted morale. Officers learned what the rank and file were thinking. Enlisted men were exposed to the complexities of command. Many of the latter had attended university and were not slow to voice opinions.

The hall resounded with laughter. Rommel, a natural kibbitzer, listened to arguments among the junior officers. This staff had a different attitude than the ones in North Africa and Italy. In the early years of the war, German soldiers took victory for granted. After the defeats on the eastern front, they had become philosophical. Here, an hour's drive from Paris, they applied for leave at every opportunity. They had become proficient at table tennis. There seemed to be a "tournament" every day.

The conversation revolved around one topic: *Where would the allies attack?* Rommel nibbled at the rich dumplings, listening. *Would the attack come at the mouth of the Scheldt, on the coast of Belgium*? No, Belgium was too far from Paris, the obvious objective. The Allies would try to retake the capital for many reasons. Psychologically, the liberation of Paris would be a big boost.

In Bordeaux, up the Gironde, or on the Mediterranean coast of France? Everyone was in agreement: *No* on both counts.

What about Cap Gris Nez?

He silently agreed with a lieutenant who replied that the rugged terrain in Brittany would inhibit an inland push. The enemy would keep to flat country.

The coastline between the Pas de Calaise and Cherbourg?

Yes, he thought, this was the vulnerable sector. Calais was closest to England and in a direct line from London to Paris. There would be several landings in rapid succession. A feint was to be expected elsewhere.

No one spoke of Patton.

Where else could one experience camaraderie like that of the mess? He experienced a heart tugging nostalgia. Young men had fresh ideas. They were forever on the attack. He was not a little bit jealous.

After dinner he asked Ruge and Speidel to go for a walk. He took his dachshund, Elbo, six months old. While the puppy ranged the park, stubby legs churning, they climbed Rommel's favorite hill. Between two ancient cedars was an excellent view of the village, red roofs thronging the country palace. The great Seine angled through green fields. French farmers did not let war interfere with their work. As panzers rumbled past, they yoked their oxen and plowed the fields. At noon they ate cheese, sipped wine and smoked their pipes. He coveted this bountiful existence. The people of Germany were starving.

For weeks the officers had met under the Lebanon cedars. The ageless evergreens fetched home by Crusaders spoke of the ancient clash of arms, of warhorses prancing and snorting. "*Who will succeed Hitler*?" Speidel picked up where they had left off.

"I thought that was settled," said Ruge. Both of them stared as if the time had come to announce his candidacy.

Before the war, Speidel, scholarly and intense, had served as military attaché in Paris. American and British military attachés in Berlin were his personal friends. He was a close associate of the Wehrmacht's prewar Chief of the General Staff, General Ludwig Beck, leader of the secret German resistance. Like Rommel, Speidel was from Swabia in the south of Germany and a democrat from birth. Like his mentor, Beck, he held a deep and abiding hatred for Hitler.

Vice-Admiral Ruge was Swabian as well. Early in the war he had been put in charge of French coastal defenses. He later served as chief naval officer in Italy. Rommel was delighted to have Ruge on his staff. He appreciated the vice-admiral's candor and sense of humor.

"When Hitler goes, you must be ready," Ruge said.

Rommel was shocked. He had no idea the plotting was proceeding so swiftly. "If we halt the enemy on the beaches, that will give us leverage to negotiate," he said hesitantly, returning to his main theme. "It all hinges on whether the Atlantic Wall holds."

Ruge complained at the use of Goebbels' phrase, his *fiction*, "The Wall," as if it actually existed. The sun was going down. The great Seine turned red, lavender and purple in swift succession.

"We must go ahead with the planning," Speidel said. "Let's assume the worst, that the enemy gains a foothold and starts to break out. We have no air force. His fighters control the roads to Paris. Our divisions are decimated, falling back. What orders does Herr Hitler give?"

"*Fight to the last man*!" Ruge exclaimed. The last man being the Führer! They'd be stuck with him until Germany was stinking rubble.

"I am against assassination," Rommel said calmly. Killing Hitler would only create a martyr. The Nazis would make a saint of him.

"Maybe, maybe not," Ruge said.

"The point is..." Speidel began.

He continued, "If Hitler won't see reason, we should have him arrested and brought to trial." A gust stirred the cedars. The puppy barked at a squirrel. He reminded them that Dr. Strölin advocated a legal remedy. After they had surrendered and Hitler was in custody, Roosevelt and Churchill could stage an international trial.

Dr. Karl Strölin, mayor of Stuttgart, had served in Rommel's unit in WWI. In February he discreetly contacted him and broached the subject of overthrowing the Führer. To Strölin's relief, Rommel admitted that he had come to this conclusion in 1942 when Hitler had ordered the Afrika Korps to fight to the last man. This in his opinion caused a loss of morale and the subsequent capture of thousands of Germany's best troops. That was when he decided to join the resistance. However, to assassinate Hitler would be to wallow in the mire with the Brown Shirts.

"All right," Speidel said, "but would you concede that we must settle on a successor to Hitler?"

"*Ja*," he said noncommittally.

They pressed their suit. Rommel was acclaimed by the German people and the West. Hitler had made him a jewel in his crown. "He has hitched his wagon to your star," Ruge said.

They were putting the wagon before the horse. "Let's give the Führer one more chance. I will talk to him about a ceasefire."

"Try not to upset him," Ruge quipped.

For months the conspiracy had sprouted like mushrooms. One by one the generals hesitantly confided in each other. They knew Hitler's fury. Who among them had not been sprayed with his spittle? When Von Rundstedt, overall commander of the western army, referred to him as "the Bohemian corporal," the mushrooms burst through concrete.

"Let me go to the Führer," Rommel repeated, "and ask permission to meet with Montgomery. I can talk to Monty, man to man. We have a common enemy in the Bolsheviks!"

Speidel was of the opinion that the Führer wouldn't listen any more than Himmler would. However, assuming a miracle occurred and he allowed Rommel to meet with Montgomery, the first question the Tommies would ask was what would the SS do?

Would they continue to fight after the Wehrmacht surrendered?

Rommel did not like the haste with which the plan was evolving, but Speidel was right. Before he went to Berlin he had to meet with Sepp Dietrich, commander of First SS Panzer. Speidel was adamant. "Call in Dietrich! If he's for it, the other SS commanders will fall into line."

His advisers were becoming dangerously rash. Here was Speidel suggesting that he meet Sepp that night in the countryside. What if the invasion were to begin *the next day*? He grudgingly told Speidel to set it up. The chief of staff turned and headed to the chateau. The dachschund began baying at something, real or imagined. "*Hier, Elbo, kommen Sie!*" What would the puppy do if it jumped a stag? He wondered if he was biting off more than he could chew.

"Do you really think we can pull this off?" he said.

Ruge was startled. "What choice do we have?"

Back at the chateau they found that the guards had captured a pair of prisoners. They wore the camouflage uniforms and padded helmets of British commandos. His aide, Captain Heinrich Lange, reported what had happened.

"These commando gangsters, *Herr Generalfeldmarschall*, were spying on our position. When they heard that this was heeresgruppe headquarters, they asked to speak with you. Strange, is it not?"

The gangsters were fine, strapping soldiers, their faces smudged with charcoal. They came to attention and saluted. Rommel, switching to English, said, "You wish to speak with me?"

"Are you Field Marshal Rommel?" one of them said.

"Yes."

A grin split the darkened face. "A pleasure to meet you, Excellency."

"Sir!" echoed the second commando, bowing.

Rose-colored optimism was common to commandos. One would think they were reporting to their own commander. What were they doing there?

"Not at liberty to say, sir."

"Assessing our strengths, no doubt."

"Begging your pardon, sir, might I be allowed a personal observation?"

"What is it?"

"When the war is over, I hope that you will be elected leader of Germany. No one better equipped for the job, *sir.*"

He concealed his curiosity. Did this soldier speak for Montgomery? Were the *Amis* responding to diplomatic queries in Madrid and Lisbon? "Do you speak for your government?"

The commando shrugged. "I speak for the chaps when I say we admire your leadership and your devotion to duty, *sir.*"

Around the courtyard, panzergrenadiers stopped and listened. The Desert Fox was famous for spot interrogation. He could learn more from a prisoner's attitude and demeanor than the intelligence service could in hours of questioning. A man's wit and clear-headedness revealed a great deal. Rommel was irritated with himself for reacting to this trivial incident. And yet he could not help wondering if Montgomery and Churchill were among the "chaps" who wanted him to succeed Hitler.

As the commandos were taken away, one of them said, "I shall return after the war." Rommel was amused. Why? The commando seemed surprised. "Because *you* were here, sir!"

Speidel laughed. "What is it, Hans?" he said.

Speidel rubbed his nose. "I wish the British controlled the Reichstag."

The commandos were marched to a truck. Lange asked where the field marshal wished them to be taken. There was a standing order that all prisoners were to be turned over to the Gestapo. Rommel slapped his gloves on his thigh. "Send them to Wehrmacht intelligence."

That night, Lange pulled off a country lane and parked the Horch staff car in a deserted field. Rommel signaled the SS motorcyclist to follow them. The passenger in the motorcycle's sidecar was General Sepp Dietrich.

"Do not speak to the general's driver," he told Lange. "This is off the record, *verstehen Sie*?"

"I understand, Herr Generalfeldmarschall."

The field was muddy. A brisk wind was blowing off the Channel. He shivered in his light tunic. The SS commander was curious and wary. They leaned on opposite fenders of the car and talked across the bonnet. Dietrich was a bulldog of a man, the son of a butcher. Instead of the black uniform of the Schutzstaffel, he wore a camouflaged uniform. Rommel got along relatively well with the Waffen SS. They were dependable combat soldiers, whereas SS security units were little more than thugs.

"I'd like you to move your division closer to the coast," he said. Allied fighter cover would dominate the battle. A counter-attack from twenty miles inland was doomed to fail when the enemy controlled the skies.

"I have orders to stay put," Dietrich said. "You know how the Führer is."

"On my own authority I have moved up some infantry and FLAK units."

Dietrich thought for a moment. "If there was a way for me to move closer to the coast..."

Rommel suggested that First SS "practice maneuvers." He thought he saw Dietrich smile. He remembered him leading his crack SS division, the "*Leibstandarte Adolf Hitler*," through the Brenner Pass in 1943, routing Italian troops which had rebelled.

"Name the sector," Dietrich said, "and First SS Panzer will be there. What the Führer doesn't know won't hurt him."

Here was the opening he had been waiting for. He summed up his argument. When Germans were fighting a one-front war, there was a slim chance for victory. Now they were fighting the whole world. Was it right for them to go on fighting in the west, while the Russians stormed Berlin?

Dietrich listened quietly, nodding when the field marshal spoke of the Russians, but he remained noncommittal. Rommel plunged ahead. Stalin could not be trusted. It would be better to surrender to Churchill and Roosevelt than Stalin. Dietrich sat unmoving on the fender. After what seemed an eternity, he muttered, "*Jawohl.*"

Suppressing his excitement, he laid out the plan. If they could hold Eisenhower and Montgomery on the beaches, he would have leverage to negotiate.

"What do you want me to do?" Dietrich said.

He had been prepared to argue until he was blue in the face. It was unbelievable that Dietrich was so forthcoming. "What would SS commanders in the west do if I surrendered to Eisenhower?" He hastily amended, "Would *you* obey my order to cease firing?"

Dietrich took off his cap and stared into the wind. Rommel

knew what he was thinking. To say *yes* was to violate the SS oath to obey Hitler to the death. When the SS terrorized the civilian population, the oath absolved them. They were not doing evil deeds but fulfilling the Führer's will. The oath allowed them to retain, if not their humanity, a sense of duty. Dietrich was a combat soldier. In a celebrated case he had hanged suspected partisans-and no doubt would answer for it if he survived the war. The fact was, *all* German commanders had innocent blood on their hands. How many nights had he waked up in a cold sweat dreaming that Hitler had ordered him to kill civilians? He had never stood people against a wall and shot them, but he had not spoken out against the practice. To Dietrich the oath of allegiance might have more meaning than to the ordinary SS sadist. If he said *yes* he would be admitting that Hitler was not Germany. If he said *yes* he would be cutting himself loose from everything he believed in.

Rommel turned his back and crossed his arms. Lange stared into space. The motorcycle driver sat sideways on his machine. The trees leaned and whispered in the wind. Rommel imagined the SS on parade, heard the tramp of a thousand hobnailed boots, the deafening *Sieg Heil*, the irresistible pull of massed troops moving as one.

"*Ja.*"

Rommel hurried around the car.

"I will obey your surrender order." Dietrich sat slouched on the fender as if he made this kind of decision every day.

"Do you speak for the SS?"

"I think my fellow officers, those who keep their wits about them, would do the same thing."

Rommel stood with arms at his sides as though presiding at a decoration ceremony. If a respected SS general was willing to obey, the rest were likely to fall into line. Dietrich stuck his jaw out. "No one in his right mind wants the war to drag on until Germany is destroyed. We honor our commitments but we are not *blind*, you know?"

Would it be possible, he pressed, for Dietrich to sound out others without asking for a commitment? "I will try, Herr Generalfeldmarschall."

His legs felt weak. In his excitement he forgot about the wind. It blew right through his tunic. He shivered but not from the cold. "I thank you for your cooperation," he said. "We all have

Germany's interests at heart."

They shook hands. He promised to send word where to bring up the First SS Panzer division "on maneuver." Dietrich got in his sidecar. The driver started the motorcycle engine. Rommel got into the Horch. In turning the car around, Lange got it stuck in the mud, rear wheels spinning. Rommel jumped out and waved his arms at the departing Dietrich.

"*Gott im Himmel, komm zurück*!"

Dietrich ordered his driver to stop. With Lange at the wheel, and Rommel, Dietrich and the SS driver all pushing, they got the Horch moving. Mud was caked on Rommel's boots and trousers. He pointed at Dietrich's spattered uniform and joked that they had fought in the trenches. To the surprise of the drivers, the general and field marshal threw back their heads and roared.

While Lange drove back to La Roche-Guyon, very slowly, without using headlights, Rommel considered his options. To know of a *coup d'etat* was to put one's family in jeopardy. He worried about his wife, Lucie, and his son, Manfred, fifteen. It had been months since he had seen them. Lucie's birthday was two weeks away. He had ordered her a pair of shoes from a French cobbler. Leather was in short supply in Germany. She had expressed delight at the prospect of new shoes.

How was he to get a message through to the *Amis*? Previous attempts to put through peace feelers in Rome, Lisbon and Madrid had been rebuffed. Speidel had suggested contacting Swiss intermediaries or possibly the Vatican.

As the Horch roared into the night, a face floated into focus, an American lieutenant squatting beside the railroad tracks in Benghazi, waiting alongside the British POWs. That was the last time he had seen Lieutenant Max Speigner, his interpreter and guide during the trip to America, a resourceful and intuitive enemy in Africa.

"Lange," he said.

"*Ja*?"

"Search the prison camp rosters. There is someone I wish to locate."

III

His captors' idea of an outhouse was two thick planks six inches apart suspended above an open latrine. No roof or walls. Occupants of said planks exposed to the stares of guards who seemed to make their rounds every time that he, Lieutenant Max Speigner, late of U.S. Army Intelligence, happened to be relieving himself. He waited with his fellow POWs in a queue at the latrine. Group Commander Hugh Rawlings, the ranking officer, inquired if he had any spare paper. In a theatre of war, the question would have been a command. Speigner replied that he had none, had not seen any for weeks and did not expect to.

"Will you speak to Commandant Schumann?" Rawlings posed the order politely. "The Red Cross regularly sends tissue. It's against the Geneva Convention for the guards to pilfer the packets!" The queue moved forward. They sidestepped as they spoke.

"I'll bring it up," he said, "but if the Germans had any, they would sell it on the black market…*Sir.*" As to the Geneva Convention, the POWs' single copy of that distinguished document had been put to latrine use. Mail call had taken on a new urgency. Letters were *paper* from home. Men sold letters from wives and sweethearts. What a bunch of sad-sacks they had become-rank body odor and skin rashes and holes in their pants-once-proud fighting men of Britain, America, Canada, New Zealand and South Africa. Every POW had a hard-luck story. This one had been captured because he ran out of ammo or gasoline. That one because his compass malfunctioned. None had been outfought or outsmarted. None, as well, had been trained to stand and wait. Being fluent in German gave him an official duty as interpreter and translator but it was a hell of a way to spend a war.

A cold shower every week. Two bars of soap for four hundred men. Those at the back of the line begging the first bathers to "go easy" on the soap. Anyone who used more than the allotted twenty seconds was in trouble. Counting as they stood shivering in line, "*One thousand, two thousand, three thousand*¾!"

Theirs was a fraternity with deep affections and violent rages. Breaking into chow line was grounds for murder. Before dawn they turned out for roll call. Did daily calisthenics as the sun came up. Waited for mess call. Ate poorly. Went back to the barracks. Squeezed into bunks a foot apart and stacked to the ceiling. Tried to stay warm in winter, cool in summer. Knew too much about everyone. Who snored. Who farted in in his sleep. Who had boils on his ass. Who hated his mother. Who suspected his wife was cheating. Who had guts. Who didn't.

When it was his turn at the latrine, he tried to ignore the pasty-faced guards watching through the barbed wire. If he ever got used to relieving himself in public, they could stand him against a wall and shoot him.

"When you see the commandant," Rawlings said as they walked bowlegged around the barracks, "please use the strongest language possible. Remind them of your relationship with Field Marshal Rommel." He wished he'd never mentioned having served as Rommel's guide in the states. Or that Rommel had subsequently captured him in Libya and packed him off to Bavaria. "Mind you ask about the soap," Rawlings added.

At the main gate the guards demanded *Zigaretten*. He replied as he had a thousand times that he did not smoke. Hitler's master race, he thought ironically. They opened the gate and he went up the neatly trimmed walk paved with gravel. Everything seemed to be in place, the Third Reich proceeding according to plan-except that the Allied invasion was no longer an *if* but a *when*. The signs were everywhere. Guards joked with POWs. The iron-fisted sergeant who ran the commandant's office as if he were Hitler's nephew addressed Speigner respectfully. *Ja*, the commandant would see him. *Nein*, it would not be a long wait. Would the *Herr Leutnant* care to take a seat? A few days ago the sergeant had made him stand at attention for thirty minutes.

"For what purpose, do you wish to see the Herr Kommandeur Schumann?"

"*Toilettenpapier.*"

The sergeant wanted to know if everyone in America spoke German as well as Speigner. He explained that his parents were German immigrants. He did not add that his linguistics skills had landed him in this stinking stalag. He had been assigned to the War Department to keep a file on the Wehrmacht. In 1937, when the German Embassy requested liaison for a group of German officers touring Civil War battlefields, he had been sent as interpreter. He later submitted an intelligence report on the visitors, one of whom was a lieutenant-colonel named Rommel.

Rommel, a rising star in Hitler's army, had been an enthusiastic tourist, roaming Civil War battlefields and asking informed questions, getting inside the heads of Stonewall Jackson, Jeb Stuart and Nathan Bedford Forrest. Max had been curious why Rommel, an infantry officer, was interested in cavalry tactics. Later, when the Germans invaded the Sudetenland and Poland, he found out.

His file on Rommel grew to several folders. In January, 1941, the British, under attack by the AfrikaKorps, requested Speigner's files. When they read that he'd predicted Rommel's "end run" in France, they asked G-2 to send Max to Cairo, where he became a respected adviser. When Rommel's panzers crossed the Libyan border to raid a fuel dump, an RAF squadron was waiting, alerted by Speigner. Spitfires and Hurricanes sent the panzers reeling. It was the first British victory in months. Later, acting on a hunch, Speigner flew to Benghazi. A FLAK battery shot down the reconnaissance plane. He was captured and briefly reunited with Rommel before being shipped off to POW camp.

"Captain Schumann will see you," the sergeant said.

The commandant greeted Max with cautious civility. He returned Max's salute and offered him a chair. "It is really too bad...about the...toilet paper," Captain Schumann said in English.

Speigner stuck to German. "Group Commander Rawlings wishes to know if the Red Cross has stopped sending toilet paper."

"Yes, I believe they have."

Schumann scratched his ear, a nervous tic. Max noted razor nicks on the commandant's jaw. The Yanks were coming-and Limeys and Canucks and Paddies and Jocks. In the meantime everyone was scratching and waiting. Where were the Red Cross supplies? Not only toilet paper, but stationery and mailing envelopes, none of which the POWs had received.

"Commander Rawlings was wondering if guards opened the

packages.

"*Nein*, impossible." Pilferage was so common it did not rate a show of indignation. They both knew that Mrs. Schumann, her family and friends, the guards and their families, had American toilet paper in bathroom cabinets, that towns and hamlets surrounding the stalag were living off the Red Cross.

"Each month," he persisted, "each prisoner is sent a month's supply of bathing and shaving soap, chocolate, cigarettes, writing paper and toilet paper."

"Protest all you like." Schumann scratched his ear. "I am told that the Red Cross inspections have been suspended."

"Why?"

Schumann avoided looking at him. Did this mean the invasion was imminent? Had it already *begun*? Why else would the Red Cross cease deliveries? The men lived for mail call. The sight of a red logo on a white truck was enough to send caps sailing. A letter told them they were missed, people were waiting, a normal existence was possible. "The lack of toilet paper," he said, "combined with a scarcity of soap, has caused skin rashes. There's no *Hautcreme*. The men are using axle grease as lotion."

Schumann neglected to ask how POWs had obtained axle grease.

Sir, we bribed the guards with Zigaretten.

There was a wail of a siren. Cars braked sharply in front of the building. The sergeant stuck his head in the doorway. "SS," he whispered. Schumann began to button his tunic. In his preoccupation he seemed to forget Max. The sergeant stood at attention. Schumann snapped to attention. "*Heil, Hitler*!" An SS colonel stood in the entrance. He gave Speigner a cursory glance. Prisoners were bugs on Hitler's windshield.

"Am I intruding?" said the colonel.

"No, no, Herr Oberst, not at all," said Schumann. "I was just finishing with this prisoner." He turned to Max. "*Dismissed*!"

Speigner started toward the door. Without looking at him the colonel held up a gloved hand. If he raised his finger a minnow-sized POW could disappear.

"We were discussing nothing of importance," said Schumann.

"What is of no importance?"

Max replied without thinking, "*Es gibt kein Toilettenpapier.*"

A prisoner was not to speak unless addressed. The colonel swelled with resentment. He addressed Schumann as if Max had not spoken. "You discuss such things with *them*?"

"I was just about to dismiss him."

"He stays." The colonel pulled off his gloves. His black tunic made Schumann's blue-gray Luftwaffe uniform seem almost civilian. The silver SS insignia on his collar winked like a set of eyes. Schumann-the POW's nemesis, tyrant, boss, purveyor of contraband tissue-was a loving uncle by comparison.

"To what do I owe the honor?" Schumann said.

"Moment," said the colonel. "The prisoner. His German is quite good."

Speigner hesitated. If the colonel had meant him to reply, he would have addressed him. He became aware of his shabby, smelly uniform. His beard stubble was three days old. His U.S. Army fatigues were patched and frayed. His web belt was gone, in its place a piece of string. After a few seconds, the colonel said, speaking rhetorically, "So, how is morale?" It was a test. Which of them was being addressed?

Schumann spoke up. "Very good, I'd say, very high."

The colonel glanced at Speigner. "Except for toilet tissue?"

He weighed the colonel's tone, fairly sure he had been addressed. "Morale is good, as the Herr Hauptmann said."

"How is it you have such excellent German?"

He looked at the colonel directly. This, too, a gamble. "My parents are from Frankfurt. They immigrated in 1933. My father is a steelworker, an engineer."

"*Ihr Name*?"

"Speigner."

The colonel drew out the pronunciation, almost lisping: *Schpeigner*. Jewish POWs were supposed to be off-limits to the SS. Otherwise, they'd be shaking down the camps whenever new prisoners were brought in. He waited in silence, ashamed of his terror. He had not been this frightened when his plane was shot down in Libya. "And the prisoners, they are well-treated?"

There had been speculation that the SS, when the Allied army overran Germany, would line up all POWs and shoot them. The war would never be over for the SS. They had sworn to die for Hitler. He willed his stomach muscles to relax. "The men held a lottery," he said.

"Oh?"

"For the top fifty places at the showers. The winners get first crack at the two bars of soap."

Schumann was horrified. The colonel turned slightly. The slanted eyes of the SS bars seemed to squint with reflected light. Schumann scolded, "Prisoners must make do!"

"We held a story-telling contest," he went on, unable to stop. "First prize was head-of-the-queue for a month. There were accusations of favoritism. Judges were bribed."

"They have a sense of humor, these Americans," Schumann said hastily. "They entertain themselves by telling stories."

"Let him speak."

"We wish to complain to the International Red Cross," he said.

"*Lieutenant, you are dismissed!*" Schumann broke in.

"I suggest," the colonel said, "that the prisoners write down their complaints. They will then be hanged. This will save much *Toilettenpapier.*" He turned to Schumann, who immediately came to attention. "Double the labor, twice the work in half the time."

"*Jawohl, Herr Oberst!*"

"And *you*, Lieutenant." The colonel almost smiled. "Lift your thoughts higher than your asshole."

"*Der Herr Leutnant,*" Schumann cried lest Speigner make a mortal error, "*ist entlassen*-dismissed!" He came to attention and saluted. Schumann flicked his hand impatiently. The colonel did not look up. Max left the office. Outside an SS motorcyclist glanced at him indifferently.

As he approached the gate to the compound, he was startled by a throaty sound. What he thought were mourning doves was actually girlish laughter. Two *Landmadden* rode bicycles past the camp. They waved at the prisoners, who clung to the fence and howled. One of the girls, blonde and buxom, yodeled at them. They went wild. The girls smiled at the scruffy *Amis* tarrying in their midst. German frauleins, it was said, were frank and bold. One asked, "Will you go to bed?" They replied *Ja* or *Nein.*

Bicycle wheels flashed in the sun. The prisoners groaned good-naturedly. Bragging aside, most of them had forgotten how to strike up a conversation with a pretty girl. Surely it would come back to them.

Until the girls came pedaling by, he had not noticed the fields in the distance. It was May, time to plant, to start anew. A farmer pushed his plow in a large wheelbarrow. There was no petrol for tractors. Wildflowers were in bloom. He had always wanted to see Europe in the spring, go to Frankfurt, look up his cousins, sample the local brew. The POWs talked incessantly of peace but how would they respond when it happened? Would the Nazis let them go? Would they open the gate and wish them *Viel Glück*? Or march them to a ditch and mow them down?

"*Los rein, Americaner*!" The guard held the gate open for him. "*Macht schnell*!"

IV

POW camp was a madhouse run by madmen. The prisoners had one faith, one religion: a sense of irony. When Speigner was called back to the commandant's office the next day, he was prepared either for an "official response" to the POWs' toilet paper complaint or an SS execution order. If the latter, he hoped Schumann would stamp "*Verboten,*" on his forehead: "*Off limits to SS.*" Sitting in the waiting room he heard Schumann's muffled voice from within. The commandant seemed to be agitated. The desk sergeant raised an eyebrow at Speigner. The door opened and Schumann bellowed, "*Wo ist Leutnant Speigner?*" He saw Max and gestured for him to come in.

An officer was waiting in Schumann's office. His uniform was not SS but Wehrmacht with a captain's insignia. The officer took an immediate interest in Speigner as if he matched a physical description. This was a combat soldier in the well-oiled *Wehrmacht*, where orders passed through the chain of command with the ease of thought.

Schumann resumed his complaints. The captain had disregarded regulations and bypassed channels. He'd never seen anything like it! The captain shrugged. The contrast was obvious. Schumann was a bit player. The captain was a front line soldier. Schumann would not authorize the request until he phoned Munich. The captain replied that there was no time to waste. The *Herr Generalfeldmarschall* had the prerogative of transferring any prisoner, anywhere, anytime.

Field marshal? Transfer? Speigner glanced at the campaign patches on the captain's uniform. He recognized the palm-tree-and-swastika of the *AfrikaKorps.*

Rumors often arrived with new prisoners-the most popular men in camp. He had heard that Rommel commanded the Atlantic Wall. It was strange to imagine the Desert Fox dug in, hunkered down behind fortifications he'd once scorned. Any fort, minefield, Maginot Line, was meant to be bypassed. Had Rommel sent for him? For *him*! Was he no longer to be flanked and bypassed?

"I will get the transfer papers!" Schumann tramped into the outer office. Cabinet drawers were opened and slammed shut, then the staccato sounds of typing.

The captain said in perfect English, "Lieutenant Speigner, I am Heinrich Lange. How do you do?"

"Very well, thank you," he responded automatically. Schumann returned, waving a triplicate form.

"This is most irregular! I shall report to my superiors." He began stamping the forms, taking out his frustration on the ink pad: *Sanktion, Sanktion, Sanktion.* The commandant's indignation had a sanguine effect. Freedom crept into Max's bones.

"May I be allowed to report to Group Commander Rawlings?" he said.

"Who?" Lange said. Schumann identified Rawlings as the ranking allied officer. Lange said he did not have time for protocol. They must leave at once. "Regrettably," he apologized.

This small gesture made everything real. In a few minutes he would be gone. The unknown tugged at his consciousness. He thought of packing his things, then remembered that he was wearing everything he owned. Under his mattress was a rusty razor, a dog-eared book of poetry, an extra pair of shoelaces (brand new, an item of exchange). Whoever claimed his bunk would inherit these treasures. Where were they going? he asked. Schumann was vitally interested. When Lange did not reply, Max added, "Commander Rawlings will think I *disappeared.*"

The implication was obvious. Schumann softened half a degree. "I will tell Rawlings you were transferred *unharmed*!" He thrust the papers at Lange. Speigner came to attention and saluted. He and the commandant were not friends, not even friendly enemies, but they had grown used to tossing the Geneva Convention at each other, week in, week out. Schumann returned his salute.

Viel Glück, Herr Leutnant.

Und Ihnen, Herr Kapitan.

Schumann followed them into the anteroom. He resumed his tirade. Regulations were in place for a reason. Rules were not meant to be thwarted. There would be an investigation. He followed them outside and watched them get into a car.

A tanker truck was parked beside a single-engine Heinkel, which he knew to be Rommel's preferred light aircraft. The pilot attended to the refueling. Lange gestured for Speigner to get into the rear seat, then got in beside him.

"Are you going to handcuff me?" he said, only half-joking.

"No, but after we land you must submit to a blindfold," Lange said. "I place you on your best behavior, Lieutenant. Don't do anything foolish."

"Are you going to throw me out at a thousand feet?"

Lange smiled. The pilot closed the door and locked it. In the closeness of the interior, Speigner was embarrassed by his body odor. His anus itched. He willed himself not to scratch. "I was with Field Marshal Rommel in North Africa," he remarked.

Lange said. "Buckle the safety belt."

The pilot put on his headset and started the engine. The noise of the exhaust drowned out thought. In moments they were taxiing to the end of the runway. Speigner felt himself tensing for takeoff. He was *out*, he was *mobile,* he was *free*. The pilot pulled the throttle and the small plane bounded over the grass strip.

As the aircraft gained altitude, he looked out the window. How small the camp seemed. His entire world was a tiny square where prisoners milled about like ants. He felt guilty. He was getting out. They were not.

They flew over the mountains of southern Germany. Then the plane turned west. To the south were the white peaks of the Alps. The pilot spoke into his microphone, calling Luftwaffe Control in Munich, filing a flight plan. Speigner heard "Frankreich."

France.

He asked the name of a large lake and was told "Ammersee." The river that flowed into it, the Ammer, was a bright blue band. Lange, in an unguarded moment, gazed at the wooded countryside with nostalgia and called out landmarks to the pilot. Speigner knew the feeling. When Lange murmured, "the Donau," he might have been saying *the Mississippi*. When he said, "Ulm, see the tower above city hall?" he might have been describing *Natchez* or *Terre Haute* or *San Antonio*. War was damned strange. Here he was, a captive in stinking rags, feeling sorry for his captors.

Dusk crept over the land. Dark lines of military convoys crawled along the highways. The pilot descended to under five hundred feet. Speigner guessed that this was to avoid allied fighters, which meant that they had crossed into French air space. Was that Strasbourg below-was that Nancy-could that be Chalons? An hour later there was an unmistakable glow on the horizon, a shimmering lake of darting light. *Paris*. Motorists and bikers were breaking curfew. Their headlights flashed on and off like startled fish leaving phosphorescent trails in the water.

Lange acknowledged that they were north of Paris. Soon, the pilot radioed the airport at Rouen. A tower operator responded in German, confirming the heading. As the aircraft approached the field, blue runway lights blinked on and off, *once*. Speigner was amazed at the ease with which the pilot landed the aircraft in the dark. He could not see a thing until hangars loomed ahead.

"*Können Sie mir bitte unser Ziel sagen?*" Can you tell me our destination?

"It is only a small village," Lange replied. "I must now place on you the blindfold."

V

The car slowed as it twisted through narrow lanes. The whining of tires echoed off walls. Blindfolded, Speigner sensed row houses with shuttered windows. He imagined French families eating dinner, opening a bottle of wine, stirring a *café au lait*, doing strange and ordinary things.

The car stopped. A man, a sentry, spoke to Lange. The car proceeded slowly as if entering a narrow lane. Lange parked the car, got Speigner out and led him along a walkway. A rusty hinge creaked. Was the secrecy for *him*? He smelled dank earth. Gravel crunched under his boots. Water dripped in a fountain. They entered a building, went down a corridor. He felt cool, airy space and smelled floor wax, an amazing and wonderful smell. The captain untied the blindfold.

They were in a large, wood-paneled room. The windows were tightly curtained. At one end was an antique desk, a lamp and a few chairs. The floor was covered by oriental carpets. Lange went to the door, spoke with a guard. Moments later Rommel entered. When he saw Speigner he accidentally stepped on a dachshund puppy following at his heels. It yelped. He stooped to pick it up. The dog started to bark. "Elbo, be still!" Rommel said. "Leutnant Speigner, you have arrived, *ist gut*!"

He did not know whether to salute or shake hands. He forgot to come to attention. By the time he remembered it was too late. Rommel held the puppy in one hand and grinned. Max heard himself saying, "*Wie geht es Ihnen*?"

"Things have changed." Rommel gestured at the paneled room as if this explained everything. "All right, Lange, thank you. Did everything go all right?"

"*Ja, Herr Generalfeldmarschall,*" Lange said. Max noted the familiarity between them.

"Bring coffee."

"Right away, Herr Generalfeldmarschall."

"On second thought, no coffee. I'd like to 'keep this quiet.'" He glanced wryly at Speigner to see if he had noticed the use of idiom. The American seemed disoriented. His clothes were patched and frayed. A string held up his trousers. And he smelled like, well, a prisoner of war. Their last meeting had been in Benghazi at the railway depot. How quickly a soldier went from fighting man to captive. Perhaps he was hungry. Yes, that must be it. Rommel cast about and noticed a bowl of candy.

"*Schokolade, Herr Leutnant?*"

Speigner accepted a chocolate. He remembered the stolen Red Cross parcels and almost checked the wrapper markings. The general petted his dog while the American devoured the sweets. "I heard a funny story the other day. When the Führer was a corporal in the army, he applied for officer training. His company commander turned him down, saying-you'll never guess what-he was *unfit for command*!" Rommel glanced at the puppy. "*Ja*, '*Untauglich für Kommando*' was printed on the application form. Hitler's historians are busy removing such embarrassing documents." Speigner swallowed his fourth candy and was suddenly thirsty. He did not know which was more unusual, his eating chocolate or Rommel's joking about Hitler.

"There is a pitcher of water on the table. Help yourself."

"Thank you," he said, "and...I wouldn't mind washing up if it is permitted?"

Rommel showed him the water closet. He went inside and relieved himself, marveling at the porcelain toilet. He could not remember the last time he had seen a clean restroom with a washstand, basin and towel. He sniffed the fragrant soap and willed himself not to steal it. He washed his hands and face, luxuriating in the novelty. He quickly unbuttoned his jacket and shirt, washed under his arms, inspected his haggard reflection.

He looked terrible. Rommel on the other hand was pretty much the same, minus the desert tan. There were lines in the field marshal's face he did not remember seeing. In Libya, he wouldn't have joked about Hitler. *Things have changed*. For the first time in his career Rommel commanded a defensive position. Fortifying miles of coastline, worrying where the Allies would attack, inspecting troop positions, a colossal drain on genius-but of course that was what most generals did, most of the time. Waiting for an invasion had aged Rommel ten years.

Speigner rubbed his jaw, wished for a razor. He also wished he could send the Hitler joke to POW camp by mental telepathy. At the camp the guards turned away when the prisoners made wisecracks about *Der Führer*. They didn't want anyone to see them laughing. Sounds came through the radiator, a familiar *tok-a, tok-a* telegraphed through the pipes. It was a noise from his childhood. As he emerged from the water closet, it came back to him. *Ping pong*. What was going on?

Rommel offered him a chair. They faced each other across a desk. The dachshund sniffed Max's shoes. The general apologized. "No, please, it's good to see a dog," he said.

Rommel began, "I don't know if you've heard since your internship. I've been assigned to France."

So that was what prison was: an internship. Someone ought to tell Commandant Schumann.

"Herr Generalfeldmarschall, it's common knowledge that you command the Atlantic Wall. Even in the camp we knew that. However, if you are going to ask about the allied invasion, I have nothing to say."

Rommel smiled. For a few seconds he was the same man who had walked the battlefields with Speigner at Shiloh and Brice's Crossroads. "That is not why I sent for you." The field marshal was about to ask him for *eine Wohltat*, a boon, a favor. What did he have to give? Air was coming through holes in his pants. The heels of his shoes had worn off. The *tok-a, tok-a* in the background confused and disoriented him. "*Wie geht's*?" he said. "Is someone playing ping pong?"

Rommel was puzzled. "Oh, you mean, table tennis. The junior officers have a table in the ballroom. *Ping pong*, that is a good one!"

Had the Wehrmacht changed that much?

"Now, let me tell you why I sent for you."

The time had come to speak of *Frieden*, of peace. Everyone knew the war could not go on much longer. Both armies had fought courageously. The Wehrmacht was a formidable force to be reckoned with, but why should soldiers fight and die so close to the end? A useless and tragic waste. This was what he wished to tell Eisenhower and Montgomery. They, the generals, had a duty to prevent further death and destruction. The pinging echoed through the pipes. Speigner felt bounced back and forth. Rommel was at his most dangerous when cornered. Was this a ploy to gain time?

"You do not believe me," Rommel said shrewdly.

Fingerspitzengefühl. Some things never changed.

"I am willing to surrender to the west before the Russians reach Berlin. What I must know, and what you must discover for me, is whether the allied commanders will accept *me* as the representative of my country. I wish you to tell Eisenhower that I am speaking for the German army and navy in the west. The air force remains under Hermann Göring's control, but as we all know, the German air force is not what it was."

His throat was dry. He reached for the water pitcher and poured another glassful. He gulped it down. *What about Hitler*? Rommel had obviously anticipated this question. "In my opinion the Führer will have no choice but to go along." He changed the subject, addressing the communist threat to Axis and Allied powers. The west was united by capitalism and industry. After the war, the communists would be the enemy. He talked about Eisenhower's leadership, how he respected "Ike" and other allied commanders, including Patton. He asked if word had reached the POW camps about Patton's *faux pas* about the Russians. "He excluded the Bolsheviks when speaking of postwar development."

Speigner had not heard this. They were getting away from the question. *Would Hitler agree to a surrender?* Rommel saw that prison had not changed Speigner. He was as alert as ever. "Do you remember the battlefield in Mississippi? What was it called, don't tell me...Brice's Crossroads. You explained to me the tactics of General Forrest? We will 'get the bulge' on the Führer. He will have no time to react. By the time he knows of the surrender, it will be a *fait accompli.*"

Was this possible? Half-digested chocolate lay on his stomach like an igneous deposit. If Rommel said that Hitler could be outflanked, he had no choice but to believe it, except-would Eisenhower believe a man with holes in his pants? "Do you have any clothes I could borrow?"

"We must not change the way you look. You have just come from a stalag."

His mind raced. He could see himself standing like a beggar before Eisenhower. *Trust me, sir. I may look like a fool or a madman but you can believe that I, a mere lieutenant, speak for the Herr Field Marshal Rommel, who speaks for Germany. Yes, sir, that's right. When you talk to me, you are talking to Germany. Forget Hitler. My old friend Rommel-you know, I was his guide and interpreter when he came to America-says to tell you, Let's get together and make up!*

"I cannot commit this message to writing. Nor can I use radio or telephone. The Gestapo is monitoring all transmissions. The only way to get through is by courier. Will you do this?"

Peace was breaking out inside him. It took getting used to. "I am honored, Herr Generalfeldmarschall, but the fact is, I do not have top secret clearance. It's possible I could get to the High Command but I cannot guarantee it."

Rommel removed an embroidered insignia from his tunic. "The oak leaves to my Knight's Cross," he said. "As a token that you speak for me." Max held the insignia gingerly. The future was racing ahead of him. "Have you a chill?" Rommel said alertly. "The Heinkel can be drafty, especially during a four-hour flight." He went to the fireplace and struck a match under kindling. As flames ate through the wood he leaned on the mantelpiece. Without looking at Speigner he said things that needed to be said, that Eisenhower and Montgomery would want to know.

"We, many of us, are ashamed to have fought in the service of a madman. We have no excuse except that we were soldiers. It was what we knew and we did it to the best of our ability. Now is the time to stop fighting, go home, repair the damage. We shall punish those responsible for terrorizing civilians, for what has been done to the Jews. We shall rebuild Germany one brick at a time. We lost our way¾" He glanced up to let Speigner gauge his sincerity. If Eisenhower could be there, at that moment, they could have stopped the war. His voice trailed off. He petted his dog. "I know nothing of espionage," he continued. "Even if I were able to contact a British consulate, I could not go through channels. I am willing to give myself up, but only after my family is out of Germany. They could be taken to Switzerland. My home is not far from the Swiss border. Everything depends on you. *You* are the key, *mein Herr Leutnant.*"

"Assuming I get through, how do I communicate with you?"

"You must bring me Eisenhower's reply in person. All you have to do is come ashore and you will be brought to me." Speigner was suddenly thirsty. He filled the water glass again. "If you are successful," Rommel went on, "once the peace process is set into motion, I will see that you are escorted back to your people. You have my word."

He raised his glass. "*Auf Frieden*," he said.

Peace was a beautiful word in any language, Rommel agreed. He looked at his wristwatch. It was almost twenty-three hundred hours. Speigner had to be across the Channel by daybreak. "We are at the Chateau La Roche Guyon, on the Seine, forty miles west of Paris. Remember that, in case you must find your way back. Show any officer these oak leaves."

He had a dozen questions, not the least of which was where to rendezvous. He could imagine a machine gun opening up as he waded ashore. Of course that could just as easily happen on the British coast. The field marshal put out his hand. He tried not to grab hold like a drowning man.

"Captain Lange will take you to the coast. The French resistance has a boat waiting. Do not say anything to the French. The less anyone knows, the better."

He hesitated. He wanted to acknowledge Rommel's vision, to thank him for trusting him, for setting him free, for allowing him to join the cause, but all he could think of was, "What am I to say when the British pick me up?"

Rommel shrugged. "Tell them you have a message for Ike."

VI

The fishing boat beat through a six-foot chop, the two-stroke engine making a steady *thump-thump, thump-thump*. Spray drenched the windshield and there were heavy patches of fog. Swaying and shivering in the enclosed pilot house, Speigner could not see anything. Powerful swells lifted the small fishing boat. The skipper gave him some bread and cheese along with a thermos of lukewarm tea. If his French were better, he would have asked where he was being taken. Was he to be picked up by a British patrol boat? Where was the nearest town?

The skipper secured the pilot wheel and motioned him to follow. Wind and spray chilled him. Fog blanketed the ocean. He listened for the sound of breakers. Two sailors lowered a dinghy and swung it over the side. It bobbed on the heaving swells. They expected him to make landfall in that little thing?

"*Maintenant*!" said the skipper, pointed at the boat bobbing up and down. Oars bumped and rattled in the oarlocks. "*Bonne chance, mon ami*."

He climbed into the bouncing boat. The dinghy bucked, slamming him down on the seat. He grabbed the oar handles. If it capsized he would have no chance. The skipper disappeared inside the pilot house. *So much for hands across the Atlantic.*

"Which way is England?" he yelled.

The skipper stuck his head out the door. "*Comment*?"

His voice was a squeaky falsetto. "*Où est Angleterre*?"

The Frenchman made chopping motions with his hand. "*Allez, allez, allez*!"

He rowed towards an offshore breeze, his only compass. Water splashed across the gunwales and puddled around his feet. The fishing boat turned around and was soon lost in the fog, sturdy little engine fading. He pulled on the oars. He could be lost in this fog and no one would know. There was a distinctive, hissing roar. He stopped rowing.

An outgoing tide turned the dinghy sideways. No wonder the Frenchman had been amused. They'd dropped him close to shore. He righted the boat and resumed rowing. He heard breakers. White cliffs rose before him. The tide pulled him to shore. He rowed hard, too busy staying on top of breaking surf to think of anything else. The bow crunched against pebbles. The moment he stepped ashore, a spotlight dazzled him. A man shouted, "Hands on your head."

British marines surrounded him. He tried to tell them who he was and what he was doing. They frisked and handcuffed him. He tried to say something. They told him to be quiet. He was taken to a stone hut. A sergeant cranked a field phone and reported the detention of "a subject" in a U.S. infantryman's uniform.

"Came ashore alone," the sergeant said. "No identification."

"I'm not a spy," Speigner said.

"What's your unit?"

"I'm not AWOL!"

"Nobody said you were."

At least they were allowing him to speak. He told them he had been released from a German prisoner of war camp and had a message for military intelligence. He didn't mention Rommel or Eisenhower. Enlisted men had more sense than officers. They might put him in a strait jacket.

"Where were you held?"

"Bavaria."

"How'd you get *here*?"

They wouldn't believe it if he told them. He asked to be taken to the nearest U.S. Army headquarters. The radio came on. The patrol was ordered to bring the subject in. He found himself in the back of a jeep driven at high speed. He thought they would be killed, then remembered that the British drove on the left. He was cold and hungry.

They turned onto a major highway. Convoys of trucks were stalled bumper to bumper. The jeep continued on the narrow shoulder. In the grey light he caught glimpses of row houses, harbors filled with ships, piers jammed with truck convoys, meadows used as staging areas, Sherman tanks as far as he could see. If he *were* a spy, his hosts were giving him a grand tour. This was not the sluggish, monolithic U.S. Army that he had joined as an ROTC graduate. Here were acres of brand new weapons and equipment, rolled steel-mesh treads, fuel pipes, steel bridging. He understood Rommel's urgency.

The jeep stopped in front of an ordinary brick building. Inside, a flurry of activity belied the staid exterior. Phones rang, couriers delivered packets, muffled shouts came from behind closed doors, WACs came and went-the first women he had seen up close in a long time except for Madame Schumann. A door opened on a map room with a weather board. A navy seaman was sticking markers on it. Another open doorway revealed desks piled with magazines and newspapers. From his days at the War Department he knew fact-sifters when he saw them. G-2 recruited college professors, lawyers, ad-men, clever types for whom coffee break was nothing without a crossword puzzle. If information were gold dust, they were born to the pan. He was among his own kind.

Coffee was brewing in a steel coffeemaker. He inhaled the aroma. "Get the lead out, Mac!" one of the MPs said. The slang brought tears to his eyes. A passing officer casually remarked, "Hi, how are ya?" A WAC yelled, "*Yoohoo!*" A down-home-soul intoned, "Well, lookee here!"

He was a legionnaire in a time machine. He caught a whiff of perfume. WACS smelled too good to be soldiers. A wake of curious silence followed him down a hallway. A major stood in a doorway. He dismissed the MPs, took Speigner into a debriefing room and asked if he would like coffee or a cigarette. He replied that a cup of coffee would be just fine.

Two captains entered the room and without a word sat down, notepads and pencils handy, younger than any captains he'd ever seen. One of them set up a reel-to-reel recorder. "You were a POW," the major began.

He sipped hot coffee. So robust it made him cough. "Yes, sir, in southern Bavaria, near the Austrian border. I was there for two years....uh, sir, I've got a message from Field Marshal Rommel for General Eisenhower!"

They glanced at each other as if to say, *Oh, well, another nut case.* He had to play along. He described the camp, the prisoners and where they were from, how some of them came to be captured. There was more to it than that, but he did not think they cared about fights breaking out over crap games. The captains pelted him with questions testing his credibility. Were the POWs well treated? What kind of facilities did they have?

"How the hell did you get out?" the major interrupted.

"Rommel sent a plane." They looked at each other. He groped in his pocket for the oak leaves insignia. "This is his. He gave it to me. It's for Ike...General Eisenhower."

They passed the insignia around.

Could have picked it up somewhere.

Maybe he stole it.

"Can I have it back?" he said.

One of the captains reluctantly handed him the patch. A WAC came and delivered a folder. The major glanced through it, then looked at Speigner respectfully. "The Brits have a file on you! You didn't tell us you worked for them in Egypt."

"You didn't ask."

The major stiffened. "Let's remember who we're talking to."

"Sorry, sir."

The captains took turns reading the file, then looked at him as if to say *Who is this guy*? "Can you prove you were in the POW camp?" said the major.

"You'll find my name on the Red Cross prisoner list. Field Marshal Rommel asked me to¾"

"How did you get out of the camp?"

"Herr General...Field Marshal Rommel had me released. Like I said, he had me flown to France."

"You flew over German territory?"

"Yeah."

Did you see convoys?

Was there much military activity?

How many troops did you see on the roads?

"It was at night. Listen, I've got to get through to the High Command."

"Sure, sure," the major said. "Where did you fly to?"

"Rouen."

The captains grabbed an atlas. "You must have flown over troop concentrations near Paris. Where are they, here...or *here*?"

"I told you, it was dark."

You must have seen something.

No, I didn't see anything.

Where's Rommel's headquarters?

In a village.

Next, they'd be asking for coordinates. If he said "La Roche-Guyon," a flight of B-17s would be airborne within the hour. He felt the field marshal's presence as if Rommel were sitting next to him.

Near Rouen?

It was night. I was blindfolded.

What kind of command center has he got? Is it a bunker or a villa?

"There were windows with curtains. I couldn't see outside. We met in the field marshal's office." He inadvertently pushed their question button.

What's the name of his unit?

Is Rommel commander of all troops in the west?

Does he command the panzer reserves?

Where are the troop concentrations, near Rouen?

Did you personally observe any fortifications?

"Rommel's *there*, okay? He commands an army. All I know is that I met with him and he authorized me to present his regards to General Eisenhower and Field Marshal Montgomery and to ask whether, in the event that he were to surrender, the High Command would accept him as Germany's chief representative in the west!"

"We'll get to that," the major said doggedly. "You were about to tell us about Rommel's headquarters. I'm surprised they aren't, well, underground."

The commander of the Atlantic Wall wanted to end the war. How did he get through? "By the way, when is D-Day?" They stared in surprise. "I saw the ships queuing at the docks. We can stop this war. It can be over tomorrow. Get me General Eisenhower, dammit! *Sir!*"

The captains, taking notes, chuckled at the notion. He had had his little joke. Now it was their turn.

Pinpoint Rommel's headquarters.

How far from Rouen is it?

How long did it take to drive there from the airfield?

"I was with Rommel for about an hour. All he talked about was *Frieden.* Do you understand? Peace!"

Nobody said anything for a few seconds. He was beginning to think he had gotten through. "Ever hear of Rommel's Asparagus?" added one of the captains.

"No."

The captain smiled. "Logs stuck in the fields to rip gliders apart. We heard Rommel designed them himself. He's planning a surprise party."

The major stared at him fixedly. "You must have observed *something* about the enemy!"

He hugged himself in frustration. "They were playing ping pong. You know, table tennis." They were dumbfounded. He felt vindicated, though not for the reasons he'd hoped.

"You're saying," the major replied, "that they don't have anything better to do? They've completed their defenses? They figure we don't stand a prayer?"

He felt helpless. "No, no, there's a general malaise among the Germans, a sense that the war is lost. Ping pong is a symptom."

"'Malaise'? Did Rommel say that?" said the major.

"I'm telling you what their attitude is. They're ready to surrender…to Ike!"

The major glanced at him shrewdly. "Playing ping pong could be a sign of how confident they are."

How many troops does Rommel have?

Where's his headquarters?

Show us on a map.

His thoughts drifted. Periodically he interrupted to ask if they would pass Rommel's message on. He remembered his parents and asked if he could send a telegram. The major glanced at his watch. "You could probably use a little sleep. How about we continue this in the morning? Maybe after some shut-eye you'll be able to reconstruct what Rommel's headquarters looks like. Then you can send mama a telegram."

"In case you dream about Rommel," one added, "we'll leave a pad and pencil by your bed."

Two MPs materialized. They took him to the lobby. A WREN motorcycle courier from the British army was standing at the checkout desk. She wore a canvas helmet and goggles. He stood like a sleepwalker while the major signed him out. He said, "Am I under arrest?" The major explained that he would be quarantined until debriefing was completed.

The WREN pushed the official pouch at the WAC behind the counter. "I really must protest. My message should have been put through right away to the High Command." Max looked up.

"Wait your turn," the major said.

"Sorry, sir. In a bit of a rush."

The courier's voice had a Highland lilt. She took off her helmet and fluffed out her hair. It was reddish gold. She had green eyes. The last time he had seen Anna McAlpin was in a sandstorm in the Sahara. She had been a correspondent for the *London Times*. She obviously did not recognize him. When one of the MPs took him by the arm, he resisted.

"Anna?"

"Come on, pal." The MP tightened his grip.

Her face lit up. "*Leftenant Speigner*! How have you been?" She glanced at his dirty tunic. "What in the world *happened* to you?"

The major handed the transfer papers to the MPs. They took him by the arms and hauled him outside. He glanced helplessly over his shoulder. McAlpin watched them take him to a jeep.

VII

Major General Speidel was delighted. Rommel had sent the American prisoner of war to Eisenhower. He congratulated the field marshal. The question was, how much had he told the American?

"All the *Leutnant* knows is that he is to establish contact with Eisenhower and Montgomery," he said, irritated at being interrogated by his own chief of staff, "and to request their cooperation. Then he is to bring me the reply."

Speidel pushed his glasses up on his nose and fussed with some papers he was holding. Could the American be trusted?

Rommel thought about Speigner's worn appearance, his beard stubble, his alert, questioning stare while he wolfed down the chocolates. "It has been a long time since I saw him. He seems little changed by prison. These Americans! Where do they get their optimism?"

"Thomas Edison and Henry Ford." Speidel glanced at his pocket watch. "Is everyone coming to the meeting?"

Neither of the generals had canceled as far as Rommel knew. He went to the door and called Lange. It was imperative to use a route that bypassed checkpoints. After a moment Lange appeared.

"This just came in, Herr Generalfeldmarschall." The aide handed him a decoded radio transmission. He scanned the sheet, then gave it to Speidel. It was a transcription of a message broadcast over the BBC radio, the first verse from Paul Verlaine's poem, *Chanson d'Automne*, which read: "*Les sanglots longs des violons de l'automne,*" the long sobs of the violins of autumn. This, according to intelligence reports, meant the French underground had been placed on alert. Speidel could not contain his elation. "The invasion could be any time, now!"

"Or two weeks, or two months. Who knows?" Rommel was irritated at his chief of staff. Hans pushed too hard. They disagreed about the intelligence. Rommel suspected that the British had planted it. They had turned the airwaves into their own "spook" division. Hadn't Admiral Canaris, head of "Abwehr," Wehrmacht military intelligence, paid an informer for this information? He would believe that the tip was valid when OKW placed Army Group B on alert. Lange reported that Fifteenth Army intelligence officer, Lt. Colonel Meyer, had contacted von Rundstedt but so far nothing had come down from OKW.

"No general alert?"

"*Nein, mein Herr.*"

An alert would keep them at their stations, forcing him to cancel the generals' midnight rendezvous. Speidel had invited General von Stulpnagel, Military Governor of France, and General von Falkenhausen, Military Governor of Belgium and Northern France. Since an alert had not yet been received, Speidel pressed him. Shouldn't they get going?

Lange went to bring the car around. Speidel telephoned Vice-Admiral Ruge to meet them. In fifteen minutes they were on their way. To avoid detection, Lange drove with the lights off.

The heavy touring car struck potholes, bounced and swayed over roads whose surfaces had been roughed up by halftracks. On either side, tall hedgerows blocked out what little moonlight filtered through the clouds.

The meeting place was a crossroads convenient to all parties. If they were discovered, their cover would be that this was a planning session. A company of panzer-grenadiers was handling security. They had been told to watch for French partisans, though it was the Gestapo that Rommel wanted to keep at bay. A tent had been set up in the forest. It had a thick black lining in accordance with blackout regulations. Red lanterns provided minimum lighting. The military governors had arrived. General von Stulpnagel, impatient as always, was anxious to get started. He was keyed up about Verlaine's poem, though the others disagreed about its significance. At the very least, Rommel observed, it lent a sense of urgency to the proceedings.

"We will speak of poetry after the war," he said. The laughter broke the tension. The old war dogs! he thought. They smelled invasion. He could see it in their faces. To be with them was like breathing oxygen. He apologized for being the last to arrive. "Fighter-bombers knocked out two bridges. We were obliged to go out of our way. I thank you for coming."

Speaking English, as was the fashion among the generals, he told them about the meeting with Sepp Dietrich. Stulpnagel and Falkenhausen congratulated him. "Dietrich is aboard! I never doubted it," Stulpnagel crowed.

Rommel came straight to the subject. "There are those who are for an assassination," he said, "but let us consider the effects. A *coup d'etat* could cause dissension in the ranks. The Eastern front could collapse, the very thing we must prevent. The Führer has promised miracle weapons–"

They groaned and complained. He raised his hand. "It's no joking matter. If Hitler can convince the officer cadre that they can battle their way to a truce, why should they support a coup? To achieve stalemate could result in an honorable surrender."

"Yes, *if* the Führer would go along, but of course he will not," Falkenhausen remarked.

Stulpnagel, who made no bones about killing Hitler, addressed Rommel as the Führer were already dead. "The people believe in you. In case of a rebellion, you would have the confidence and esteem of the German people."

He was against assassination. "Let us not make a martyr of Hitler. If he were arrested and brought to trial, the German people would see that he is guilty of war crimes and subject to international law."

Stulpnagel's ironic laughter cut him off. He imagined the sentries outside saying, Those generals are *verruckt*–crazy! Stulpnagel said, "The little corporal is doomed and he knows it."

Speidel observed that if the Führer showed *any* sign of going along with a surrender, they could proceed at once to contact western leaders. Rommel saw that Hans was a brilliant actor. No one in the room suspected that initial contact had already been made.

"The Führer has agreed to see me," Rommel said. There was a respectful silence. "I am flying to Berlin tomorrow. Among other things, I intend to ask for command of all reserve divisions in France."

Falkenhausen asked him to emphasize the military and political realities. "Tell the Führer we must have land-sea-and-air coordination. Also, access to the latest intelligence."

Stulpnagel renewed his tirade. "He'll *never* give up control. Divide and conquer is his meat and potatoes. None of us commands more than a few divisions. Rundstedt says that the only order he can give with confidence is to relieve the sentry outside his door!"

He told them not to give up hope. He would do his best to bring Hitler around. The Führer claimed to be all things to all people. On a good day he had been known to give his generals what they wanted.

VIII

Berlin traffic stopped for the Desert Fox. A driver rolled down his window and asked for an autograph. Motorists did not seem to mind waiting for him to cross the street. Not a horn was honked. Always it was "*Rommel will see us through! Rommel will save us!*" A modern Siegfried had risen to save Germany. Hitler and Goebbels had turned him into an icon. The tragedy was that the people swallowed such propaganda.

He entered the Reich Chancellery. The taint of death was everywhere. The polished marble floors reminded him of a mausoleum. He took the stairs two at a time. Hitler's staff stopped what they were doing. He returned their salutes and reported to Hitler's charge d'affaires, an SS lieutenant who invited him to take a seat in the waiting room. The Führer was receiving phone calls and would see the Herr Generalfeldmarschall as soon as he had finished.

In the waiting room he paced back and forth, drawing stares from a well-dressed couple. A pall of trouble hung over them. He avoided their furtive glances, afraid they would tell him that their relatives had been sent to a concentration camp, or how much it had cost to buy their way into Hitler's presence. The woman kept staring as if she wished to say, "My dear General, would you help us?" It was unusual for private citizens to gain an audience. The man looked like an industrialist, perhaps a banker. Rommel feigned interest in a news magazine, flipping pages only to discover a picture of himself on the beach in Normandy. In the background were the bewildered French girls.

Until now he had never requested a private meeting. Hitler would be suspicious. His favorite pastime was outsmarting his generals. He lived to control OKW and keep them guessing. For Rommel to approach him was like placing an advertisement in the *Berliner Morgenpost*.

"Herr Generalfeldmarschall, come this way."

The distraught couple tried to catch his eye as the SS lieutenant ushered him into an inner office. After a few minutes a door opened abruptly. Hitler came striding into the room. Rommel saluted like the gladiator he was. "*Heil, Hitler*!" The Führer greeted him effusively, smiling and pulling on his ear in a show of goodwill.

Greetings, Herr Field Marshal, so nice to see you. How is Frau Rommel?

Very well, thank you, mein Führer.

"It has been too long since we were together." The dark circles under the Führer's eyes said otherwise. Was he expecting Rommel to ask about the resettlement camps, or what was happening to the Jews? The Führer looked like a raccoon, furtive and wild.

"Would you like something to eat or drink? A coffee, perhaps?"

He shook his head, smiling, playing the golden boy. Since the campaign in Poland, Hitler had showered him with promotions, praise, medals. Then the defeat in North Africa. Hitler had sent him home on indefinite leave. When given the chance to command the western defenses, he'd jumped at it. The Führer had never mentioned North Africa again but spoke only of the future. The present with any luck would slide by before people caught on.

How is the mine-laying going?

Very well, mein Führer.

Are you getting what you need?

What the Führer needed was something to enthuse over. Rommel reported laying Czech mines, millions of them, from Denmark to France. Furthermore, he had mounted thousands of French artillery rounds on posts in the surf. Anti-glider obstacles had been constructed of timber from the forests of Brittany and Normandy.

"*Gut, gut, wunderbar.*"

He neglected to mention that if there had been adequate supplies, he would not be forced to improvise. The eastern front was funneling off desperately needed munitions and vehicles, but back to good news.

"I have built two dummy fortifications for every real one!" This tactic had served him well in Africa, though he could not speak of that continent. "It is a quite efficient way to draw off the bomb attacks. It makes our defenses appear twenty percent larger. The enemy is bombing these empty artillery emplacements even as we speak."

Were there any other successes, limited or otherwise? Hitler's eyes never left his face. All he could think of was the breakdown in the chain of command. If communications were not streamlined, when the invasion came there would be chaos–something the mad corporal knew a great deal about.

Speidel, on the hill overlooking the Seine, had asked, "*Who* will succeed Hitler?" And Ruge looking pointedly at Rommel had replied, "I thought that had been settled."

"The only thing I'm certain of is that the attack will not come at the Pas de Calais." Hitler seized on this popular topic. Were not he and the Desert Fox fellow strategists? He went to a map table. Maps did not talk back. If only generals were as polite. Rommel noticed the Channel Islands on the map. He could not hold back a grievance.

"*Mein, Führer,* I am opposed to garrisoning these uninhabited islands. They have no strategic value. The allies will wipe out our troops, and for what purpose? Those units are needed elsewhere."

Hitler changed the subject. He had been much encouraged by the progress of jet plane manufacture. In a few months the sky would be filled with a thousand jet fighters. The Luftwaffe would launch an aerial blitzkrieg *the likes of which the world had never seen*! He paused as if acknowledging the roar of the masses.

Don't let him smother you with half-facts, Speidel had warned.

"Speaking of the Luftwaffe," Rommel said, remembering his promise to Falkenhausen, "how are we to call in air strikes during a battle? We must have coordination between the Luftwaffe and Panzer divisions. We lack even the most rudimentary radio call system!"

Hitler clasped his hands behind his back. The subject did not interest him. He remarked that this was best left to Göring.

"Perhaps we might stage a joint training maneuver to practice coordinating air/ground attacks–"

"How is the morale among the ground troops?" Hitler interjected.

He admitted that it was fairly good, considering how few battle-tested troops he had. Some poorly equipped infantry divisions reminded him of the First World War when the army relied on horses for transport. In a combat situation they would be, practically speaking, immobile. Hitler took a deep breath, hanging on. "Our jets will wipe out their air force in a week. Then you will be all smiles. *I can tell you that.*"

Don't discount the faith the people have in you, Stulpnagel had said.

Hitler turned to the map. There must be something on which they could agree. Rommel noticed how close the V-bomb launching sites were to the Allied staging areas on the south coast of England. He suggested that the V-rockets might be fired at the enemy launching docks to disrupt preparations for the invasion.

No, no, the rockets are not accurate enough to hit the docks. We must use them only against a large population area.

It might make them think twice.

If we targeted the docks, the rockets would fall into the sea. The enemy would see that we cannot control them.

Stulpnagel had been just as persistent. "In case of a rebellion the Herr Generalfeldmarschall will enjoy the confidence and esteem of the German people."

He indicated where reserve divisions were stationed, then pointed to coastal areas where he wished to move them. Hitler refused to look at the map. It was proving treacherous. Guderian and Geyr von Sweppenberg wanted the panzer divisions stationed inland.

Divide and conquer, Stulpnagel said, Hitler's meat and potatoes.

The panzer reserves had to be held back. There was no other way. OKW, the Führer argued, had agreed with von Rundstedt's plan to wait until *after* the landings to counterattack in force. He reminded Rommel that in the beginning he had been willing to position reserves near the beaches. Had he not given Rommel command over Panzer divisions 2, 21, and 116? "Guderian and von Sweppenberg were opposed to letting you have them, but I did not listen!" he added magnanimously.

Guderian, in Rommel's opinion, had made a mess of preparing for the western invasion. His experience at the Russian front had not prepared him for what was happening in France. In Russia, Guderian enjoyed air superiority. Now the Americans and British controlled the skies. Without the Luftwaffe, Guderian's theories were hogwash. Of course, there was nothing to be gained by dredging this up, though he felt obliged to warn the Führer that the reserves would be pinned down by constant bombardment.

Hitler spun on his heel, went to the window. The rooftops of Berlin were gray with dust and debris. Even here, the bombing was becoming frequent.

The corporal is doomed and he knows it, Stulpnagel had said.

He was gathering his nerve to broach the subject of *surrender* when the Führer launched into a discussion of the eastern front. The Russians could be vulnerable to an all-or-nothing counter-attack!

No one in his right mind wants the war to drag on until Germany is utterly destroyed, Sepp Dietrich had said.

In dealing with men and gaining their loyalty Hitler was a genius. When a general agreed with him the Führer invited him to a staff meeting, and at the right moment would casually ask how he felt about strategy. When the general said what Hitler wanted, the Führer would disagree, playing devil's advocate, saying what all the other generals were thinking. The general would then press his case, with Hitler reluctantly conceding: *I have been afraid to take that step, but if you are so strongly in favor I suppose I shall have to go along.* If he had been a general in the regular army, Rommel thought, his specialty would have been strategic withdrawal.

He suddenly burst out, "Exigency plans must be made for a surrender." He could not believe he had said it.

"*Horseshit*!" Hitler said with his back turned.

He hurried on before he lost his nerve. "Why not negotiate a surrender in the west with the provision that we be allowed to defend our eastern boundary? That is the logical thing to do."

Hitler jerked as though stabbed.

"I am not saying we should *do* it," he said diplomatically. "Only that we should discuss it."

Hitler began to sway tipsily. He tottered to the table and beat the treacherous map with his fist. "*Nein, nein, nein*!" Then he turned to the window as if nothing had happened.

What was it the British commando had said? "When the war is over, I hope and trust that you will be chosen the new leader of Germany. There's no one better suited..." (Suited or *equipped*?)

"My generals desert me in my darkest hour." Hitler rushed on before Rommel could contradict him, "Don't they know that their Führer has Germany's interests at heart? Have we come so far to falter now that our goal is within reach? Our scientists and arms manufacturers slave day and night to produce miracle weapons to turn the tide. Germany surrender? *Niemals, niemals, niemals*! Never! Talk of surrender is rank insubordination. I forbid it, do you hear? Traitors must be shot. No, they do not deserve shooting-too easy-they must be flushed like rats from the gutter and poisoned."

How many of our people must die? Stulpnagel had said.

Hitler stared out the window, hypnotized by his own rhetoric. Rommel saw that the frenzy was a hoax. Here was Hitler's miracle weapon. It had to be used sparingly. He had to ration his frenzies.

"If I thought I had let you down," Rommel said, "I would tender my resignation."

Rage pooled behind the flat gaze, sank beneath the surface, sub-rosa, gathering force. "*Get out, leave me. I have nothing more to say.*" Rommel bowed and left. In the outer office, voices echoed in the hallways. Clerks calmly went about their duties. They had to have heard the Führer screaming, yet here they were, filing papers, following routine, mindless fury all in a day's work. He went down the double staircase. Here were heroic sculptures and soaring archways. Swastikas were plastered everywhere. There had been a time when such trappings excited him.

In the beginning, his star on the rise, all that mattered was to join the Führer's circle. They had become close, or what passed for close, back-slapping that ceased the moment the door closed. After the invasion of Poland, Hitler had given him a panzer division. He had allowed himself to believe that the Führer was a visionary, capable of restoring Germany to its former glory. Was that not what they were fighting for, to set European geography, unnaturally altered at Versailles, to rights? Like a draft horse plowing a straight furrow Rommel obeyed orders, fought for his country, asked no questions. Now he knew there was a higher responsibility. *I think I speak for many of the chaps when I say we admire your leadership, sir.*

IX

Before the MPs locked him into "Quarantine," a barracks run by counter-intelligence, he was issued a safety razor, soap, towel and a change of clothing including underwear and socks-all olive drab except the towel. The abundance overwhelmed him. He got high on the smell of new cloth. How could the supply sergeant take such bounty for granted? He felt guilty having a whole bar of soap to himself. There was a shower stall at the end of the corridor next to his room. *There was nobody else in there!* He stayed in the shower so long an MP knocked on the stall and asked if he was okay. After he toweled off and changed, he remembered that time was against him. He would not sleep until the message was delivered to Eisenhower. The bed however with its clean sheets, real pillows, a mattress from heaven, was a magnet. As soon as his head hit the pillow, he plummeted... *down.*

A tapping began. In the POW barracks someone was always rattling the straw, turning over, scratching, cursing lice. This tapping had a persistence all its own. He opened one eye, half-expecting to see a woodpecker or squirrel. A face appeared at the glass transom over the door. *Anna.* He got up, dragged a chair to the door and climbed on it. "What are you doing?"

"Standing on a telephone stand."

"How did you find me?"

"Open the transom. There's a latch on your side."

He opened it. They shook hands through the narrow opening. She asked if he could open the door from the inside. He asked if she were kidding. They were immediately on their old footing as fellow mavericks. McAlpin, a reporter for *The Times*, had been the first female correspondent at the Egyptian front. He had been assigned liaison duty with Eighth Army primarily because he had known Rommel before the war. Having spent a night in the desert with her, he did not find it strange to resume their acquaintance through a transom.

"Did the *Times* fire you?"

"I volunteered for the Women's Royal Navy Service. It's not as if millions of readers awaited my next column!"

"How did you get past the guards?"

"My sexy WREN cohort is chatting up the white helmets. They think I'm in the loo. What sort of fix are you in?"

He pulled his thoughts back to the present and told about the POW camp, Rommel springing him, sending him across the Channel to contact Eisenhower. Unfortunately he had run up against a stubborn major. He thought she would be pleased at the prospects of a ceasefire, perhaps even offer to help. She frowned, unpredictable as ever. "It's still a game, isn't it! One would have thought that being a POW would have improved, or perhaps seasoned, your outlook."

Once, in Cairo, they had taken a taxi to the pyramids. It was a long ride past the villages clustered along the Nile. They got out and walked across the sand and stood under the hulking mass of Cheops. He thought he might get lucky. Instead, she had lectured him about the war. Two armies fought, ate and slept under the same sky as if it were a sandlot game of football. Desert rats and foxes couldn't see the war for the sand. He saw that nothing had changed. She was still a burr under his saddle.

"I'm in a helluva bind." Not knowing what else to say, he started to climb down from the chair.

"Wait, you know *me*," she apologized. "Not exactly the world's most diplomatic person. Go on, tell me the rest."

He pushed the oak leaves decoration through the transom.

"Rommel gave me this patch right off his uniform, as identification. If it could be shown to a general…"

"Which one?"

"Eisenhower, preferably. Failing that, anything above major."

She examined the insignia, turning the patch over as if critical of the stitching. The night when they stood under the great lion's head rearing up out of the sand, she had observed, *Rommel makes a game of war. He makes war seem an honorable affair, a chess match in the desert, when in fact it is a vicious circle of mayhem and death.*

Remembering this, he said as if picking up where they'd left off, "Rommel has changed. He wants to surrender to the west. He wants to save his country. The Germans are terrified of Stalin."

"I don't see what *I* can do." She returned the patch. He pushed it back.

"Show it to a general."

"Max…"

"I don't have the right to ask, but they're not letting me go until they get tired of grilling me. In the meantime, a lot of men are going to get killed. You have a knack for getting into places you aren't supposed to be."

She gave him a skeptical glance. A woman called from downstairs, "Anna, are you coming?"

She looked at Rommel's patch again. A small grin tugged at her mouth. Encouraged, he said, "You can do it. Just be yourself, the world's most stubborn person." He was remembering a night in a pup tent, lost in the desert. He had not realized until that moment how starved for ordinary conversation he was.

"I'll see if I can talk my way into SHAEF."

"What's shafe?"

"You *have* been out of pocket! It's where Ike hangs his hat-Supreme Headquarters Allied Expeditionary Forces. Near Portsmouth. I can motor there in an hour."

He knew she hated war and everything about it but she was his best hope. "You don't think Rommel is sincere. Believe me. He's ready to end the war." She started to get down. He called to her, "If not Ike, find another general."

"Right, no majors!" She jumped off the stand.

"Rommel sends his regards and asks Ike to accept him as spokesman for the German army in France!"

In the Libyan desert, their vehicle had hit a mine stranding them fifty miles behind enemy lines. They had no choice but to start walking with half a canteen of water, the sun scorching. She had struck out across the dunes as if going to a picnic. He watched her through the transom as she put on her courier's helmet, tucked her hair inside it and disappeared down the stairwell. From the bottom of the stairs came a disapproving murmur. The guards had figured out where she'd been. Heavy footsteps sounded on the stairs. He closed the transom, stepped down and placed the chair beside the bed.

X

She parked the motorbike in front of Southwick House and went in. Sentries in white helmets, belts and leggings, accustomed to seeing WREN couriers, allowed her to enter with only a cursory check. She reported to the SHAEF reception desk. She took off her helmet and shook out her hair. The sergeant behind the counter looked up. "Which heaven did you fly down from, sweetheart?"

"One man's heaven is another's hell." She held the pouch

close. “Message for General Eisenhower!” The sergeant wanted to sign for it. “The general’s eyes only.”

He pushed the courier ledger at her. For “receiver” she wrote *General Eisenhower.* For “assignee” she wrote *8th Army MI.* He waved her through. She pretended to know where to go, though she’d never ventured past the reception desk. At the end of a long corridor, she blindly turned left and chose a door with a sentry. The sign over the door read “SHAEF - Chief of Staff.” The MP obligingly opened the door. She entered. A captain seated behind a desk glanced up with a frown that told her no WREN courier had ever been inside.

“Message for General Eisenhower.”

He motioned to her to put the pouch on the desk.

“His eyes only!” She used her most official tone.

The captain seemed irritated. “Who from?”

She forgot what she’d written. “G-2, sir!”

“It says here 'Eighth Army Intelligence.'” The captain pushed his swivel chair back and regarded her uniform and insignia. “Open the pouch.”

“General’s eyes only!” she pleaded. “Number One Priority.”

He rose, towering over her. Just then a major, less imposing, emerged from an inner office.

“Delivery for General Eisenhower!” she repeated.

“Ike’s eyes only,” the captain said sarcastically.

“I’m General Smith’s adjutant,” the major said, adding, “General Bedell Smith, Chief of Staff. Can I help you?”

“Priority delivery.” She looked him straight in the eye. “Marked immediate attention, *sir.*”

“This is cockamamie,” the captain complained. “*She* can’t barge in here…”

“What’s in it?” the major said.

If she refused to open the dispatch, they might turn her away, or call the MPs. She unbuckled the straps and opened it. The major peered inside. There was a single letter-sized envelope addressed simply: *General Eisenhower.*

“Is it from Eighth Army or G-2?” the captain said.

“General Eisenhower is in a staff meeting,” the major said casually.

Here she was talking to a major despite Speigner’s instructions! She took a deep breath. She was delivering a special item for General Eisenhower from *Field Marshal Rommel.* Before they could throw her out, she told them that the item of interest came from an impeccable source, a U.S. Army intelligence officer whom Rommel personally released from a POW camp.

The captain threw up his hands. "What a *crock*!"

"Can you prove any of this?" the major asked. She appreciated his courteous manner. All majors were not alike.

"Please, sir, ring up 8th Army and ask for Research Section, Intelligence. They can confirm that the POW's name is Leftenant Speigner. He worked as a liaison officer with 8th Army in Cairo. That's where I met him. I wrote a story about him for the *Times*. I could dig it up for you, but at the moment it's very important to–"

"The *press*!" the captain said. "Always pushing to see the general."

"So, are you with the *Times*?" the major said.

"No, sir," she said anxiously. "Women's Royal Naval Service. I have identification. Would you like to see it?"

"These reporters will do anything," the captain muttered to himself.

"Please, you're jumping to conclusions. I was reporting for the *Times* in Cairo, but I signed on with WRNS after returning to Britain. *Sir*."

"Let's buzz security," the captain said.

She glanced hopefully at the major. The higher the rank, the more imagination. "That envelope," he said. "Is it sealed?"

She had left it unsealed for this possibility. She gave him the envelope. The captain peered over his shoulder. Rommel's oak leaves were inside. "What the hell?" the captain said.

"Less than twenty-four hours ago, that patch was on Field Marshal Rommel's uniform," she said with an air of authority. "He sent it with Leftenant Speigner as proof of his mission."

The captain pushed a buzzer. "This is Garrett at Chief of Staff. I need security on the double." She stared. What was this? The major had seemed so accommodating.

"I think I recognize this..." The major turned the patch over. "The oak leaves cluster to a gosh-darned Knight's Cross!"

"No way it's for real," the captain said. She suggested that they give it to General Eisenhower. Let him draw his own conclusions. The captain smiled without humor. "What do you think *we're* here for?"

"I must see General Eisenhower!" She raised her voice. "Him

or his chief of staff."

The major held the patch against his chest as if to see how it looked against olive drab. He and the captain both wore the flaming-sword patch of SHAEF. Heavy boots sounded in the hallway. Two MPs ducked their six-foot-plus frames under the low door frame. She began yelling at the top of her lungs, "*General Eisenhower, General Eisenhower*!" The MPs seized her by the arms, but she would not be silenced. "I have a message for General Eisenhower from *Field Marshal Erwin Rommel–*" The MPs started to haul her off. "*Message for Ike from the Desert Fox*!" she shrieked.

The door to an inner office opened. The MPs held her above the floor, feet dangling. A colonel came into the room, followed by a general. Both wore the flaming-sword patch. "I must see General Eisenhower right away!" she exclaimed, writhing between the MPs The major began apologizing to the general.

"What's going on out there?" a voice called. She recognized the famous, midwest accent. The officers squared their shoulders and stood at attention. Dwight D. Eisenhower appeared in the doorway. He looked smaller than he did in the newsreels. "What the heck is this?" he said.

The MPs set her down. The captain took responsibility. He hated to bother the general with a minor matter. This woman was not what she appeared to be. She was probably with *The London Times*. Dwarfed by the MPs, she awaited Eisenhower's ruling.

"What do you make of this, sir?" The major presented the oak leaves insignia. Eisenhower examined it, then gave it to his chief of staff.

"German," he noted. "I've seen it somewhere but I can't place it."

"Knight's Cross, highest commendation for valor the Nazis give," the major explained, pleased with himself. "The oak leaves cluster to the Knight's Cross."

"By golly, that's right," Eisenhower said thoughtfully.

"The courier claims Rommel sent it," the major said, cutting off the captain's protest. "According to her, this leftenant-I mean, *lieutenant*, one of ours-allegedly brought it from France."

Eisenhower studied the patch. "You know, Auchinleck warned the Eighth Army to stop thinking of Rommel as some kind of superman. They were giving away a psychological advantage before the first shot."

"I remember," General Smith said.

"Rommel had them against the wall," Eisenhower added.

They were chatting as if she were not present. This was better than being thrown out but just barely. It irritated her to see them clucking over the patch like headhunters with a shrunken head. "Where is he?" Eisenhower said.

She said, "Pardon?" as the major simultaneously said, "Excuse me?"

"The *lieutenant*."

This simple question took the captain and major by surprise. They had not thought to ask.

"He's being interrogated by U.S. counter-intelligence," she said, realizing as she spoke that this could get Speigner in trouble. "They are housing him in a...secure area."

He's under house arrest?

It's only temporary.

He crossed the Channel?

Yes, sir.

Alone?

I think so.

When?

This morning before daybreak. Sir, he has an urgent message...

"General, I apologize for interrupting your briefing," the captain broke in. "We can handle this."

Eisenhower nodded at McAlpin as if to say, Let her finish. She told him that Field Marshal Rommel sent his regards and wished to know if General Eisenhower would accept him as spokesman for the German army.

"For what purpose?"

"Surrender...*sir*."

Eisenhower dismissed the MPs. After they had left the room, he turned to her and said, "Young lady, are you sure this patch actually came from Rommel himself?"

Hope made her dizzy. "If the general would bring the Leftenant here, he could deliver the field marshal's message himself and explain everything, *sir*."

The major pulled a reference book off a shelf and was thumbing through it. "Here you go, sir!" he told Eisenhower. "It's the oak leaves to the Knight's Cross."

The generals examined the book and compared the illustration to the patch. Eisenhower turned to her. "When Rommel says 'accept *him* as spokesman,' does that mean he's operating on his own? Without Hitler's approval?"

Speigner had not gone into this. "Sir, you'd need to ask the Leftenant."

"Jodl and Rundstedt run the Wehrmacht," General Smith observed. "Assuming this is on the level, I don't think Rommel could go over their heads, certainly not without Hitler's approval."

"Sir, assuming this patch did come from Rommel, the message could be legit," the major said. "On the other hand, Rommel could be stalling. He's not one to surrender unless there's no way out."

The captain stood on tiptoe to get everyone's attention. "What about the SS? They're not under the field marshal's command."

Eisenhower asked Smith how many SS divisions there were. "In France?" Smith said. "At least three that I know of."

Who did these big, arrogant Yanks think they were? She had placed the olive branch at their feet and they were stamping on it. These saviors of planet earth-overfed, oversized, oversexed-held England's fate in their hands! They had not seen half as much death and destruction as the British yet here they came with their industrial might and gross national optimism. Maybe this was the only kind of warrior who could defeat Hitler. One who had never known defeat. General Eisenhower reminded her of John Wayne, the screen actor, riding into one of those vast American sunsets that stunned the imagination, *clippity-clop, clippity-clop*, wind in his face, cool and cocksure, polite to a fault-the innocent, arrogant champion of western civilization.

He said, "Tell your lieutenant we'll take it under consideration, but Counter-Intelligence is better equipped to handle enemy contact."

He turned to go. His staff stood at ease.

"Please, sir, may I have the patch back?"

The major, who was comparing the patch to his reference book, looked up. "*Why*?"

"I'd like to present it," she said regally, "to the Prime Minister."

There was surprised silence. Eisenhower chuckled. They burst out laughing. The generals returned to their inner office.

The major returned the patch, the captain watching ironically, his arms crossed. He opened the door, leaned into the hallway and spoke with the guards.

"The MPs checked out her story," he reported. "The lieutenant is under house arrest but there ain't no record that the little lady speaks for him."

"I assure you I am not making this up!" she said.

The captain wanted to detain her and inform the Royal Navy. The major, irritated at losing the patch but still courteous, opened the door. She was free to go. As she left, the captain called after her, "Give my regards to Sir Winston!" Their laughter echoed down the corridor.

XI

The meeting of general officers was being held at La Roche-Guyon. Its central location made travel convenient for all of them except Falkenhausen, who was driving from Belgium. Air travel was too dangerous. OKW had issued a directive that no generals were to fly. Stulpnagel was coming from Paris, Geyr von Steppenburg from Abbeville. It was crucial that they be of one mind. The *Kriegsspiel*, in which they matched wits and tried to predict the Allied landings, was a ploy. The real reason for the meeting was to discuss the ceasefire.

"Why bring in Geyr? He'll only argue against a coup." Speidel was poised to scratch von Steppenburg off the list.

"If push comes to shove, I want him on my side," Rommel said.

Ruge seconded Speidel's reservations. He was worried about including Falkenhausen, given his record of shooting Belgian hostages. That was regrettable, Rommel said, but they could hardly proceed without the military governor of Belgium. Later they could give him a lesser role. He hated these deceptions but such was politics. Hitler's divide-and-conquer strategy-limiting generals' authority and keeping them off balance-had made politicians of them all.

The *Kriegsspiel* had been set up in his study. A map of western France was laid out on a table. A second table was for hats, batons, swagger sticks and briefcases. A third was set with a silver coffee service and refreshments. As he waited for the officers, he checked the latest information on allied troop movements. A Luftwaffe pilot reported increased activity from Portsmouth to Weymouth. Many ships had been seen massing offshore. The invasion was days if not hours away.

"I will take you all on," he greeted the arriving generals. "Consider me the Tommy High Command." Falkenhausen and Stulpnagel were in high spirits. They teased Rommel for "hogging" the British command structure. *Shall we call him "Monty"?* Geyr greeted him perfunctorily. Both were Wurttembergers but with deep differences.

Tall, elegant Leo Geyr von Sweppenburg was a member of the Wehrmacht's old-boy club, a *grand seigneur* like Field Marshal von Rundstedt. A cavalryman famous for competing in horse races, he was one of the first panzer commanders when the German cavalry converted to armor. Along with Field Marshal Guderian, he was Rommel's major rival on the general staff. Rommel held no brief against Geyr or any of the noblemen, yet it rankled when Geyr was given command of Panzer Group West, a reserve force. Guderian supported Geyr's view that a central force should be held in reserve between Paris and the coast to counterattack after the landings.

On March 29, in his first meeting with Geyr after assuming command of Army Group West, Rommel lost his temper. "I am an experienced tank commander. You and I do not see eye to eye. I refuse to work with you, anymore. I propose to draw the appropriate conclusions." The aristocratic Geyr, always correct, saluted and left. Neither had forgotten.

"Erwin prefers to attack," Falkenhausen mocked. "I think he would not mind fighting alongside Patton."

"Why must we fight with one hand tied behind our back?" Stulpnagel complained. "The Bohemian corporal will never give up command of the reserves. We will not be able to defend France until we solve the problem in Berlin."

Rommel did not want Stulpnagel to get started. He would talk all night about Hitler. An intellectual, a debater and political strategist, Stulpnagel had been the chairman of the German-French Armistice Commission after France fell in 1940. He commanded the 17th Army during the invasion of the Soviet Union in 1941. A year later he was appointed military governor in Paris, and promptly crossed swords with the Nazi regime, protesting seizure of Jewish property by Alfred Rosenberg, Reich Minister for the Eastern Occupied Territories. From the beginning Stulpnagel had been a firebrand in his opposition to Hitler.

Falkenhausen, at 66 the senior member of the group, was more discreet. Bald, wearing rimless spectacles, he, too, was an aristocrat. Like Rommel he had won the Pour le Merite for extraordinary courage. After the Great War he commanded the School of Infantry at Dresden, where Rommel had been one of his students. From 1934-39 he had served as military adviser to Chiang Kai-shek.

Stulpnagel tried to draw Ruge off to one side and engage him in a one-sided discussion about Hitler's folly. Rommel started the map exercise. "Gentlemen, deploy your forces!"

Falkenhausen and Geyr positioned their infantry and panzer divisions, placing flags along the coastline from Belgium to Cherbourg. The flags had weighted bottoms and could be moved like chess pieces. Speidel was the referee. Rommel, getting into the spirit of the game, advised him to take into consideration Allied air supremacy when the reserves were committed. Geyr protested that the invasion had not begun and already "the British" were trying to subvert the reserves. He complained that Rommel was using his influence with the referee. Stulpnagel moodily pushed flags about as if he would rather be sticking pins in a voodoo doll of Hitler.

As Rommel expected, Geyr held Panzer Group West back from the coast, whereas 12 SS Panzer (*Hitlerjugend*) was scattered inland and 2 Panzer was fifty miles from the vulnerable Somme sector. The Allied bombers would cut them to shreds before they reached the embattled coastal defenders. He could see the battle raging. Instead of flags he envisioned tanks, artillery emplacements and panzer-grenadiers dug in and waiting. He knew the conditions of the roads, where the vulnerable intersections were, which divisions were short of equipment, which were under-manned.

"I shall split my forces and move these divisions south into

Normandy," Falkenhausen proposed. Rommel reminded him to look out for Patton. "His army is poised across the Channel from the Pas de Calais. Can half your force stop him?" Falkenhausen moved his flags nearer to Calais.

Rommel asked Stulpnagel if he were ready for the invasion. Had he not positioned 116 Panzer and Panzer Lehr divisions too far inland? Stulpnagel protested that he was only following von Rundstedt's orders. These divisions could counterattack and turn the tide.

"I doubt it!" Rommel said. "Hitler would have to be convinced to release them, and that takes time."

"Hitler is the noose around our necks!" Stulpnagel burst out.

Geyr could not hold back. "I am most afraid of an airborne landing deep inside France. My forces must remain in a position to crush the paratroopers before they link up with the main force on the beaches."

Rommel took his time replying. "In my experience, we have destroyed enemy airborne troops every time they landed behind our lines. It is better to concentrate all forces on the *coast* and keep the enemy from landing his armor. As long as we hold the coast, the airborne assault, though it may have some incidental effect of disrupting communications and inhibiting troop movement, must end in the destruction of the enemy paratroopers. They will be cut off from their main force."

"I *know* the British," Geyr said stiffly. "I worked with them before the war. I believe they will attack here, farther inland, with airborne glider troops."

"Excuse me, general," Rommel responded. "You knew the British in peacetime. I knew them in war. They are winning because of their *airpower.* Enemy air supremacy makes it *impossible* to send massed panzer reinforcements into the battle!"

"I shall move my tanks at night."

"If you had been in Africa you would know that the British have flares that burn like a midnight sun." Geyr remained silent. "Let us proceed!"

When their flags were all set, the others stood back and waited for him to place his battle markers denoting the allied divisions. He walked around the table and picked up a British Eighth Army flag. No jokes or sarcastic remarks, now. Where the Allies would attack was everyone's greatest concern.

"The invasion begins here..." He planted the flag on the coast south of La Havre, near Bayeux. "In *Normandy*!"

Stulpnagel snorted with amusement. Falkenhausen rapped the table impatiently. Geyr shrugged. Rommel pointed at their flags. No reserve division was in position to counterattack at the stretch of coastline he had selected.

"You did not anticipate this," he said.

He began to narrate the *faux invasion* in the clipped voice of a "Movietone News" commentator:

"*Zero hour. The allies begin their naval bombardment. Their landing boats stream in toward the beaches. The German panzer divisions are pinned down and helpless, their infantry cowering in their bunkers and foxholes. On the beaches, Allied demolition squads efficiently blow up the underwater obstacles, one by one.*"

"How can they, when they're underwater!" Geyr protested.

He grinned. "Pardon, we came at low tide."

The others started moving their flags toward the critical sector. He quickly brought to Speidel's attention that the necessary routes were covered by Allied fighters. Their convoys would be bombed and strafed to pieces. Speidel advised Generals Geyr and Stulpnagel to stop moving their flags forward.

"Their divisions were too far inland," Rommel observed mildly.

Stulpnagel exploded, "If Hitler were dead, we would not have that problem!"

Rommel resumed a Movietone narration: "*The English and Americans continue to flood ashore. The beach batteries are overrun. Russian troops are surrendering in droves. They were boiling tea in their samovars and doing laundry when the attack commenced. The allied infantry is pouring inland. There is nothing the Germans can do about it.*"

"Shall we surrender?" Falkenhausen said.

Rommel crossed his arms in embarrassment. In his enthusiasm to win the game he had neglected the real reason for the meeting. The generals listened as he informed them of his intentions to present to von Rundstedt, at the earliest opportunity, a detailed plan to overthrow Hitler. He had drawn up a list of general officers qualified to negotiate with the Allies. The team would consist of Stulpnagel, Geyr, Speidel and Ruge. They were to offer the following terms:

1) An immediate armistice, the German army to withdraw within its own borders and cease hostilities with the west.

2) The Wehrmacht would be allowed to hold a defensive line in the east against the Russians.

3) The Allies were to suspend their bombing.

4) Hitler would be arrested and tried for war crimes, the German population to be informed by radio.

5) The temporary head of government might be one of the two main leaders of the anti-Hitler resistance, either General Beck or Lord Mayor Goerdeler.

They murmured their approval. A few applauded. Stulpnagel expressed reservations that it could prove difficult to arrest Hitler, whereas *killing* him would save time. This was received in skeptical silence. Falkenhausen asked why he was not on the negotiating team. Rommel assured him that he would play a major role in the surrender.

"The Führer is not the only one with secret weapons," he said, tongue in cheek. "I have Ruge and Speidel!"

It would be bad luck to mention Leutnant Speigner. He had ordered his patrols to watch for an American "double agent," though he could not alert the entire Army Group. Such an order would filter back to Berlin within hours. There being no further discussion, Speidel noted that it was nearly 2300 hours. They all were no doubt ready to get back to their commands. "Wait," Rommel said. "We didn't complete the exercise. *Meine Herren*, are you willing to concede defeat?" He pointed at the map. "The invasion is twenty-four hours old. Are you beaten or not?"

Falkenhausen renewed his attempts to move 15th Army south to meet the threat, saying that since this was no feint he no longer needed to protect Calais. If Patton attacked, it would probably be a secondary attack. Rommel was pleased to remind him that General Salmuth was in command of Fifteen Army and was *still waiting* for Patton. Falkenhausen thought of 19 Panzer Division, stationed in Holland. He picked up the flag but before he could reposition it farther south, Rommel again intervened.

"Clausewitz," he reminded his former teacher, "*never* split his forces. You will not be strong at either end. Move all or none."

"*Wo ist Patton*?" Falkenhausen said irritably. "You have to tell us. Is First Army attacking in Normandy?"

"I do not have to tell you."

Falkenhausen stayed put. Neither Geyr nor Stulpnagel

could devise an alternative strategy. They watched helplessly as Rommel enlarged his beachhead, pushing inland in a wide front stretching from Carentan to Bayeux. Stulpnagel sluggishly moved up his reserves. Rommel intoned:

"Movietone News presents: 'Too little too late.' The airborne Tommies and Yanks hold the connecting roads while their fighters strafe the panzer convoys at will. The invasion has succeeded brilliantly. Berlin ponders what to do next!"

"Time is up," Speidel announced. "The Allies have established a beachhead."

"Element of surprise, *meine Herren*," said Rommel.

"Surely, weather and tide and moonlight will determine when they land," Stulpnagel argued. "The *Amis* have never invaded from the sea except at full moon and fair weather."

He would risk bad weather and high seas to get his forces ashore. Wouldn't Eisenhower? Geyr seized on the weather factor. "Cloud cover also aids my panzers in moving up to support the coastal defenses! Your British fighters are of no use without visibility."

"How long do clouds last?" he shot back. "The fighter pilots may get lucky if they circle long enough."

Stulpnagel said, "*Ach*, I thought your motto was shed sweat, not blood!"

Rommel thought of the American, perhaps on his way back at that very moment, on foot and alone. He jammed his hands in his pockets. "It helps to be lucky."

XII

The thick walls of Number 10 Downing Street muted the noise of street traffic. For all its aura of power and prestige the prime minister's office was more modest than she had imagined. Alone in the waiting room she looked at framed mementos: a picture of King George, a map of France, an honorary Ph.D.

degree from a Canadian college. She was just about to sit down when she smelled cigar smoke.

"*Sir*!" She came to attention and saluted.

The Prime Minister returned the salute with an airy wave. "I hear you have a report for me, young lady," he said, offering her a seat. She expected him to sit behind the desk, but he pulled up a chair facing her. She plunged into Rommel's message and how the field marshal had chosen Speigner to be his messenger. She avoided looking directly at the prime minister lest he observe her nervousness. She showed him the oak leaves patch. He examined it, chomping on his cigar.

"The Germans must use the same manufacturer for their medals as the French. Rommel is up to his tricks. He's given us fits, I can tell you. It's all we can do to stay abreast of new toys such as his 'Asparagus!' Since Hitler put him in charge, the Atlantic Wall has stiffened considerably."

She waited in respectful silence.

"You say the American was with Rommel. How do we know this?"

"He knew Rommel before the war and was captured while fighting the Germans in North Africa."

"I'm told this Speigner chap worked with Military Intelligence in Cairo."

"Yes, sir."

"You knew him?"

"Yes, sir, we met in Cairo."

"You can vouch that this is the same man, physically."

"Absolutely!"

He glanced at her in amusement. She caught the inference and pointedly added that she and the lieutenant had served together in the line of duty. He puffed on his cigar. It had gone out. He soberly picked at tobacco bits. "Weren't you reporting for the *Times*? I seem to remember a 'McAlpin' byline from Africa."

She was thrilled. "Yes, thank you, sir, that was me, I mean, that was I...yes...sir!"

"So you were acquainted with this American lieutenant," he prompted.

She explained how Speigner helped arrange clearance for her to tour the front lines, adding impulsively that she was the first female correspondent with the Eighth Army. "I confess I sometimes get awfully put out at the way men take to war, like ducks to water, especially the generals."

"Oh?" He took the cigar out of his mouth.

"Lieutenant Speigner and I had to cross a stretch of desert on foot. Our half-track hit a mine and we were stranded for twenty-four hours. We got into this heated argument about Rommel and General Auchinleck and everyone else. To them, the desert was a chessboard, a level playing field. War was only a game."

Churchill conceded it did appear that way, sometimes, and yet a game of the highest stakes. "Well, then, I am only a pawn," she said before she could stop herself.

"Not at all! This is vital information. I wouldn't have seen you, otherwise."

"Thank you, sir." She reached into her pocket. "Here is a dispatch from the *Times* in 1942."

He unfolded the newspaper clipping and swiftly scanned the contents.

YANK DIRECTS AMBUSH
OF AFRICA CORPS

by

Anna McAlpin

The Yanks have landed in North Africa, or at least in the person of Lt. Maxwell Speigner, U.S. Army Intelligence. Speigner enjoys the distinction of having met Field Marshal Rommel in America before the war. Rommel, then a colonel, was traveling with a small group of German general staff officers studying Civil War battlefields. Lt. Speigner escorted the German visitors to the battlefields of Shiloh and Brice's Crossroads. According to Speigner, the Desert Fox showed an especial interest in the flamboyant Confederate cavalryman, General Nathan B. Forrest, sometimes called 'The Wizard of the Saddle.'

A memo by Speigner anticipating Rommel's tactics during the invasion of France in 1940 received belated attention from British military intelligence. By comparing Rommel to Forrest, Speigner was able to predict some of the maneuvers Rommel used in the German march to the sea.

Sent to Cairo as a military observer, the American had an immediate impact, accurately forecasting the Sept. 14th raid on British supply dumps along the Egyptian-Libyan frontier.

> RAF fighters consequently were successful in bombing a panzer division caught in the act of loading captured materiel. The ambush was the first of several in which Rommel's Africa Corps was foiled, boosting morale of Western Desert Forces.
>
> In one of the odd coincidences of the war, the paths of these two soldiers who met in a neutral country have crossed again. Lt. Speigner is the toast of Cairo society and continues to advise the Eighth Army.

Churchill grunted as he read. He handed her the clipping. "Does your lieutenant believe Rommel wants to surrender?"

"He wouldn't be here otherwise, prime minister."

"There was a time," he confided, "when I was so obsessed with defeating Rommel that I considered it a personal test of wills. I long ago conceded that he was an audacious and brilliant general. Parliament received that remark with skeptical silence!" He added with a smile, "In war one is not encouraged to praise one's enemy. Well, what did General Eisenhower say?"

"Sir?"

"You reported this to Ike. What did he say?"

"Sir, he was not as forthcoming…"

"*He turned you down!* Ike is to be applauded for his prudence." Her heart sank until she realized the prime minister was expressing his view of human nature. "*However,* one can be too cautious. The times require us to consider every option."

She smiled hopefully. "I agree, Mr. Prime Minister."

He thought for a moment. "You were with the *Times* but now you've volunteered for courier duty. How is that?"

She replied honestly that she could be of more service in the WRNS than behind a desk.

"Rather partial to the navy, myself. Your lieutenant knows his man, does he?"

"Sir?"

"Rommel."

"Oh, yes. The Eighth Army chaps told me, in Cairo, that he knew more about Rommel than anyone."

"Fluent in German, I take it."

"Yes, sir. His parents are German."

"He was born in Germany?"

"In America. His family immigrated after the Great War."

He stood up heavily and went behind his desk, searching

in drawer after drawer, cigar clenched between his teeth. She could not believe she was not only at Number Ten Downing Street but that she felt at ease. Compared to the reception she had received from the Americans, Churchill was Father Albion-attentive, sympathetic, chomping on an unlit cigar.

"You wouldn't have a light? I suppose not." He flopped into his chair. "Rommel wants to end the fighting. Still, I imagine Herr Hitler will object strenuously. Where were we?"

She recounted what Speigner had said about Rommel appealing to the west because he feared Stalin.

"Don't trust the old bear, myself. Wouldn't it be spectacular if Rommel were to surrender before we invade France! I'm going to take a chance." He grabbed a memo pad and scribbled on it. "Take this to Eisenhower. I'll telephone him to say you are coming. Do you know where Special Services Branch is located?"

Her heart was pounding. Yes, she had delivered official pouches to Special Services. Churchill began to discuss logistics. How could Speigner be returned to France without alerting suspicion? If Rommel were operating on his own, he would not want the German army–the SS, especially–to intercept the American.

He stood up as if he thought more clearly on his feet. "Rommel is vulnerable. Can't trust the Nazi spy network. Word might get back to Berlin. He's downwind of Hitler but none of them are free of the stench. Truth be told, if Germany had enough tanks and aircraft he would probably fight on. That's all he knows. All any of them know. Point the gun and pull the trigger. What are the poor sods going to do when it's finished!"

"Whatever soldiers do in peacetime." She could not keep the irony out of her voice.

"Special Services Branch is taking agents in and out of France every day. I think I can convince Eisenhower to release the lieutenant to Special Branch. After all, he served as liaison to Eighth Army. Wasn't that his previous assignment? That means he belongs to *us*!"

The prime minister took a business card out of his pocket, asked her to spell "Speigner" and scribbled a second note. "I can understand why General Eisenhower hesitated to act on uncorroborated evidence. I'm inclined to agree, except–" He looked over his spectacles at her. "–you came to me regardless of your obvious opposition to the war." He handed her the card. "Tell your lieutenant to give this to Rommel and *godspeed*. I'll be happy to meet with Rommel, anywhere but Berlin!"

She wrung her hands in delight. It wouldn't do to hug a prime minister. There was just one problem. "I fear I'm in hot water. I made up a false delivery in order to see General Eisenhower."

Churchill said that he would take care of it. They shook hands. She left, her palm warm and glowing. Outside in the courtyard, she paused beside her motorbike and examined the prime minister's card. It smelled of cigar smoke. On the back he had written in a heavy scrawl:

To Marshal Rommel,
The bearer of this card, Lt. Speigner, speaks for me.

W. S. Churchill

XIII

The Special Air Service base was located in a heavily forested area. The driver stopped the jeep to let a company of commandos jog past. They had a look of anonymous determination. Max was taken to what appeared to be a basic-training area, complete with obstacle courses, balancing beams, rope swings. His instructor, a drill sergeant with a neck like a bull, was waiting. *We're going to put you through the short course, sir. Ever jumped before? No? That's all right then. No problem.*

The instructor fitted him out in zippered jump suit and padded helmet. He shrugged into the overalls, feeling like a stuffed panda. He began to sweat inside the helmet. A few hours earlier he had been napping in his room after his first meal in a U.S. Army mess–spuds and mystery meat that a POW would kill for. McAlpin came to his room and explained what had happened at SHAEF, that General Eisenhower and his aides seemed more interested in Rommel's patch than in his message. "After Ike brushed me off, I gained an audience with the prime minister with the help of God, Jesus and Saint Mary."

He had food and a clean bed. New fatigues and boots. A Gillette razor. A tube of Burma Shave. His own, personal roll of toilet paper. He had been expertly conditioned–by the Nazis, no less–to sit and wait. Now, just when he was getting used to normal living, or what passed for it, the Brits were telling him to go *back*!

Churchill's support of Special Services and commando spy operation was well known, she went on. The prime minister wished him Godspeed and promised to meet personally with Rommel if a ceasefire could be arranged. He told her to take it from the top. How had she managed to see Churchill?

"I rang his executive secretary and said I had a message from Rommel delivered by an American lieutenant who'd escaped from a POW camp." She slapped his knee. "I only fibbed a little. The Prime Minister had a brilliant idea."

He was afraid to ask.

"Since you are still 'on loan' to Eighth Army, Sir Winston has ordered you to report to duty. The British have reassigned you."

She gave him Churchill's card. He rapidly scanned it. *Lt. Speigner speaks for me*. He glanced up. How fast could he get this to France? She kissed him on the cheek in a proprietary way. "How do you feel about parachutes?" she said.

The instructor laid out a chute on the ground and demonstrated how it was folded. Not so that Speigner could fold it himself-*I'm told this is a once-only jump, sir!*-but to show how the thing worked. He learned how to strap it on and how to leave the aircraft with knees tucked. "Now let's do a PLF, sir." *A what?* "Sorry, parachute landing fall." How to hit the ground and roll. He imitated the instructor's example. "That's the ticket, sir!"

The jumpmaster led him to a wooden platform six feet high and made him jump and roll until his whole body was sore. "Now then, we've built a tower to let chaps like you get a feel for it. Not to worry, we'll hook you to a cable."

He felt for Churchill's card hidden inside the sleeve of his jacket. Anna had turned the jacket inside out, made a tiny tear in the cuff and slid the card snugly inside. "You expect me to be captured?" He meant this as a joke but it came out lame.

"Nothing of the sort! You wouldn't want to lose the card, eh?"

"Before I forget…" She reached into her pocket and taken out Rommel's patch. "The prime minister hated to give this up. It might help in case you get picked up." He had forgotten the insignia. She was right, of course. It could save his life. She stuck the oak leaves patch in his pocket. "If you show it to the French Resistance they will take you to the field marshal. I'm sure you've thought of that."

"No," he said in a small voice.

"Special Branch will get you there."

"Special what?"

"Commandos, my dear."

She hooked her arm in his. They went to a car in front of the quarantine barracks. MPs stared at them. He forced himself to think positively. Rommel would want to know Churchill's intention, his mood. What else had the prime minister said?

"That he would be delighted to meet with Rommel. He wasn't surprised that Rommel hated Stalin. He doesn't trust Stalin himself! And...he admires Rommel as a soldier."

Bit out of condition, eh, sir?

He panted in the jumpsuit and harness. They were ascending the tower. How high was it? *High enough, sir.* They came to the jump-platform. He was stunned by the view. From here he could see the harbor. There were hundreds of ships: battleships, cruisers, destroyers, troop transports. Tiny figures crowded the decks. The English Channel stretched to the horizon. Beyond the murky boundary of sea and sky France was waiting. The instructor hooked a demonstration chute to a cable attached to a crane.

"Here's where students find out if they've got the nerve," the jumpmaster said. "Though in your case, sir, I understand you've no choice."

Was it two days ago that he had stood in the prison yard listening to POWs bitching? Queuing for a meal. Fighting over a frayed copy of Dickens' *Great Expectations.* As the instructor tightened his parachute straps it occurred to him that no prisoner, not even Commander Rawlings, had asked for lessons in German. He thought of McAlpin hooking her arm in his, the port city pulsing with traffic, horns bleating, tires squealing. She leaned in close. "You'll do splendidly. You always have."

"Meet me at Big Ben and we'll have a Highland fling."

She laughed and curtseyed. He'd never seen her show

emotion, not even when she encountered badly burned soldiers in North Africa. "I'm sorry what I said about the Americans!"

"What did you say?" He got into the jeep.

She shouted over the street noise. "Oh, you know, gross national optimism and all that! You're not so bad, you Yanks."

As the jeep sped away he twisted in the seat and looked back. She was standing in the road, motorbikes swerving around her. She took off her cap and threw it in the air, a compact, determined redhead in a dark blue uniform.

Don't worry, sir, the grass is quite thick. It will cushion the impact. This won't be nothing like a real landing.

He was told to imagine that he was sitting in the open hatch of a plane going 175 knots, or just over 200 mph. Could he make himself jump out of an airplane? Could he put his life in the hands of an anonymous, gum-chewing girl who packed chute after chute? "The cable jump demonstrates the sensation of the chute opening and, of course, the shock of landing. Remember, bend your knees and roll. Tally ho, sir!"

He was startled by a gentle pressure on his back. It was as if Rommel, not the instructor, were urging him on. Glimpsing the harbor where tens of thousands of soldiers were poised to board ships, he consoled himself with the thought that he was not alone.

XIV

Until that morning the bomb crater had been a *Schein-batterie*, a dummy artillery emplacement. Allied planes were bombing fake positions like this one, leaving real FLAK batteries untouched. The device had been successful in North Africa. Why not in Normandy? Pilots and bombardiers could not distinguish dummy from real. He congratulated the battery commander who had put up the now-demolished counterfeit.

"*Jawohl, Herr Generalfeldmarschall.*" The artillery officer was delighted.

He asked if any patrols had picked up an American *Oberleutnant.* He waved vaguely toward the English Channel. "I heard a rumor that a double agent might be sent over. It would be a shame if he were shot."

"I will order the patrols to watch for him," the officer said.

Rommel returned to his car and took the wheel much to Corporal Daniel's consternation. The field marshal liked to go fast. Rommel accelerated, the speedometer rapidly climbing to 100 kph...110...120. Speidel, riding in the back seat, complained that they had outdistanced their escort, a platoon of panzer grenadiers in a truck. Rommel's response was to pour on the speed. He passed a freight train running parallel to the road.
"You missed the turn!" Speidel shouted. "Back there, at that railway crossing."

He hit the brakes. At that moment there were explosions. Seconds later American planes thundered overhead. They had strafed and bombed the train that Rommel had just passed.

"Drive under those trees," Speidel said.

"Of course, do you think I'm crazy?" No one mentioned that if he hadn't beaten the train to the crossing, they, too, might have been in the bombardiers' sights. After a few minutes he drove back to the crossing. The train had derailed. Black smoke boiled from burning coaches. The grenadiers' truck arrived. He ordered his men to assist the wounded passengers.

Men and women wandered in a daze, weeping, talking to themselves. When civilians were caught in a combat zone he felt responsible. In the back of his mind was the knowledge that he had contributed directly or indirectly. There was nothing he could do except order his men to observe all courtesies.

"*C'est Rommel, c'est Rommel*!" a man cried. Others took up the shout, echoing it down the tracks. Everyone wanted to see the man who had ridden roughshod over France. Perhaps he could stop the American and British pilots from bombing them. Faces turned to him against a backdrop of burning coaches. The defeated stood and gawked. He was embarrassed. The example of their commander in his belted overcoat going among the wounded, helping a woman out of a coach, had a powerful effect on the German soldiers. They typically remained detached in such situations and let French police handle civilians. With no less than a field marshal setting an example, the panzer grenadiers began to carry dead and wounded from the coaches. A Wehrmacht field hospital was set up to assist *la Croix Rouge.*

A woman told Rommel, "*Merci beaucoup, Monsieur le général*!" He nodded and walked on. Only a hypocrite would pretend that what had happened was an accident. The pilot had mistaken the train for a troop transport. Like his dummy positions, the French passenger train had been randomly targeted. This had to stop. How much longer were people to suffer? Jet aircraft and more FLAK batteries were not the answer. As he walked among the devastation, the wounded crying piteously, the dead contorted and silent, he wished Adolf Hitler could see this.

A woman's corpse covered by a blanket lay on the tracks. All that was exposed was her high heeled shoes. He thought of the shoes he had ordered for Lucie. In the Great War, the French army terrorized Germans living on the border. Before that, Napoleon laid waste to Europe. Before Napoleon there was Charlemagne. Before Charlemagne there was Caesar. War was the razor's edge of history–but whom would history hold responsiblc for a Frenchwoman dead on the tracks?

Lucie believed in what he was doing. She and Manfred were his future. He would write her, tell her about what had happened, the two separate but interconnected bombings, two targets, the *Scheinbatterie* and the train. ("The French suffered heavy civilian casualties but the Atlantic Wall took no direct hits.") She would understand. She would not judge.

An hour later they were back on the road. Rommel rode in the rear and listened to Speidel report on his meeting in Freundstadt, where he had seen Baron Constantin von Neurath, the former foreign minister, and Herr Dr. Strölin, mayor of Stuttgart, the founding fathers of the German Resistance. While Daniel drove, they held onto their hats and talked. "Strölin's main concern," Speidel was saying, "is that after Hitler is arrested, people will have to be enlightened. Otherwise there will be civil war. Neurath does not think we could force Hitler to go on the radio and say that he was resigning from office. He thinks Hitler will have to be removed by any means, along with Himmler."

It was encouraging that von Neurath and Strölin, high-minded Germans in positions of authority, were ready to act, but Rommel did not agree with *any means.* "I don't want you committing me to something without my approval."

"I would never."

"You do not speak for me in matters such as that."

They were on their way to a meeting with Sepp Dietrich and other SS commanders. Rommel wanted to look them in the eye. Only then could he be sure they would obey his orders. He was gambling on German common sense. Dietrich had been a sergeant major in the Bavarian cavalry. His rise was due, it was said, to a personal friendship with the Führer. For a dyed-in-the-wool Nazi like Dietrich to agree to a ceasefire was a sign that the end was in sight.

The Waffen SS generals for the most part were hardworking, middle-class overachievers. The difference was party affiliation. Rommel had advanced in the Wehrmacht without joining the Nazi Party. In the SS, party membership was a given.

There were three German armies: The Wehrmacht, with 258 divisions, the Luftwaffe field infantry, six divisions, and the SS–Hitler's Schutzstaffel, or "protection staff"–twenty-one divisions. The Wehrmacht general staff was a mix of patrician and bourgeois. Rommel, whose father was a Wurttemberg schoolmaster, was middle-class and proud of it. He resented the Prussian aristocracy which had dominated the Wehrmacht for too long. Many of his disagreements over strategy with the "army vons" arose from his distaste for class distinction. This had caused him early in his career to reject an invitation to the elite Staff College and consequent initiation into the OKW's magic circle. His promotions resulted from hard work and front line service. He would not have had it any other way.

During the battle for North Africa he had ignored Field Marshal Jodl's order to attach an SS battalion to the Afrika Korps. When his son, Manfred, then fifteen, had expressed an interest in joining the Waffen SS, the military branch of Hitler's *garde du corps*, Rommel said it was out of the question. ("You'll join the same service I did thirty years ago.") Manfred innocently argued that the SS had the best weapons and smartest uniforms. Rommel sat him down and said, "I have reason to believe that Himmler has been carrying out mass killings. By such actions, men like Himmler are trying to burn the bridges of the German people behind them." Besides, he said, the Waffen SS was not what it was cracked up to be. The recruitment surge of 1943 to replace men lost in combat resulted in less qualified soldiers. "My son," he concluded, "stay away from the SS."

The SS generals were fanatical patriots–but of *which* Germany? What kind of country would they leave behind? A divided land torn between radicals, communists and capitalists or a unified Germany ready to resume its place as a member of the European community? Even the battle-tested Dietrich, whom Rommel trusted up to a point, was an unknown commodity. During the northern Italy campaign, he had been ashamed when Dietrich's SS troopers looted Milan and other cities.

Like the Wehrmacht, the SS were the products of intensive training and political indoctrination. Both armies, military and political, had sung the same barrack songs, gotten drunk in the same beer halls and sworn to die for the fatherland–but in SS *Walhalla* storm-troopers sang "Deutschland über Alles" from the open turrets of panzers as they crushed civilians under the treads.

Before he addressed the SS generals, he needed a common denominator. Courage in battle? Loyalty to the cause? Obedience to the Führer? Every time he had fallen into disfavor with Hitler he had come crawling back. That was a fact. He could not deny it. After he failed in Tunisia, he had jumped at the chance to command the Atlantic Wall. He not only sat at Hitler's side, the prodigal returning to his insane father, but considered himself fortunate. The SS generals would obey his ceasefire order not because he was right, or because they respected his leadership, or because they preferred ceasefire to self-immolation, but because they were doing what Hitler *should be doing*. That was it! They were helping Hitler do the right thing.

Arriving at 12 Panzer headquarters he left Speidel in the car and went to meet the generals. They snapped to attention and gave a Nazi salute. He returned a hand-salute to show them that Hitler had nothing to do with what was about to happen. He shook hands first with Dietrich, then with Colonel-General Paul Hausser, 64, commander of 2 SS Panzer. Hausser was a builder and shaper of the Waffen SS from its earliest beginnings, having been first director of training to the Field SS, in 1934.

Lt. General Georg Keppler, 48, was another seasoned SS veteran, first commander of the SS Standarte "Deutschland," and now heading the "Reich" division. He was known for his strict training and especially the Reich tradition that every man was to be trained as a skilled individual fighter.

The host for the meeting was General Kurt Meyer, 33, the youthful commander of 12 SS Panzer (*Hitlerjugend*). Rommel joked that Meyer did not look much older than his tank men, whose average age was eighteen and a half. "*Herr Generalfeldmarschall,*" Meyer responded earnestly, "I must ask your help in getting some replacements. My division is not up to combat strength. Instead of a hundred tanks I have only forty-three in working order..."

He shook his head. "Another time, General."

The SS generals were on edge. For men who slept in starched pajamas, for whom arrogance was a way of life, nervousness was a sign that they felt vulnerable, perhaps for the first time in their lives. Meyer offered them coffee and biscuits. Rommel suggested they get started.

"Gentlemen, I would like to give you my assessment of our chances when the invasion comes," he began. "First, I put this question to you: Should we fight on here, in vain, while leaving Berlin to the Russians?"

They shook their heads uncertainly. *Nein, nein.* All felt guilty about abandoning Berlin. All would rather be defending the homeland against rape and pillage, but what could they do?

"It is physically impossible, given our limitations of manpower and equipment, to defend the entire coastline from Holland to Bordeaux. In some places Herr Goebbels' Atlantic Wall is a picket fence. It has gaps. It has holes. If the Allies choose the least-defended place to attack–and why shouldn't they? Wouldn't *you*?–they will establish a beachhead. That is a mathematical certainty.

"Now, what happens next? Will we rally to the point of attack and push them into the sea? I have told the Führer himself, on several occasions, that the prospects for a counterattack are not good. The Allies control the air and the sea. They can bomb and lay down a naval bombardment at will. Our reserves will in all probability be trapped."

He waved his hand dismissing their arguments. "There are various points of view to be sure. Von Rundstedt is betting everything on a single counterstroke. My point is, after we do the best we can, which is to slow down and hinder the enemy's advance, *what next*? Do we manage a fighting withdrawal all the way to the homeland, taking hundreds of thousands of casualties only to bow, inevitably, to a superior enemy? Or do we negotiate a conditional surrender as soon as possible? I myself would bet that the *Amis* would welcome the latter! My feeling is that this is the only realistic course to save Germany from being overrun. The point is to negotiate a truce in the west so that we can concentrate all our efforts on beating back the Russians in the east. The western leaders don't trust Stalin any more than we do."

He paused, letting them see the risk he was taking.

"I wish to act in behalf of the Führer and of the people of Germany. I believe he would come to the same decision *if he were behaving rationally*. Now, if I give the order to surrender, will you obey?"

In Berlin, they would have drawn their pistols and shot him. The SS thought as a unified army, each man a part of the whole. His best chance was to break them down individually.

Keppler?

I will obey.

Hausser?

Jawohl, Herr Kommandant, ich auch.

Meyer?

Jawohl, and twenty-thousand Jugend along with me.

Und Sie, Dietrich?

"You have but to give the order, *Herr Generalfeldmarschall*," Dietrich said quietly. Trying not to show how relieved he was, he shook each general's hand. He assured them that by pledging their loyalty they had done their country a great service.

"Discuss this with no one, *meine Herren*," he told them. "I will keep you informed of any development. I am in contact with the Allied High Command. If, however, the invasion begins before a ceasefire can be arranged, we must hit the enemy with everything we have and force him to the peace table."

Tough diplomacy was more to their liking. He turned to leave. They snapped to attention and saluted. None, he noted, gave the Nazi salute. As he went outside, he motioned to Dietrich. "Have you heard of an American lieutenant being captured?" he said when they were alone.

Dietrich was puzzled. "Have commandos landed?"

"No, it's not that. Never mind." He returned to the Horch. Speidel jumped out and held the door.

XV

The plane was a twin-engine Lockheed Hudson. On the outside of each of the twin tail sections was an identification number, "T-9465." The slim aircraft had green and brown camouflage paint on the sides and black underneath, with five windows and a gun-turret atop the fuselage. The door opened behind the wing and was roomy enough for a parachutist to exit. There was a crew of three: pilot, co-pilot/navigator and gunner. The pilot told Max that the Hudson was the aircraft of choice for transporting agents to France. He and his crew had been based in East Anglia. With invasion imminent they'd been assigned to Special Services Branch. Short flights to France were routine. He had two flight plans: one for dropping commandos behind enemy lines, another for landing and picking up agents. "Or politicians on the run," he added with a wink.

What about the Luftwaffe?

"No fighter problem to speak of. We watch for ack-ack. We know the positions of FLAK batteries around the towns. It's not too difficult to avoid them."

The pilot introduced Max to the commandos who would escort him into France. He had encountered British commandos in North Africa. These two exhibited the same quiet confidence. "It's nice not to be going solo," he said. To them, he was simply "Leftenant." Eric and Dan were sizable lads who inspired confidence. They spoke French and had trained to operate with the Resistance. This was their first mission. "Not to worry," Dan assured him.

The navigator asked the location of Rommel's headquarters. Speigner faced a decision. He wanted to get close but exact directions could lead British bombers to the chateau.

Near Rouen.

Which direction?

South, along the Seine.

There are a fair number of villages. The anti-aircraft fire in that sector is hot. We call it Ack-Ack Alley.

Sorry, don't know which village.

Right, then. We'll drop you in the area. The rest is up to you.

The commandos assured him they had names and locations of *Maquis* contacts. The codeword for the mission, Dan said, was "*Violet*...or violent without an *n*."

They checked his parachute and gear. He had been given camouflage fatigues. His First Lieutenant's bar was pinned inside his T-shirt. While the pilot and co-pilot underwent preflight inspections, the heavily armed commandos ticked off an equipment check, beginning with the .45 automatic pistol in canvas holster. *Check*. The unaccustomed weight on his hip was both intimidating and reassuring. *Check* for plastic poncho, torch, first aid kit, canteen, candy bars. *Check* for sheath knife strapped to his leg, four extra ammo clips. *Check* for metal gadget called a "Cricket" which the 82nd Airborne had loaned Special Branch. It was to be used for identifying oneself. A click was to be answered with two clicks.

"Strange old thing," Eric said.

Dan checked Speigner's chute, tightened the straps and whacked him on the back. *All set*! Eric rubbed black camouflage paint on his face. He followed the commandos inside the narrow interior of the ten-seat plane. The pilot mentioned that his last assignment had been ferrying a general and a couple of "high muckety mucks." Max nervously joked that he was neither. He sat behind the commandos, encumbered by equipment, unable to lean back comfortably. The gunner climbed into his swivel chair, checked the ammunition belt and opened a paperback. Max found his bored expression heartening.

The plane's engines turned over. Dust kicked up around the windows. The co-pilot spoke into a throat-mike, words drowned out by noise and vibration. The Hudson took off into the dusk and rose swiftly over the Channel. Below, thousands of ships rode at anchor. Speigner craned his neck to look out the window while the commandos slumped in their seats and went to sleep. The navigator suggested that he do the same.

Flak explosions lit up the sky. The light plane tilted violently. Tracer bullets were white arcs in the darkness. He started, surprised he had fallen asleep. The nervous energy had worn off. He was bone-tired. Over the door a red light blinked on. The pilot's voice crackled over the intercom: "Five minutes."

Eric said, "Stand up and hook your static line to the cable over the door." He tried to stand. His helmet bumped the ceiling. He almost fell as the plane swerved to avoid flak. He reached out blindly and caught the back of a seat. "One minute!" the pilot called.

He tried to imagine what it would be like. What if the chute did not open? "Go to your reserve," Eric said. Dan cheerfully contradicted this. They would be jumping too low to employ the reserve. In a regular combat jump, they hit the silk at 500 feet. Tonight, they were jumping at 350 feet. The distinction had not registered until now. "You won't have time to worry about the chute with all the ack-ack," Dan said as he slid the door open. A cold wind rushed through the plane. White tracers searched the sky. Dan stood in the doorway. When he jumped, Max and Eric were to follow as fast as possible. If Max hesitated, Eric was to "assist" him. Any delay could spread them out and lead to confusion on the ground.

He checked his static line as he had been taught. It was securely fastened. The straps reaching under his crotch had been uncomfortable during the flight. Now, the tighter the better. He wanted to be connected to something that floated. The red light changed to green.

"*Go*!" yelled the pilot.

Dan disappeared in silence. "*You don't announce your arrival*," the jump master had said. He was at the door, the wind blistering his face. He had never wanted to stay anywhere more than inside this plane. Eric pushed. He tumbled into space. After a few agonizing seconds the chute opened with a blessed, terrifying shock. The straps cut into his groin. He experienced the miracle of weightlessness. For a second he caught sight of the commandos' chutes silently descending below him. The dark earth was coming up fast. Instinctively he grabbed the risers attached to the canopy. He struck ground and tried to roll. Instead he landed hard on his side. The fall knocked the wind out of him. He lay still until he got his breath back. He stood up and shrugged out of the harness. His right side was numb from shoulder to hip. He rotated his arm to get the feeling back. All around were tall hedgerows. The commandos were rolling their chutes. He gathered in the cumbersome silk, wedged it under some brush and duck-walked to where he had last seen them.

Hearing a "click" he reached for his Cricket. Which pocket was it in? "It's all right," he whispered frantically. "It's *me*, Speigner."

Shut up, Leftenant.

There was a sound he had not heard since North Africa. Small arms fire. German soldiers were taking potshots at the plane. He thought of the pilot and navigator, their faces lit by the glow of instrument lights, ignoring the ground fire, charting a new heading. All in a day's work. Squatting beside him, the commandos were equally efficient. Dan shielded a green penlight with his hand and took a compass heading. Eric spotted a road. "Keep to the woods and stay parallel to the lane," he whispered.

"The Seine is *that* way," Dan said confidently. Which way had he pointed? Max heard a cowbell and smelled manure. He was startled when Eric nudged him. The commandos unslung their sub-machineguns and moved out. Taking advantage of the dark they crossed a pasture, then went at right angles until they found a gap in a hedgerow. Like a mouse in a maze, he scurried after the others. They moved at a steady pace. It seemed that hours, not minutes, had elapsed since Dan checked his compass. He plodded along. On his hip the .45 automatic felt light. They waded into a shallow creek, perhaps a tributary to the Seine. How far they were from the river was anybody's guess. A mile. Ten miles. The splashing of their boots sounded like pistol shots. The commandos stopped and listened. He waited, cold water oozing into his boots. They went forward, stopped, listened, moved on. This time he heard it. Someone was speaking German.

There was a light-colored mass in front of them. At first he thought it was a cliff, then realized it was a bridge. A red dot glowed. He caught a whiff of cigarette smoke. A sentry was having a smoke. The commandos debated whether to leave the creek bed and go around the bridge or float under it. They decided to go around.

He followed them into the woods, ducking branches, trying not to stumble. Dan accidentally stepped on his heels, tripping him. Eric pumped his arm, signaling him to hurry up. There was a whine of truck wheels, a roar of engines. Headlights bobbed up and down, raking the fields with light.

Running at a crouch they crossed the road. Soldiers sprayed the woods with bullets. Leaves fell on them. They ran, no longer quiet, blundering through the trees. Truck brakes squealed, chains rattled. A tailgate slammed down. Dogs barked and yelped. Spotlights penetrated the woods, turning the stream into a gleaming band of silver. They followed the meandering creek. Momentarily the trees shielded them from the light. Dan cocked his machinegun. Eric followed suit, shaking his head as if embarrassed not to have done it first. Max suddenly felt afraid for them. They were hardly more than teenagers. It was his fault they were here.

"Why don't I give myself up?" he whispered, thinking that Rommel's patrols would take him to La Roche-Guyon.

"They'd shoot you on sight," Eric said.

Dan pushed him. "Keep going! We'll cover you."

The creek bed was hard and rocky. He splashed along, then plunged into shoulder-deep water. The commandos jumped in after him. The creek flowed into a culvert covered with dirt. A trail crossed over the makeshift bridge. The commandos pulled him toward it. Dogs barked. Shafts of light licked the trees. Eric was saying something to him when a green flare exploded over the trees. He instinctively dived under the water. Bullets whacked the surface. He swam a few strokes, scissor-kicking wildly, then resurfaced under some reeds and branches. Eric and Dan were floating face down. At first he thought it was a commando trick. He reached out and turned Dan over, then Eric. They were both dead.

Bullets erupted in the water. He sank under the branches. There was a piercing pain in his right thigh. He took a deep breath and went under, feeling for the bottom with his hands and pulling himself along, rock by rock. Lights flickered over the surface above him. He came up for air. Everything was black. He was inside the culvert. There were splashing noises, yelling and cursing. The soldiers had found the bodies.

He made his way down the culvert, not stopping until he emerged at the other end. He was fifty meters upstream before the flashlights found him. He crawled up the bank on his hands and knees. Pain shot through his leg with every step. Shouts and barking came from the creek. He had maybe ten seconds–literally a lifetime–to get away. He saw a cow trail in the trees and followed it. After perhaps a quarter of a mile he heard jeeps and motorcycles scouring the woods.

He came to a pasture surrounded by hedgerows. Cows were huddled at the far end. If he went back, the Germans would find him. There was nothing to do but keep going. As he limped forward, the cows shied away. These Guernseys knew where they were going. He followed the bells. The cows slipped through a narrow gap in the hedgerow. He could have searched all night and never found it. The small herd, which now included a limping human, emerged into an open pasture. He was afraid the tinkling bells would attract attention. A barn loomed out of the darkness. His bovine companions were taking him home. While the cows congregated at a watering trough, he went into the barn and crawled behind a bale of hay. Dizzy from loss of blood, he groped in his pocket, forgetting the first aid kit in his pack. He found a handkerchief monogrammed "S.A.S." The jump master had given it to him.

He pressed the cloth against his leg. The pain was not as bad as when he was walking. It was a flesh wound but would become infected if he did not tend to it. The tinkle of bells was soporific. He lay back in his soggy uniform. His eyelids weighed a ton. The soldiers could not be far behind. A short nap would not do any harm. As he drifted off he saw Dan's face, pale in the water.

He jerked awake. Someone was standing over him, the smallest soldier in the Wehrmacht. The tiny German was dwarfed by his steel helmet. Was this the master race? He struggled to sit up.

Il est allemand.

Non, Anglais!

The diminutive soldier spoke to a little girl. She opened his pack and shook it. The contents spilled onto the straw. The boy took the canteen and a candy bar.

XVI

He had just stretched out for a nap when the call came in. *Two British commandos killed, a third at large in the countryside near Brionne.* The American! He got dressed immediately, awakened Daniel and asked him to calculate the fastest route to Brionne, some fifty kilometers west of La Roche-Guyon.

"Send a bulletin," he told the desk sergeant. "Take the third commando alive. I don't want him killed, *Verstehen Sie*?"

He hurried to his car, telling Daniel, "*Mach schnell*!" They drove without lights. The tires struck potholes. The road curved. Dark shapes loomed. A convoy of tank retrieval vehicles. Daniel hit the brakes.

"Why are they blocking the road?" Rommel fumed. He could not get OKW to move the *panzer* reserves to the coast and here they were releasing *tank-retrievers*. He ordered Daniel to cut through a field. As usual the heavy Horch with its innate self-destructiveness homed in on the softest ground. Before Daniel could react, the car bogged down to the axles, wheels spinning. *Stupid, stupid, stupid car!* Rommel jumped out and kicked the tires. It was like El Alamein when his tanks had given out of fuel. He could remain cool in battle, make decisions under fire, but what he could not endure, what made his blood boil, was inertia. He heard a motorcycle coming. He ran between two huge, flatbed trucks and flagged it down. The cyclist hit his brakes, amazed to encounter a field marshal. "Where are you going?" Rommel said.

"Second SS Panzer!"

"I must borrow your vehicle. My car is stuck and I am in a hurry."

"Herr General, *bitte*, I have my assignment."

"Well, take your pouch and go."

The surprised courier exclaimed, "Second SS is a hundred kilometers from here!"

The instant the courier stepped off the big bike Rommel gripped the handlebars and swung his leg over the leather seat. He twisted the throttle, comforted by the throaty rumble.

Es ist ein Daimler, ja?

Jawohl, Herr General!

He walked the machine around so that it faced the opposite direction, kicked the gear lever into first and let in the clutch. Before the war, he had owned a motorcycle similar to this one. He blasted around the convoy, passing the trucks, cursing anything in his path, accelerating to 60...70...80 kph. He did not need headlights. He could see perfectly well. The wind felt good. The speed, the power, relaxed him. Peace was just over the next rise. Peace within his grasp. Peace for him and Lucie and Manfred.

In fifteen minutes he arrived at Brionne. MPs directed him to the sector where the commandos had been killed. He stopped to ask directions. Sentries were startled to see a field marshal on a motorbike. If his face had not been so famous, they might have asked for identification. He wanted to see the commandos' bodies. The corpses were lying in the back of a truck. A sergeant illuminated them with a flashlight. Neither face was that of the American. He was vastly relieved. The sergeant held the light on the bodies. "Turn it off," Rommel said.

He spoke with a battalion commander. Patrols were fanning out over twenty square miles. He suggested that the search be confined to farmhouses within a mile of where the commandos had been shot. He received directions to the nearest farm and mounted the Daimler. The battalion commander couldn't resist asking why he was riding a motorcycle. He replied that it was emergency transportation.

When Speigner woke up he was in bed, The little boy was no longer wearing the souvenir German helmet. He and the little girl looked on solemnly while a woman cleaned and dressed his leg wound with sulphur. She picked up his first aid kit to indicate where she had gotten sulphur powder. His right trousers leg had been split and rolled up above the wound. The man of the house checked the bandage.

"*Vous êtes Americain*?"

"*Oui.*"

In broken French he tried to explain that he was an American officer and needed their help. "I would like to reach the French Underground," he said, forgetting the codeword. "*Les Maquis, comprenez-vous*?"

The husband glanced at his wife, then shook his head. "*Oui, mais nous n'avons de rien faire avec les maquis.*"

In every village the *Maquis* functioned like a civil defense network. If these people were not members of the Resistance, surely they could get in touch with them. He remembered the codeword.

Violet?

Comment?

Violet?

The woman tied off the bandage and pulled down his torn trousers. The codeword having failed, he did not know what to do. He tried to sit up. The mother spoke to her daughter, who ran to the kitchen. In a moment she returned with a cup of tea. She held it while he drank. It was hot and sweet. The girl smiled shyly. He tried to explain that he was an American lieutenant and had parachuted into France. He pointed to the sky and imitated a parachute descending with his hands. The two British soldiers with him were *mort.* "I have come to arrange peace with the Germans," he said. "*La paix.*"

The woman looked dubiously at him. She shrugged and pointed at a cross on the wall. The only *tranquillité* possible, she said, was *en bas,* below ground. He asked her to speak slowly. The farmer interrupted to say that the Germans would be there soon. The *Americain* had to *aller.* The little girl gave him the last of the tea. A dog started barking.

Les Allemands!

Soldiers beat on the door with gun butts. He struggled out of bed. The farmer gave him his backpack, the .45 and holster. The wife moved a table, pulled back a rug and opened a trapdoor. "*La cave sortie au dehors*!" she whispered. "*Adieu, le monsieur lieutenant. Allez vite...vite!.*" The little girl handed him a walking stick before her mother shut the trap door.

He climbed down into a cellar. The woman had said there was a *sortie,* an exit. He stumbled over a basket. Dusty pots clattered to the earthen floor. He willed his eyes to adjust to the dark. He shrugged into the loops of his pack, fastened the holster to his belt and picked up the walking stick. Upstairs men's voices asked questions in German-accented French. Had the farmer seen any enemy paratroopers? The man obviously was saying that he knew nothing.

Outside, Rommel rode up to the farmhouse. Soldiers were searching everywhere. Flashlights beams danced over the grass. This was the third place he had come to. At the other farms he had questioned soldiers at checkpoints. Nobody had seen a third commando. He switched off the motor and leaned the bike on its stand. A dog started barking. A soldier kicked it.

"No need for that," Rommel said. Other squad members, some seven or eight military policemen, came to attention. He asked who was in charge. The lieutenant who had been interrogating the civilians came forward.

"We have searched the premises," the lieutenant said.

"Perhaps you did not look hard enough," he said. Someone emptied a wash pan out a window. He looked inside and saw a woman making up a bed. "Search it again!"

The lieutenant sent his men back to the house. They grabbed the farmer and threatened to beat him. The little girl started to cry and hid in her mother's skirt. The wife stared straight ahead. Rommel sensed that she was tougher than her man. He was vulnerable because he had his family to protect. The woman had lost hope. There was an empty tea cup beside the bed. Where was the cellar door? The lieutenant drew his pistol and aimed it at the farmer. "Put it away," Rommel said.

He addressed the farmer, speaking French, "Tell me the truth. Was there a commando here? I will not harm your family. Tell me if anyone was here. Was an American here? Was he wounded? What was his name?"

The farmer shook his head. "*Non, non*!" He was terrified.

Rommel asked politely, "*Montrez-moi la cave, s'il vous plait*!" The farmer glanced at his wife as if to borrow courage. Rommel lost patience. "The cellar door! Tell me, or by God I'll burn the house down!"

Max crept through the cellar, feeling his way, the stone wall damp to the touch. There was a narrow tunnel. Steps carved out of stone led to wooden storm doors. Using the walking stick, he pushed the hatch open. There was no one behind the house. He was not afraid of the soldiers. He thought about this and realized it was because he was ready to surrender. However, he wanted to get away from the house. He didn't want the family to suffer. Germans shot civilians who collaborated with the enemy.

The farmer revealed the trapdoor. Rommel took a flashlight and climbed down the ladder. The beam touched on shelves, tools and sacks, illuminated the exit tunnel. Speigner, meanwhile, was heading to the barn. He could hear men talking on the other side of the house. Using the walking stick he hobbled around the barn and kept going. Behind him the storm doors banged open.

Rommel climbed out of the cellar and stood in the wet grass. The flashlight revealed nothing. For all he knew, Speigner was still in England waiting to see Eisenhower. He circled the barn and turned the light on tall hedgerows. "Search the fields," he told the lieutenant, who was obviously relieved that no harm had come to the field marshal. "Pass the word to your troops to hold their fire. I want the commando taken alive. *Verstehen Sie*?"

On the far side of the hedgerow Speigner slid into a drainage ditch. He made his way along the bottom, blessing the little girl for the cane. The ditch led to a clay culvert. He squirmed through the narrow opening, taking off his pack and pushing it ahead of him. On the other side he made for the woods. He crossed an open field, using the walking stick to propel himself. Shouts came from somewhere. The search party was not far away. He hobbled through the trees until he came to a leaf-filled ravine. He burrowed under a deep pile of leaves. Moments later he heard voices. He pressed his face into the earth. His wound throbbed. A beetle climbed on his hand.

XVII

It was nearly two a.m. when he returned to headquarters. He took off his shoes and slept for two hours. In Africa that had been a full night's rest, but back then all he had to worry about was the British.

By four he was awake. He telephoned units in the area and asked if an American had been picked up. The answer was no. He buzzed his aide to send up coffee and a roll. He unfolded a map and put his finger on Bourg-Achard. The two commandos had been killed near there. Why so far from La Roche-Guyon? The pilot must have mistaken the Vire for the Seine. If the *Leutnant* walked all night he could make the Seine by dawn. That would put him fifty kilometers downriver from La Roche-Guyon. However, if he avoided roads and villages, it would take him another day. Perhaps he was moving parallel to the river. Perhaps he had been wounded. There was a knock at the door. Thinking it was Lange with the coffee, he said, "*Herein*."

Speidel came in buttoning his tunic. "You're up early for your trip!"

"Oh, that. I will not be going home."

"What about Lucie's birthday!"

"I will send her the shoes."

It was obvious Speidel was afraid that he would miss the rendezvous with Strölin and Neurath for which Lucy's birthday was to provide cover. Rommel had been dreading the meeting. The last time he met with Strölin, the mayor of Stuttgart had spoken openly of the death camps in the hearing of Lucie, exclaiming, "Are we men or animals? This cannot go on. Hitler must die or we are lost!" Rommel asked Herr Oberbürgermeister Strölin to refrain from stating such opinions in the presence of his wife.

He had to be in La Roche-Guyon when Speigner was found. What was more important than hearing from Eisenhower and Montgomery?

Speidel was desperate. "I will phone you the minute the American is picked up. I will have him brought here. As far as the invasion is concerned, the Navy says we are in for some terrible weather. A gale is kicking up in the English Channel. The Americans cannot launch an attack for at least a week, perhaps a month. You know, if I thought the invasion was imminent, I would not have invited guests for dinner."

If one listened to Speidel, the invasion hardly mattered. Why should one defend the French coast when a more pressing duty was to host a dinner party? He stared at the map, the positions marked in red-battalions, divisions, reinforcements, tanks, supplies-all useless against their real enemy, the *Führer.*

His strength as a tactical commander was to out-think the enemy. In Africa he had constructed tanks of wood and mounted them on Volkswagen frames, then ordered FLAK batteries not to shoot down British reconnaissance planes so that they could report the sham forces. After estimating German strength at twice its actual size, the British postponed a major attack. *Shed sweat, not blood.* Now Germany was shedding a Führer.

What to do? Stick to his guns, look to his troops, or go home and see Strölin and Neurath? Strölin might be useful in getting Lucie and Manfred out of Germany. That alone would be reason for going. "All right, I leave for Herrlingen."

Speidel made no attempt to hide his satisfaction and abruptly left the room. Rommel remembered that the British had not yet broadcast the second part of the Verlaine poem: "*Blessent mon coeur d'une langueur monotone.*" The completion of the poem would signal that the invasion was to begin in two weeks. Until the second verse came over the airwaves, he had time to get his family to safety.

He shaved and packed. The puppy jumped on his bed, wagging its tail. He never left Elbo behind. Lange came and said the car was ready. General von Tempelhoff had asked if he could hitch a ride to Germany. Speidel went out to see him off. Tempelhoff was waiting. "I almost forgot Lucy's shoes! Hold Elbo for me." He ran back inside. After a minute he emerged holding a package. He told Speidel confidentially, "The minute you hear about the American call me."

Speidel clicked his heels. Rommel had never seen his chief of staff happier. Corporal Daniel shut the door and went around to the driver's side. An orderly came and reported that waves in the Channel were between five and eight feet high. "Even our cautious friends at OKW," Rommel said to Tempelhoff as they got in the car, "would consider the seas too rough for a landing."

Daniel drove through the village. Tempelhoff observed that many staff members were taking the day off. Some area commanders were going to Rennes for a *Kriegsspiel*. Hitler was resting at Berchthesgaden. He had allowed Admiral Donitz to go on leave for the first time since the war began. Rommel glanced at passing houses, thinking of people preparing meals, complaining about the weather. *Where there was life, there was hope.* He would give Hitler one more chance. Negotiations would proceed more smoothly if he could assure Eisenhower that he was acting with the Führer's approval. When they reached the Rouen-to-Reims highway he turned up his collar. The puppy crawled into his lap. It was a ten hour drive to Germany.

XVIII

The house looked the same but everything had changed. He sensed this while riding through Herrlingen. The town was silent, windows shuttered, curtains drawn. At least the curtains in *his* house were not drawn.

The two-story, Alpine-style house surrounded by fir trees, had been owned by an "immigrated Jew." Until now he had not let himself dwell on what had happened to the owner. It was commonplace for senior officers to live in confiscated villas. When he and Lucie moved in, they'd felt a palpable presence, angry and sad. Time had not diminished the feeling. War destroyed everything it touched. He vowed to restore the property rights to the family. What was the owner's name? *Rosen…Abraham Rosen?*

She came sailing out to meet him. Her terrier, Ajax, eagerly sniffed Elbo. They embraced with dogs lolling at their feet. Lucie Mollin Rommel was part Italian and part Polish-German. She had dark hair and brown eyes, a Mediterranean temperament mixed with Prussian backbone. He had been at military school in Danzig when they met. She had been a language major. In personality, taste, learning and thinking, she was everything that he was not. People said the marriage would not work. Her family were Catholic landowners in West Prussia. He was *Evangelisch*, the son of a landless schoolmaster. Thirty years of happiness had proved the skeptics wrong. He took her hand and followed her inside. Ajax and Elbo stayed underfoot, almost tripping him. He remembered the shoe box wrapped in brown paper.

"Happy birthday, *meine liebste Lu*!"

"You are my gift," she laughed, hugging him.

She invited him to inspect the quarters. This was a game they played. He dutifully made a mock inspection. She followed him, smiling. He touched a table surface for dust. For a second she was taken in. On the dining room table there was a freshly baked cake with a single candle.

Only one?

Who's counting?

Do you not wish to open your gift?

Later.

In his study everything was as he left it. Eight months before, when Hitler relieved him of command and ordered him home to "recuperate," he retreated into a study with these same books and diaries and mementos. There was a glass container with different-colored sands of the Sahara, a minie-ball from the American Civil War, a portrait of Stonewall Jackson. He admired Jackson, God's warrior who knew no fear. The trick in battle was to stand like a stone wall. Now that he was on the defensive, he appreciated Jackson more than ever. Leadership rose from the heart. If a commander was ready to lay down his life, his soldiers would follow him to hell and the Sahara. The irony was that Jackson had fought for a losing cause, a civil war about slavery, pitting brother against brother. He feared that Germany, too, would be split in two. He could not let that happen.

The furniture smelled of beeswax and lemon juice. Lucie had waxed the floors to a high gloss. He thanked her for welcoming him to such a lovely home and apologized for not having brought flowers. She threw back her head and laughed. There were none to be had. This surprised him. "What, no fresh flowers at the shops?"

"You could comb the country, my love, and not find a florist."

No flowers in Germany. The war had followed him home. "The house seems empty without Manfred," he complained. She assured him that their son would arrive the next morning.

"How is he?"

"Healthy enough, but I worry that he will learn rough ways from the soldiers. He is too young to join!"

"Anti-aircraft is a good spot for him. Imagine what people would say if he had joined the Waffen SS."

She gave him a Prussian look, stern and appraising. "He knows better than that."

"Well, he always went his own way."

"Of whom does that remind you?"

He begged her to open the parcel. She preferred to open it when she had time. Neurath and Strölin would be arriving shortly.

"I'm sorry. The meeting will not take long."

She shrugged, her dark eyes impenetrable. "It's a special

occasion-a 'Get Hitler' party."

He was shocked. "I thought you liked Strölin."

The mayor of Stuttgart had plied Lucie with theatre tickets, complimentary limousines, accommodations at luxury hotels. He had even commissioned a portrait of Rommel as a housewarming present. When Strölin talked politics, Lucie listened, up to a point. She went into the parlor, poking cushions and rearranging chairs. He sheepishly followed her. Ajax and Elbo crept under a table. She said, "I cannot believe you would allow such a meeting to take place in our house!"

"*Bitte*, do not worry. Strölin will help you and Manfred get out of the country."

"'Do not worry,' he says! You know the Gestapo is investigating Strölin and probably Baron von Neurath. They have been anti-Hitler from the beginning. Only their connections have kept them out of prison."

"Hitler would not dare!"

"They are not above suspicion and neither are we!"

Embarrassed to have caused a row, he was about to retreat to his study when a car pulled up in the driveway. She looked at him in amazement. "Five minutes you have been here." Car doors slammed. She put her birthday present away. Rommel went to receive his guests.

Politics made strange bedfellows. Baron General Constantin Freiherr von Neurath was a stiff-necked blueblood. An ambassador to Rome and London before the war, he was a member of the powerful "cabinet of barons" when Hitler came to power. The very next day, Jan. 31, 1933, Neurath joined the Nazi party and was made a general in the SS. Rommel was not absolutely sure about Neurath, even though he had already confided in Sepp Dietrich and other SS generals. Dr. Karl Strölin, a jovial bear of a man, also had joined the Nazi party and with its backing won a mayoral election. Despite his party affiliation, he had fought from the beginning against Hitler's resettlement of the Jews. Rommel was not surprised that his comrade from the Great War was a leader of the resistance.

He respected both men as soldiers, the highest accolade he could give. They were men of character, ready to sacrifice themselves for the common good. They came inside and bowed to Lucie. She went to get refreshments. Rommel took his guests into the parlor. Strölin closed the blinds at once. This automatic gesture shocked Rommel. Had the Gestapo followed them? Lucie had a right to be concerned. If a man as well-connected as Dr. Karl Strölin was hiding behind closed blinds, a field marshal would do well to take precautions. Neurath took up a discussion that he and Strölin had been having. "We cannot decide how it is to be done, you see."

How what was to be done?

Strölin shrugged as if they had been talking for years of killing Hitler. Rommel saw that the assassination was a *fait accompli*. "We thought you might advise us," the *Oberbürgermeister* added.

"What would I know about that!" How could he tell them that he had decided to give Hitler another chance? Embarrassed and indignant, he argued that Himmler was more to blame for crimes against the Jews than Hitler. Perhaps Himmler should be their primary target.

"*Bitte*, we've heard all that!" Neurath said. Rommel felt a rising irritation. Did they think he was out of touch?

"Let's be realistic," Strölin said. "How else can Hitler be stopped?"

A man should be allowed to make up his own mind, especially where his family's safety was concerned. Had they thought of the consequences?

"You mean, if we should fail?" Strölin said.

"I think he means if the coup *succeeds*," Neurath observed.

Germany was split down the middle. Though Waffen SS commanders in the west had agreed to support a coup, Himmler's death squads and palace guard were certain to rally around Hitler and turn Berlin into a fortress–not against the Russians but German nationals. With the Wehrmacht divided, the eastern front would collapse in days. "Think of what could happen," he told them. "Russians pillaging the country. Germany annexed as a communist state along with Poland, Czechoslovakia and Hungary."

"The *Amis* would never allow it," Neurath said.

"How can they stop Stalin, short of invading Russia!"

Strölin went to the window and peered through the curtains. Rommel had a sudden urge to throw them open.

"If Hitler were assassinated without warning," Strölin said, "the SS would have nothing to rally around."

Neurath enthusiastically agreed. Denied an ideological center the SS would crumble. Rommel found it otherworldly to hear an SS general speak of his army's disintegration. "But… would Himmler not take the Führer's place?"

"Himmler will be dead!" Strölin exclaimed just as Lucie brought a tray of refreshments. She froze. Rommel motioned for her to come in.

If it took the rest of his forty-eight-hour leave, he would make it up to her. She sliced the birthday cake. Rommel saw that she had thrown the candle away. What a birthday! While the men ate the cake, she chatted about the weather, asked about the drive from Stuttgart, if there was much bomb damage. Strölin, the consummate politician, changed the subject. Where had she found chocolate and sugar? "It just goes to show the resourcefulness of the German *Hausfrau*, may you be crowned in heaven!"

"Nothing to it," she protested, tongue in cheek. "I only began hoarding in January." As soon as they finished, she collected their plates and left the room.

"So we are agreed, Hitler has to go?" Strölin resumed

Rommel pointed out that this was no simple matter. The Führer had been guarding against assassination since the day he came into office. Apart from the prospect of a civil war, killing Hitler was a tough assignment. "I don't want to get into actual planning, nor do I expect to be included, but speaking theoretically, how could it be done...by sniper? Infiltrating the Reich Chancellery is out of the question. No one gets into the Eagle's Nest. How would you go about it? A suicide mission?"

"A bomb." Neurath's tone suggested that the method had been determined. Rommel had a sense of shadowy figures plotting. He did not want to know any specifics. "You asked how we would go about it!" Neurath shrugged.

"I was speaking hypothetically."

"Well, there is no reason you should know," Strölin said. "However, we will call upon you as soon as *they* are out of the picture."

He stared at his boots. They wanted him to commit to succeeding Hitler as minister-president, a verbal commitment that they could report to the Resistance. If they failed to kill Hitler, such compliance on his part would likely mean a death sentence. "A smooth transition is of utmost importance," Neurath pressed.

He would prefer to see either General Beck or Dr.

Goerdeler as the Reich Chancellor. They praised his modesty but emphasized that he was the unanimous choice to lead post-war Germany and negotiate with the *Amis*. Democratic elections could be held after a period of military rule. He was silent. It was an irrevocable step. Talking about it with Speidel and Ruge was one thing. This was the German Resistance. After a moment he tried again to soften their position. "If we surrender to the west, the Führer will have no choice but to accept it. Let me arrange a ceasefire. Let the *Amis* handle Hitler."

"That is naive, *Herr Generalfeldmarschall*." Neurath stood ramrod straight. "Hitler will fight on!"

Strölin added that if Hitler remained in power much longer, eventually the SS generals would talk about Rommel's ceasefire proposal. He would be denounced as a traitor, his family sent to one of the notorious camps. Jews were being put to death by thousands. There were gas chambers. He felt a coldness in his gut. Was *this* what he had been fighting for? Was this what his magnificent *Afrikans* had died for? His men had fought too long and too bravely for Hitler to take them down with him. "You may count on me to whatever is needed after the...." He could not bring himself to say *assassination*. "There is one condition. You must get my family to Switzerland before this takes place."

"Absolutely," Strölin said. "Do not worry."

He asked them not to treat the matter casually. They had to act when Manfred was on leave. He was coming the next day. Could his wife and son be taken to Switzerland immediately? Strölin said the details could not be worked out that quickly, but assured him that it would soon be arranged.

Lucie returned with coffee. "If you were discussing disposing of Hitler, do not mind me," she joked. He looked at her with such tenderness that she accidentally filled a cup to overflowing. She turned her back, wiped tears from her eyes. The guests pretended not to notice.

After their visitors had left, Lucie prepared a light supper. They ate quietly. He did not tell her what had been said, and she did not ask. Instead he asked about Manfred's schooling. Lucie replied that he was not getting as high marks in mathematics as he had the previous year. Rommel blamed the war. The best teachers were in the army. "With you gone, I can't do anything with him," she said. Both took refuge in the normal, the ordinary, in Manfred's school work, in sharing a meal.

He tried to soothe her anxiety. "Let me push the Americans and British into the sea. Then we will have it out about his math scores."

It was almost midnight when they went to bed. He stripped down to shorts and undershirt, ignoring the pajamas she had laid out. She was in her slip, putting her dress on a hanger. "It's been too long," he said.

She slipped inside his arms. "*Ja, zu lang.*"

"So much is happening."

"I know."

"We have to be very careful."

They held each other and talked. As always, she was his touchstone, confirming his deepest feelings. She told him what people in town were saying. No one had confidence in Germany, not just in Hitler-whom they of course avoided mentioning-but in the future. They remembered Versailles. Surrender would be worse, this time, because of what had been done to the Jews. Everyone was saying Germany would be punished "*but please God, don't let it be the Russians*!"

The Red Army was a rising tide. Patton's disgust for the Russians was well known. Surely Eisenhower would see the logic of combining forces to defeat the communists. Career military men among the *Amis* knew that not all Germans were monsters.

"No more talk," she said.

No, they had to speak while they had the opportunity. He wanted her and Manfred out of the country. Strölin would find a way. She should be packed and ready to go at a moment's notice. She sat up. "When?"

"The next time Manfred is given leave." He tried to sound confident. The army kept a close watch on soldiers. There were many desertions. How was Strölin to snatch Manfred from under his commander's nose? What if he were caught? The Gestapo shot deserters. He stroked her hair, kissed her cheek, told her not to worry. Strölin and Neurath had powerful connections.

"I shall not leave without Manfred!"

"Shhhh. You won't have to."

Who would come for them? Would they travel by car? Would they be required to walk across the border?

He advised her to pack light. Just a few overnight things.

She asked if she could give her silver and china to her friends for safe-keeping.

"No, that would alert the Gestapo. We can buy more things. Now, do you remember the young man I met in America, Lieutenant Speigner?"

He explained about sending Speigner to Eisenhower. With any luck, by the time he returned to La Roche-Guyon a reply would be waiting. She said mischievously, "Your *Leutnant* is a gem you picked up at a prisoner-of-war sale." They laughed, savoring the closeness. He remembered the shoes. She switched on the bedside lamp and unwrapped the parcel, exclaimed over the handsome pumps. She stroked the grey suede. The color was perfect. How did he know? She took out the paper wadding and tried on a shoe. It did not fit. He could not believe it. "*Damn the French*!"

"It was sweet of you to remember."

"I'll get you another pair, a half-size larger."

She turned off the light and got into bed.

XIX

The road curved. In the dark he could not tell if he were headed toward the Seine or away from it. Rain was falling intermittently. He was drenched to the skin, thirsty and hungry. *Damn those kids for taking the poncho and canteen.* He swung his bandaged leg stiffly. The entire right side of his body, ribcage, arm and shoulder muscles, burned like fire.

Dark clouds scudded past. Trees shifted and swayed in the wind. What day of the week was it? To lose track of time was to give up one's sanity. Keeping up to date had been the first order of business at POW camp. "*Wednesday*!" someone would shout as they turned out for reveille. Time flowed ahead of him, measured not by hours or days but events: *tick* Anna's face at the transom; *tock* leaping off the training tower; *tick* the green light coming on; *tock* Eric and Dan floating in the creek.

During the day he had hidden in a thicket. The pain in his leg had subsided to a steady ache. He peeked under the dressing. The bullet had cut a shallow gash about three inches long in his right thigh. Wearing a plastic helmet liner, pants leg flapping where the Frenchwoman had torn it open, he set out at dusk, keeping to the woods where possible. Hedgerows and stone fences forced him back on the road. Luckily, there was little traffic. The weather was bad. Eisenhower would be crazy to launch the invasion in this storm. Pilots could not locate drop zones.

He stopped regularly to listen and sniff the air for engine fumes or cigarette smoke. It was important not to blunder into a sentry post. The rural countryside was startlingly silent. Even the birds seemed intimidated. He came to what appeared to be a huge cemetery, grave markers in neat rows, hundreds of them. *Why a graveyard in the middle of nowhere?* The dark meadow was more swamp than pasture. What he thought were tombstones were actually logs embedded in the wet ground. This must be "Rommel's Asparagus," the anti-glider obstacles the G-2 captain had mentioned, tree trunks poised to rip gliders apart. *I am Rommel. Look upon me and despair.*

Was the Desert Fox using him? The intelligence officers suspected the ceasefire offer as a stall. He was betting his life the field marshal was sincere, but in twenty-four hours anything could have happened. Rommel himself could have been arrested.

He came to a crossroads. Amfreville-la-Camp was to the right, le Gros Theil to the left. Elbeuf straight ahead. He tried to picture the map. Elbeuf was on the Seine. La Roche-Guyon was twenty-five miles upstream. Engrossed in these calculations he did not hear wheels whirring. A *Kübelwagen* was running without lights. He dove for the ditch. Tires crunched wood. His cane lay broken in the road. The engine noise faded. He sat up and wiped mud from his face.

Without the walking stick he was reduced to a slow shuffle. He was beginning to look for a place to rest when a moist, fecund scent caught his attention. The Seine! He would steal the first boat he saw. He kept going.

Wood smoke drifted through the light rain. A church steeple knifed into the sky: *Elbeuf.* Under curfew and blackout restrictions, houses were dark and silent. He skirted the town, crossed a plowed field. It was slow going but the pungent scent of water was getting stronger. East of town he came back to the road, which gradually sloped down to a bridge. He climbed a fence and made his way down the river bank, passing a house suspended on stilts. An unexpected sound made him freeze. A man was singing.

Two soldiers were on the bridge, one singing, one listening. It was a sad song as if the singer knew the end was coming. Under the steel arch the Seine surged in whispery silence. The guards sat on the railing at the far end. He thought of approaching them with Rommel's insignia. He could surrender and ask to be taken to army group headquarters. Then he noticed a boat tied to a bridge piling. He decided to row upstream, get as close as he could to La Roche-Guyon. Extending his stiff leg, he slid down the slick clay bank.

At the base of the bridge were two boats. The one he had seen was too large for a single oarsman. The other was a fifteen-footer. He searched for oars under the gunwales. He removed two with exquisite stealth and climbed into the smaller boat.

Was ist das?

Ein Blitz?

He froze. The sentries were not talking about him. Downriver there was a sudden glow. Ripping explosions followed. He gave thanks to the RAF and pushed off. Staying close to the shore he rowed upstream. The men on the bridge were silhouetted against the glowing horizon as they watched, gripping their weapons helplessly. There was a droning vibration of hundreds of aircraft. The trees shook. FLAK batteries opened fire. Anti-aircraft tracers disappeared into the heavens. An .88 milimeter gun hidden in the trees began to fire methodically, *ack-ack-ack-ack*. The flash of anti-aircraft fire lit up the river.

D-Day.

No wonder Eisenhower didn't give a damn if Rommel wanted to surrender. Above the clouds American and British paratroopers were standing and hooking up. Ahead of them came wave upon wave of B-17s. The shrill scream of bombs ceased a split second before they exploded. By all rights he ought to have been terrified–but he was laughing.

XX

The phone rang. He groped for the receiver. "Yes?"

"*Hans hier*!"

He swung his legs over the bed. Lucie put her hand on his back.

"We are getting enemy activity," Speidel said calmly. "It may be nothing but I thought you would want to know."

"Have the *Amis* landed?"

"There are conflicting reports. Enemy paratroopers have been spotted east of the Orne, around Breville and Ranville, and along the northern fringe of the Bavent Forest. It could be a feint or an attempt to form the Resistance into battle groups. I don't think there is a need for alarm."

He stood very straight, receiver against his ear. Had they built hundreds of fortications only to turn their backs? "Of *course* they would send in paratroopers first," he said impatiently. "Have you alerted Group B?"

"Fifteenth Army has been placed on full alert."

"What about Seventh Army?"

"I was waiting until I spoke with you."

Speidel's first order should have been to put *both* armies in Group B on alert. He wanted to know why this was not done.

"Fifteenth Army was the first to report enemy activity in our area. General Salmuth would have placed them on alert, I imagine."

"You imagine!" Something was wrong. Fifteenth Army's sector extended from Belgium to the Somme River. Eisenhower could well be landing there. "Have you spoken with General Dollman?"

"Not yet."

"Do it now!"

"*Jawohl.*"

Speidel's sluggish response was inexcusable, his heady *Jawohl!* suspicious. Why so cheerful? With the receiver in one hand he pulled on his tunic with the other. He strapped on his wristwatch, noting the time: 0130 hours. Lucie got up and went to make coffee.

When did it happen?

About an hour ago.

When, precisely?

I would say around midnight.

Before committing his reserves, he had to be certain where the main attack was taking place. Hitler would, of course, hold back the four SS divisions as well as Panzer Lehr division. "Telephone Dollman and call me back," he said. Speidel responded with another enthusiastic *Jawohl*! He hung up and went downstairs. Moments later the phone in his study rang.

Speidel said, "Airborne landings are being reported in the Cotentin peninsula near Caen. However, no one takes these landings in Normandy seriously."

"What do you mean 'no one'?"

"Well, besides myself there is vice-admiral Ruge, Captain Lange and of course Colonel Staubwasser."

"Has anyone actually *seen* an enemy soldier?"

"There have been reports of straw dummies attached to parachutes." Speidel seemed strangely ebullient. "I asked to have one brought in. Use of dummies indicates this is a diversion, which reinforces my belief that the real invasion must come at Calais."

"Keep me abreast."

"*Jawohl.*"

The idea of a straw dummy attached to a parachute made him want to wake Daniel up and drive to France using headlamps all the way. To hell with the RAF! He wanted to be with his staff. Soldiers coming and going. Phones ringing. Speidel insisted there was no cause for alarm. "Everything is under control. I myself am going back to bed."

Rommel was incensed. "*Das ist verboten*!"

"Truly, *Herr Generalfeldmarschall*, there is nothing more that I can do."

"Call me back in twenty minutes." He hung up before Speidel could object. He missed Alfred Gause, his longtime chief of staff whom Speidel had replaced. If Gause had been in charge, he would have alerted all units. He paced back and forth under the sober gaze of Stonewall Jackson. Lucie brought him some coffee. "What is the matter?" she said.

"I am not being given all the facts. There should not be so much confusion. Something is clogging up the intelligence network. Either the allies have invaded or they have not." The phone rang and he snatched it up. Anticipating another burst of temper, she left the room.

"It appears that this is a local matter." Speidel's casual tone continued to perplex and confound. "I believe that bailed-out airplane crews are being mistaken for paratroopers."

"May I remind you of what I have said all along? For the counter-punch to be effective, it has to be made swiftly and in precisely the right place. *Mein Gott*, I should be there to make these decisions. I should drive to the coast at once."

"No need for that!" Speidel was genuinely alarmed. He promised to call back with more information, then abruptly rang off. Was he more afraid of being "invaded" by his superior than by the enemy? Before Rommel could dwell on this, other generals called in. U.S. paratroopers had been captured. Both the 82nd and 101st Airborne had units scattered all over the Normandy coast. German intelligence was unsure whether this was a major attack or a probe. His coffee cold and forgotten, he studied a map of France, trying to imagine battle lines forming. Something told him this was the moment to counterattack.

There is no cause for alarm. Why had Speidel not issued a full alert? Was it nerves? Despite wide experience in military planning, Hans had never commanded a unit larger than a company of infantry. *Go home*, he had begged Rommel. It was all about the meeting with Strölin and Neurath. Hans was pushing him into the conspiracy.

At 0215 hours, the chief of staff of Seventh Army, Maj. Gen. Max Pemsel, phoned to complain about Speidel's foot-dragging. "Get it in his head," Pemsel said, refreshingly blunt, "that this is a major operation. Of that there is no doubt. Hans will not face facts! Paratroopers, gliders, light vehicles and anti-tank weapons are on the ground and being deployed. We need reinforcements on the coast between La Havre and Cherbourg."

He promised to see what he could do. Pemsel knew as well as he did that OKW would not release the reserves until it was clear where the main attack was occurring. He hung up. It was all too clear. Speidel had downplayed reports that the invasion was imminent. He had made a point of countersigning the official report, June 3, by Rommel's intelligence officer, Colonel

Staubwasser: "The increased transmission of alarm phrases since June 1 sent to the French Underground by enemy radio is *not* to be interpreted as an indication that the beginning of the invasion is imminent." Hans had sent Rommel home with assurances that the weather was too bad, the seas too high. He had said navy intelligence *guaranteed* that the allies could not attempt an invasion.

"How could I be so stupid!" He savagely struck his palm against his knee. They were all in it together-Speidel, Ruge, Stulpnagel, Falkenhausen, Neurath and Strölin. The meeting with the latter may have been arranged to keep him at home when the invasion came. Speidel had encouraged him to pose for Goebbels' cameras, saying, "The publicity will backfire on the Führer. He in effect is selling you to the public as his successor." Outwitted and manipulated by his own staff! He had no one to blame but himself.

"The invasion has begun," he told Lucie, "and here I sit in Herrlingen when I should be directing a counterattack. The Allies are on the beaches. Our army was not placed on alert until an hour ago."

"How could that happen?"

"You may well ask."

He should have made Speidel swear an oath. To negotiate from strength was their only chance for an honorable surrender. With their backs to the wall, it was imperative that Lieutenant Speigner bring him a positive response from Eisenhower.

"Would you like more coffee?"

"What?"

"Never mind."

She went out and shut the door. He thought of his troops, FLAK batteries manned by middle-aged gunners, the Russians' laundry festooning the cannon. Bombarded and strafed, outflanked, outmanned, they would soon be running for their lives. All his preparations were for naught. If the Channel was a "moat around Fortress Europe," his own chief of staff had let down the drawbridge. Perhaps he *wanted* Speidel to fool him. Perhaps his subconscious had let him down. What positive note could the great master-of-illusion, Goebbels, put on this catastrophe?

MOVIETONE NEWS REPORTS: ROMMEL VACATIONING IN HERRLINGEN NEAR ULM. HELPS WIFE CUT BIRTHDAY

CAKE. HAPPY SMILES ALL AROUND AS THE DESERT FOX HAS HIS CAKE AND EATS IT, TOO.

At daybreak Speidel phoned to say the invasion was definitely on. Rommel had been wondering how long it would take him. "I had to wait until I was sure," he insisted.

"Of course," he said coolly. He did not want to sack Speidel over the phone. "*Wo ist der Amerikaner*?Alert all patrols to pick him up."

"*Jawohl!*"

He turned his mind to the battle. It was fortunate that Rundstedt, in defiance of OKW directives, had dispatched elements of 12 SS Panzer to the coast and ordered Panzer Lehr division to proceed to the emergency assembly areas. At 0445 Rundstedt phoned to say that he had requested that OKW release the strategic panzer reserves. Rommel agreed wholeheartedly. Despite the enemy bombers, the tanks had to be moved up without delay. It still was theoretically possible to beat back the invasion, though 12 SS Panzer could not reach the coast in less than twenty-four hours under the best of circumstances, or Panzer Lehr in less than forty-eight.

"It is a disaster," he told Lucie as he dressed. She handed him his belt and a pair of clean socks. He suspected that Speidel had created a desperate situation so that the generals-not only Rommel but Rundstedt, Geyr, Dollmann and the rest-would go along with an assassination attempt. "German soldiers are being sacrificed for political *expediency*!" He shrilled the word as if expediency were the worst obscenity he knew. "It's not fighting. It's not soldiering." No hills to capture. No rivers to cross. No enemy divisions to cut off.

"I'm sorry, my darling," she said quietly. "It is the only solution. Everybody but you sees that." He went downstairs in a fury. At the bottom of the stairs he paused. She was right. Hitler had to go. There was no way around it. He buzzed Daniel on the intercom and told him to bring the car. Lucie brought his suitcase. "You never unpacked," she said sadly.

As he was going out the door, she begged him to wait until Manfred arrived. "He should be here in an hour. I want him to see you!"

She usually kept her emotions under control. He pulled his mind back from what was happening in Normandy. "Tell him I'll spend time with him when we are in Switzerland. We will work on mathematics, *ja*? Tell him I promise!" Daniel was holding the car door open. "I must go. We will celebrate your birthday next time. Here's to better days." Each goodbye could be their last. She looked at him with a sad, sensitive gaze.

XXI

Allied bombs were falling somewhere to the east. Misting rain smelled of cordite. Feathering his strokes, he rowed under a railway bridge. A sentry fired a warning shot. Speigner shouted *merde*–the only French profanity he knew. The sentry laughed. The crazy fisherman had picked the worst time to check his lines. Another soldier called out, "*Keine Kugeln verschwenden*!" Don't waste bullets! In the rain they did not notice that he was wearing a uniform.

By dawn he was five miles upstream. His blisters had blisters. He saw a steeple through the trees. Columns of black smoke rose from burning buildings. With daylight at hand, he had no choice but to give up. He rowed to shore, pulled the boat up on the muddy bank and climbed the levee. The rain had stopped but the footpath was slick. His bad leg gave out and he fell down the steep slope. He struck his head against a tree and lost consciousness. When he came to, it was twilight. He struggled to the top of the levee, dizzy, weak from hunger and thirst, his leg throbbing. Two German soldiers spotted him. "*Faire halte*!"

He raised his hands. One covered him with a machine pistol while the other skidded down the the bank. He saw that the soldier was very young, sixteen at the most. There was a death's head medallion on his cap and SS on his collar. He had heard about the *Jugend* division, Hitler's master race in embryo. The Waffen SS was robbing the cradle. When they reached sixteen, Hitler Youth traded their armbands and Swiss army knives for *Schmeissers*. He could not ask these baby faced assassins to take him to Rommel. He would be lucky to survive the interrogation.

"*Was für eine Uniform ist das?*" one of the Jugend said. The other replied, "*Amerikanisch*!"

"No, they can not have advanced so far," the first said. "He must be British."

The one on the levee sported a mustache and was perhaps a year older than the other. Speigner sensed that the younger one was more dangerous. The Afrika Korps grenadiers who had captured him in Libya had been seasoned professionals. *Jugend* were children with a license to kill.

"Hands on your head!" Cherub ordered in English. He marched Speigner to the top of the levee. When pain in his leg caused him to hesitate, a *Schmeisser was* rammed in his back. They marched him along the levee.

What if he tries to escape?

Shoot him.

He almost said, *Nein, nein, Ich werde nicht fliehen*...I won't escape! They were marching him along the top of the levee when it occurred to Mustache to disarm the prisoner. He snatched the .45 automatic out of Speigner's holster. They examined it with interest. Mustache stuck it under his belt.

Cherub said, "It is not yours."

"I will show it to the sergeant."

"You will *give* it to him."

"Only to examine. Then it is mine."

Cherub frisked Speigner and found the knife which Max had stuck under his shirt. "Knife for me," he said. "If he runs I will cut him in half."

They took him to a checkpoint next to a drawbridge. Horse drawn wagons, Citroens and three-wheeled motorscooters were stopped at the one-way bridge. SS troopers were searching civilians, men, women and children. A dead man lay on the side of the road, a blob of mud lodged in one eye. At first Speigner thought the corpse was wearing an eye-patch. The *Jugend* ignored the body. Refugees were bags of bones. An enemy commando, on the other hand, defeated and stripped of his dignity, was worth a promotion. Cherub shoved him into the bridge keeper's hut. A *Jugend* sergeant, maybe nineteen or twenty, sat at a table operating a radio.

"We captured an American!" Cherub declared.

"Or a Britischer," said his comrade. The sergeant glanced at Speigner with the air of a veteran. "Your papers!" Speaking

English, Max answered that he had no papers. He started to state his name, rank and serial number. The sergeant interrupted. "*Kommando*?"

He shook his head. Mustache handed over the pistol. The sergeant inspected it, then noticed the knife in Cherub's belt. He crooked his finger. Cherub grudgingly relinquished the souvenir. They were loathe to leave their prisoner, but when the sergeant raised an highbrow they left. He asked Max's name. When he told him, the sergeant let his excitement show. Speigner had heard that the Jugend were always looking for Jews. When they found them, they either killed them or used them as slave labor. "Are you with main invasion force or advance party?"

He shrugged. The sergeant hit him with closed fist in a businesslike manner. His ears rang. The SS shot commandos. He could be dead in a few minutes. The sergeant had discovered Rommel's insignia and was staring at it in astonishment when an SS captain entered the hut. "What have we here?"

"A commando gangster, Herr Kapitän. His name is Speigner."

The officer, perhaps nineteen, gave Max a searing glance. "Shoot him. We are moving out."

He forced himself not to react. At the POW camp a bomber pilot shot down over Germany had told him about the *Hitlerjugend*. Its officer cadre came from 500 non-commmissioned officers selected from Waffen SS units. This captain had probably been promoted from corporal or sergeant. He was surprised that the captain was not interested in the oak leaves insignia.

"*Sprechen Sie Deutsch?*"

"No."

"Your name is German."

"I am an American."

"He is British, not American." the sergeant said, speaking German.

"Are you a Jew?"

He shook his head. In terms of actual religious practice, he was telling the truth. The fact was, he was half Jewish on his mother's side. The sergeant said, "British glider troops have been reported in the area!" The captain asked what was found on the prisoner. The sergeant displayed the weapons and waited to see if the captain would take them. The captain half-cocked the .45, checking if a round was in the chamber. He yanked up

Speigner's split trousers-leg and peeled back the bandage. "Who shot you?" he said in English.

"German soldiers."

"Where did it happen?"

"In the woods."

The captain poked him with the .45. He stared at the floor. "Empty your pockets!" Speigner laid out an ammunition clip, the "Cricket" and the five hundred-franc notes that Special Branch had provided. The captain pocketed the money, then examined the Cricket.

"It may be some kind of clip or fastener," said the sergeant.

The captain was not about to let the sergeant take over the interrogation. "Show us how it works!"

He hesitated. There might be paratroopers in the woods using the gismo. The sergeant hit him again, speaking German and watching to see if he understood, "Let me shoot him."

"Look at this!"

Finally the captain noticed the oak leaves cluster. "Where did you get this?" The sergeant slapped off his helmet liner. "I ask you once more. Where did you get it?" The captain cocked the .45 and pointed it at his temple. He started to make up a story, then thought silence might allow him to live a few more seconds. A motorcycle pulled up outside, its engine revved with authority and then shut down. "*Heil Hitler*" was shouted. A middle-aged Waffen SS general entered the hut. The Jugend stood at attention. The general glanced Speigner in mild curiosity. Here, said the captain, was their first enemy captive. He waited to see if the *Herr Gruppenführer* would seize their prisoner.

"Does he speak German?"

"He says not. His name is Speigner. He is probably a *Jude*. In any case, he must be shot."

"Was he carrying anything of interest?"

The captain took the oak leaves patch out of his pocket. The general looked at the insignia, then told his subordinates to go outside while he interrogated the prisoner.

Herr Gruppenführer, it may not be safe.

I will take responsiblity.

This is not standard procedure...

Outside!

When the sergeant and captain had left, the general said in perfectly good English, "You are a lieutenant?"

"Yes, sir."

"American?"

"Yes, sir."

"Do you know Field Marshal Rommel?"

He had seconds to make up his mind. The general had spoken the name *Rommel* with respect. "I met him before the war."

"Are you the one he sent to England?" The general's gaze bored into him. He was afraid to answer. "I will see that you are taken to Rommel, but you must say nothing to anyone, do you understand?"

He felt a wave of relief. The general called the captain back and ordered him to release the prisoner to Army Group B for interrogation.

But, my general, we have been ordered to turn all commando-gangsters over to the Gestapo.

He is not a commando.

How do we know that?

Tie the prisoner's hands behind his back.

Jawohl, mein Herr Gruppenführer.

Send him to Heeresgruppe B at once. Use my vehicle.

The captain said, "I will have one of my men deliver him."

"My driver will do it. I will stay here until he returns."

The general took him outside and spoke to the driver, who saluted and started the engine. The *Jugend* sergeant shoved him into the motorcycle sidecar. The captain, obviously frustrated, could only watch. The French corpse with the one-eyed stare lay in the road, vehicles passing within inches, driving without lights due to the blackout. Max flinched when a truck ran over the dead man's hand. The general noticed him looking at the body. "It is being left there to discourage saboteurs," he said.

XXII

When he arrived at his headquarters, nothing was happening. No vehicles parked in front of the chateau, no couriers delivering messages, no sign of life except for two guards sneaking a smoke. They stubbed out their cigarettes and came to attention. Gripping his baton he strode through the entrance. The eighteen-inch gold baton was covered with red velvet, gold eagles and black swastikas, and weighed three pounds. He wanted to bash someone with it.

At the front desk a single enlisted man jumped up and came to attention. Where was everybody? The telephones ought to be ringing off the hooks. Had the ballroom been converted into a strategy room? Where was that *taka-taka-taka* noise coming from? He grimly entered his office. Lange was placing folders in a filing cabinet. He saluted. "Welcome back, *Herr Generalfeldmarschall*."

"What are you doing?"

The aide looked puzzled. "Filing field reports. They are starting to back up. General Speidel said..."

"I don't want them filed! Take them upstairs."

"Where, sir?"

"To the-" He was afraid to ask if a strategy room had been set up. He stamped up the wide staircase. The *taka-taka* sound was getting louder. At the top of the stairs he flung open the double doors. The chief of staff and naval advisor put down their paddles and stood at attention.

"We were waiting for you to get back," Speidel said.

"You have time for games?"

Speidel gave him a naked glance. He took this as a sign of guilt. "Where is my war room?"

"I was waiting for confirmation from OKW."

He could hardly trust himself to speak. Ruge laid his paddle on the table and edged away. "You may be excused, Vice-Admiral Ruge," he said. Ruge bowed and left. In the hallway, voices echoed off the high ceilings: *On your toes, the Herr Generalfeldmarschall is back.* He hugged himself in his misery. "Why, Hans?"

Accusations poured out. Speidel wanted him out of the way, encouraged him to go on leave, delayed putting the army on alert, downplayed early signs of an invasion. Did he think he was dealing with a fool? "I may turn down the chancellorship."

Speidel was horrified. "*Bitte*, you are the future of Germany!" Rommel, he stuttered, was a patriot. Could not go back on his word. Could not ignore his responsibility.

"*I could have pushed them into the sea.*"

"Fate would not have it so."

"Fate had nothing to do with it! Our best chance for a negotiated peace was to stop the enemy cold, pin him down on the beaches, and only then to call for a ceasefire."

Speidel accidentally knocked his paddle off the table. In the silence it clattered violently. He stooped to pick it up. Speidel wanted to know about the meeting with Neurath and Strölin. What about the Führer? Had the resistance leaders divulged their intentions? Rommel looked at him askance. Speidel knew *their* intentions. What the chief of staff wanted to know was whether *he* had committed. He could not sack Hans now, even if he wanted to. They had to work together.

"With half an army, the Führer will not last long." He was offering his chief of staff a carrot. Yes, he had committed to Neurath and Strölin. Yes, he had offered to lead his country out of war, though he would like to think that he had made the decision himself.

"We had no chance to stop the enemy in the sectors where they landed. At Vierville our batteries inflicted heavy casualties. Elsewhere–" Speidel shrugged. "The Allied strategy was well-planned and perfectly executed. There was nothing we could do."

He wished he were crawling under barbed wire with .50 caliber bullets whizzing overhead. He wished he were anywhere but here, safe at his headquarters, far from the front lines. "Were Neurath and Strölin 'in on it'?"

Speidel frowned. "On what?"

"The plot."

"What plot? There was never any plot. How was I to know that the enemy would attack? The weather-"

"Was ideal for an invasion!" He whacked the table with his baton. It felt good to hit something. He sensed arrested motion throughout the chateau as soldiers stopped what they were doing. *What was going on in the ballroom? Had the field marshal struck General Speidel?* "You have 'played your cards close to the vest.' You have come very close to losing my trust, Hans."

"We both want the same thing." Speidel hid the offending paddle behind his back. "To save the fatherland!"

There would be no apology. He went away and raged at his staff. In half an hour he had a war room with telephones, a wireless operator, codebook in hand. Phones started to ring. *This was more like it.* He spoke with General Feuchtinger. Had 21 Panzer Division been committed? It was the only armored division near Caen. He was relieved to hear that Feuchtinger had ordered his tanks into action at 0730 hours. How had 21 Panzer fared? "I am sorry to say," Feuchtinger reported, "that the attack failed and we were forced to withdraw." He explained that his division was too widely dispersed.

He rang off, beside himself. *Widely dispersed! Who ordered 21 Panzer to split its forces?* Speidel was saying in his precise, scholarly way that Feuchtinger had placed four grenadier battalions on either side of the Orne. *What was the point of that? Who told Feuchtinger to split his forces?* He suspected that this, too, was another of Speidel's "strategies," but did not ask lest he fly into a rage. He dug into the field reports. Was the defensive perimeter holding? How many casualties had the 716th taken? As he assembled the reports he saw that the battle was lost-and that he was a pawn in a madman's game. *Everybody sees that but you.* In Tunisia, even in retreat, he had been his own man. He had lost but it had been *his* battle to lose.

Radio transmissions were interrupted by bombing. It was impossible in some cases to contact his division commanders. He sat waiting to re-establish connections. Gradually, the big picture emerged. The Allies had established five separate beachheads with an estimated hundred thousand troops. Twelfth SS Panzer was counter-attacking, though one division would not be enough to turn the tide.

All the work, the preparations, inspections, improvisation, had been for nothing. Yet with the Neuraths, Speidels and Stulpnagels working at cross purposes, was it not inevitable that Germany would find a way to lose?

Lange brought him the puppy, Elbo, which barked when it saw its master. He took the little dachshund and asked why his aide had brought it. "I was told the Herr Generalfeldmarschall wanted his *Hund.*" Lange coughed discreetly behind his hand.

"Who told you?"

"Herr General Speidel."

What kind of sentimental fool did they take him for! Field Marshal Jodl once said that Rommel's pessimism about the war stemmed from his *Afrikanische Frankheit*, or "African sickness." Did Speidel believe he was growing melancholy? In all his years of command, he had never been so frustrated. He needed support, not distraction and manipulation. The Americans had taken Bayeux. The British were moving toward Caen. Why should Eisenhower and Montgomery accept anything less than unconditional surrender? He thrust Elbo into Lange's hands.

"General Feuchtinger calling." The radioman handed him a receiver. He took the call. Under attack, with no time for encoding, Feuchtinger shouted over the radio waves, "*We are taking a beating.*"

Rommel held the receiver away from his ear. "Can you hold out?"

"*Only if we receive reinforcement.*"

He heard firing in the background and was stung by envy. He wanted more than anything to be in the field, dodging bullets. "You must hang on! Twelve SS Panzer is trying to get through."

Feuchtinger begged for Luftwaffe support. Rommel thought at first he was joking. There was a moment of silence. He promised to support 12 Panzer as best he could and rang off. It was like putting one's finger in a dike. Wherever he committed his forces, the *Amis* broke out somewhere else. He had to reinforce the divisions that were the hardest hit. Lange handed him another phone. *Gruppenführer* Dietrich was on the line.

"*Guten Abend, Herr Generalfeldmarschall.*" Dietrich reported that 2 SS Division was still fighting but only had enough ammunition and petrol for one major engagement. If he were ordered back into battle he wanted it to count. Before Rommel could reply he added, "By the way, a *Jugend* patrol picked up an American lieutenant. Near Louviers. I did not know there were any Americans in that area, did you?"

Rommel suppressed his excitement. "What is the American's name?"

"Speigner, I believe."

"Is he all right? I mean, was he wounded?"

"Shot in the leg but not too bad."

"Send him to my headquarters at once."

Dietrich said that his driver was bringing Speigner to La Roche Guyon. They should arrive momentarily. He hesitated. "*Herr Generalfeldmarschall*, the SS must not be compromised."

"Don't worry."

"The lieutenant had an oak leaves cluster to the Knight's Cross. You are not missing yours by any chance?"

Dietrich had happened upon the American and saved his life. The SS did not take prisoners. Rommel thanked providence. "You know the problem we discussed? I am working on a solution."

"I thought as much," Dietrich said.

Danke schön, Herr Gruppenführer.

Gern geschehen.

He hung up and went to look for Speigner.

XXIII

An SS motorcycle with an American officer in the sidecar attracted much curiosity at the chateau, especially when the commander of Army Group B seemed to be expecting him. Rommel ordered the prisoner taken to his quarters. Speigner gave no sign that he knew his captor. Hands tied, limping, he followed the guards into the chateau. He realized that previously he had been brought to the field marshal's study by a side entrance. Rommel took a close look at the American and called for his surgeon. Speigner's news would have to wait. He was wounded and exhausted. The surgeon slit the cords that bound his wrists, had him sit down, then removed the dirty bandages. Rommel waited.

"A deep laceration," the surgeon said. "Inflamed but not infected." He swabbed the wound and put on fresh bandages, then gave Speigner a shot for pain. "You will have a...what is English for *Narbe*?"

"Scar," Speigner muttered.

"*Ja*, scar!" The doctor was delighted. Everyone, Max thought in a morphine rush, was speaking English. As the surgeon went out, another officer appeared. He wore the red-striped trousers of a general and rimless spectacles.

"Were you taken in by a French family?" Rommel spoke as if resuming a conversation.

"Yes."

"Near Brionne?"

"Somewhere below the Seine." Morphine whispered in his veins.

"You escaped through the cellar?" A few moments sooner and he would have discovered the American. If that had happened, things might now be different. He certainly would not have abandoned his post and gone home. He might have even been able to contact Eisenhower. Somewhat grudgingly he introduced his chief of staff to the American.

Speidel said, "How you do, *Herr Leutnant*."

Despite the languorous effects of the drug Max remembered his message. Floating under a parachute he called as he descended, his voice blown away by the wind: *Churchill agrees to a ceasefire*!

"What did you say?"

The morphine grappled with him like a powerful genie. "Prime Minister Churchill...will meet with you…to discuss *Frieden*."

Speidel asked if he had anything in writing. He took off his jacket, turned the sleeve inside out and tore open the slit in the cuff. When he tried to remove Churchill's card, it came apart. He ripped out the seam and retrieved half of the saturated card more or less intact. They were afraid to touch it. He held it in his palm for them to read. It was impossible to decipher Churchill's message, but the printed logo was legible: *10 Downing Street, London*.

"I fell in the water," he apologized. "The message said, 'To Marshal Rommel, The bearer, Lt. Speigner, represents me,' or words to that effect, signed 'W. S. Churchill.'"

"You met with Churchill?" Rommel said.

"A friend spoke with the prime minister on my behalf. I was under house arrest."

Rommel was disappointed. "Are you certain Churchill is in favor of a ceasefire? Can you be certain?"

He tried to reconstruct what McAlpin told him. "He doesn't trust Stalin. He said he would meet with you to stop the fighting. Anywhere but Berlin."

"*Und Eisenhower*?" It was frustrating that the surgeon had given the American morphine.

Rommel's face swam in and out of focus. The information spurted out of him in fragments. Eisenhower had been too busy. Sir Winston on the other hand was willing to cut through red tape. "It was awful about the commandos–" His voice trailed off.

"The two commandos who were killed?"

He wanted to buy Dan and Eric a beer. Were they old enough to be served alcohol?

When a personal courier of the commander of German forces in Western France crossed the Channel on a mission of this importance, the Allied High Command made time for him! Was Eisenhower really "too busy" or had he in fact rejected the offer? "Can you say whether Eisenhower wants to meet with me?"

There was air under his chute, a warm updraft. He felt himself rising. He dimly recalled that it was the U.S. Army that put him under house arrest. What did it matter? That was a minor detail. When Rommel spoke, Eisenhower damn well better listen. "*I shhink it is a dishtinct possibluity*," he muttered.

Captain Lange knocked discreetly and handed a communiqué to Speidel, who showed it to Rommel. While the generals discussed the dispatch, Max played tug of war with sleep. He was thinking of Anna's face and her soft hands. Someone knocked at the door. An orderly delivered a meal on a tray.

"Give my dinner to the prisoner," Rommel said.

What Lange had brought was a captured enemy document detailing the Allied battle plan. As Rommel and Speidel discussed it openly, Max dug into the potatoes and sausage, oblivious to what they were saying. U.S. strategy apparently was to break through to the west coast of the Cotentin peninsula and capture Cherbourg while the British attacked Caen. Cherbourg was a deep water port. Hitler was determined to hold it. "Has the Führer ordered Cherbourg to prepare for a siege?" Rommel asked.

"Fight to the last man, what else?" Speidel shrugged.

Hitler had done the same thing in Tunisia. The Afrika Korps with little fuel or ammunition had been thrown to the Eighth

Army and shot to pieces. Should he send word to Churchill? Arrange a meeting? Or wait and see if the German army could hold? The Wehrmacht needed a victory before he called for a ceasefire. The best bet would be to drive a wedge between the bridgeheads and prevent the Americans and British from linking up. That would be Geyr von Schweppenburg's job.

He and Speidel talked under their breath, their backs to the American. OKW expected a second Allied landing. Intelligence reports said Patton had forty divisions standing by in England. Would this second wave strike at the Pas de Calais? OKW was holding back 15 Army units north of the Seine, including two panzer divisions with 300 tanks. Rommel wanted to take these fresh troops and attack between Cherbourg and Caen, splitting the *Amis* in half, but the order had to come from Berlin.

Speigner's stomach was full. The drone of aircraft overhead was comforting. Air raid sirens sounded cheerful. He would throw a morphine party. Everyone was invited! He was mildly curious when vehicles braked outside. Doors slammed. There were shouted commands. *Heil Hitler!* Warmed by drugs and food, surrounded by his protectors, he waited patiently.

Speidel was for contacting the *Amis*. They should not count on any victories. Berlin would not release the reserves. Rommel was aghast. "You want to push ahead with a surrender before Schweppenburg counterattacks?"

"If he fails, we would have less leverage than we have now," Speidel said.

He reminded the chief of staff that Manfred and Lucie had to be out of the country before he gave a ceasefire order. Strölin needed time to set up an escape. Could they put it off? Speidel argued.

He could not believe what he was hearing. Was Hans crazy? Did he not understand what would happen to Lucie and Manfred? The captured enemy documents gave him a slight edge. There was no mention of a second invasion. With every passing hour it seemed less likely that Patton would attack at Calais. He decided to concentrate his forces and cut off the enemy vanguard.

Speidel insisted that they send the American to set up a meeting with the British. While that was happening, they could see to Rommel's family and the army would try to slow the allied advance. Rommel appraised his chief of staff. What Speidel was saying made sense. Time was of the essence. "All right, we will make the *Amis* an offer. I will send the American."

Pleased, Speidel fiddled with his glasses. Rommel shook Max's shoulder and told him what he must do. The British, or at least their prime minister, had shown a willingness to negotiate. He was to get through to Montgomery and tell him that Rommel was standing by to give a ceasefire order.

Speigner yawned. "Sure, anything you say."

"How is your leg?"

He hated the thought of walking, but at least his leg had stopped hurting. He struggled to his feet and saluted. "Sorry to eat and run!"

"I should have stopped that injection!" Rommel muttered. It was also too bad that Churchill's card had disintegrated. He needed something to show the generals. At the same time, it was too dangerous for him to commit himself to writing. He shook the drowsy American and dictated a message. Wehrmacht forces in the west were ready to cease firing. The next step would be the formal surrender of all German forces in occupied France. He would personally coordinate the process and announce the ceasefire on the radio. In addition he would advise Hitler to surrender to the British and Americans. "Have you got that? Ceasefire, then formal surrender, I give the order by radio. You may contact me by telegraph. Say only where and when to meet. If it is with the Americans, say 'Proceed to Point A.' If the British, 'Proceed to Point B.' Identify yourself as…"

"Violet?" Speigner muttered.

"You mean, the *color*? Yes, 'violet' it is."

He helped Speigner up. The ripped trouser-leg flapped open above the fresh bandages. Max noticed Rommel's steadying hand. He took this as a sign of friendship. He did not want to leave his friend just when they were getting along so well.

"We're going to send you over the wall," Rommel said. "Get out fast and keep going. You have in your hands the future of Europe." Speigner stared at his hands. Just then Captain Lange came in. The Gestapo was at the main gate.

XXIV

They were Rommel's men. Nobody crossed them. Not the Gestapo. Not the SS. Still, they were relieved when the field marshal came to see what was going on. The lieutenant in charge of the detail saluted. He reported that when he stopped the Gestapo they threatened to put Army Group B on report. They had information that an American officer was inside. They demanded to interrogate him. "I told them to go fuck themselves." The lieutenant grinned while standing at attention.

Rommel touched him with the baton as if knighting him. Men in black leather coats waited behind the iron gates. He paused to let them know he was in no hurry. The Gestapo fed off the fecal matter of the Reich. His grenadiers, machine pistols slung loosely across their chests, stood their ground. Their commander's defiance of the Gestapo was well known. He refused to allow a political officer to be attached to his staff though this was standard procedure elsewhere in the *Wehrmacht*.

The leader of the Gestapo detail identified himself as Herr Edel. He was so furious he could hardly speak above a whisper. "We want the American," he said.

What American? Rommel thought these bastards were too cocky by half. Time they were brought down a notch.

Edel shot back, "He was picked up by *Hitlerjugend*. We have orders to interrogate all commandos. The *Herr Generalfeldmarschall* will hand over the prisoner."

There was a distant drone of enemy bombers. Rommel paid them no attention. He casually repeated, "*Es gibt keinen Amerikaner hier*!" The agent was astounded. The Gestapo had it on the best authority. An American had been brought to *Heeresgruppe B*. An SS captain had reported it.

"He may be wandering around somewhere. Who knows? Prisoners of war are paroled all the time. My advance units in Tunisia let British prisoners go when circumstances required it."

"What circumstances?"

He savored the irony. "If you'd served in combat you would

know."

Edel rammed his hands in his pockets. "Very well. When was the prisoner released and where?"

He turned to the lieutenant of the guard. "Was there an American here?"

"To whom is the *Herr Generalfeldmarschall* referring?"

Smart fellow. Rommel made a note to promote him. He told Edel he would have his staff look into it. Now, if there were no more questions?

"Do I understand correctly, you are disputing the Gestapo's right to search your headquarters?"

Rommel smiled. "Damned right!"

Edel looked at the military police and their machineguns and took his hands out of his pockets. The other agents followed his example. When he took a step back, so did they. "This violation of procedure will be reported immediately!"

Rommel's style when winning was to harass and pursue. Did the Gestapo outrank a field marshal? This was a combat zone. The *Wehrmacht* was in control. He ordered the lieutenant not to admit anyone. Double the guard if necessary. He turned on his heel. "The matter is not concluded," Edel called after him. "We have authority here!"

He had selected the chateau for its defensive perimeter. The main building backed up to a hill. Its grounds and outbuildings were surrounded by a high wall. It could only be approached from the front. Unfortunately, the security worked both ways. The Gestapo needed only a handful of men to check all vehicles. Getting Speigner out would not be easy. He returned to his study and told Speidel what had happened.

They want the Herr Leutnant.

We must hide him.

If the Gestapo finds out?

They won't.

Speidel began to speculate. Was the *Leutnant* more trouble than he was worth? Were they were pinning too many hopes on him? Rommel exploded, "Stop talking nonsense!"

"It is a matter of objectivity!" Speidel the scholar was bent on proving his theory. "In Africa, the *Leutnant* proved a worthy opponent. He possessed an instinct for the counter move. Perhaps you saw him as a brother in spirit–yes, a younger brother who made you want to live up to his hero-worship? Consequently your expectations are, well, overly optimistic?"

He was furious. "If you had not kept me from my command on the day of the invasion I would not be so dependent on him. I have no choice but to go hat in hand to the British and Americans. Unless Geyr's counterattack succeeds–which is very much in doubt–we have little chance for a negotiated surrender. If I cannot bargain from strength, do me the favor of not muddying the waters. Speigner is my *messenger*, not my 'brother.' Do you think me capable of such conceit?"

Speidel began to apologize. *Nein, bedaure, bitte...Herr...*

"And *stop* using titles! Call me Erwin."

"*Danke*, Herr...Erwin." Speidel pronounced the name as if he had marbles in his mouth. "If Berlin orders us to admit the Gestapo, what will we do about the American?" Accustomed to complete control, Rommel was at a loss. Speidel remembered a storage space above Rommel's study. He had studied the blueprints. The attic apparently had not been opened in some time.

Max was sound asleep. He stirred, hearing voices. People were talking, discussing a place to hide. He had not played hide-and-seek for years! Who better to play with than the Desert Fox. Stay on the move. Keep the enemy guessing.

"Wake up, lieutenant!" Rommel shook him.

What was the field marshal saying? Something about the Gestapo. The main gate was being watched. He understood. When he come through the gate, he had noticed how well it was watched. He sat up straight. This was no game. "When do I deliver the message?"

"We will see about that."

Captain Lange came to the door and announced the Duke of Rochefauld. The owner of the chateau came in. He nodded curtly. Rommel responded with more deference than usual.

Monsieur le Duke, comment allez vous?

Tres bien.

He offered the French noble a chair. He had been careful to maintain a working relationship. No one liked to make a man a prisoner in his own house. Now he needed the duke's assistance. He explained the situation, identifying Speigner as "the man the Gestapo is looking for!"

"What is it that you require?" said the duke.

Encouraged, Rommel began by assuring him that he and his

family would not be compromised. He was wondering, however, if there were any secret passages. There were none, the duke said. He crossed his arms and stared at the field marshal. Rommel concealed his impatience. He was going to have to reveal his plans. "*S'il vous plait*, consider this information confidential."

With a glance at Speigner–as if to say, *I have no choice!*–he explained about the American's mission. The desire for peace was genuine and shared by Rommel and every man on his staff. "The Gestapo will be here in a minute or two. If you would advise us where the American could be hidden, we would be in your debt. Suffice it to say, this is in your country's interests."

Rochefauld's demeanor changed. Rommel had deferred to him as *seigneur*. Without further delay he removed a wall panel and revealed a small door. It opened onto a narrow chamber with a ladder leading to an attic. Leaving Speidel with the American, Rommel followed the duke up the ladder. Rochefauld opened a trap door. Fine dust showered down on them. They entered an attic storeroom filled with furniture, paintings and statues. There was another entrance at the far end of the attic but the objects covered with sheets and canvas tarpaulins blocked access to where they stood.

The attic had been used for hiding at least once that the duke knew of. One of his ancestors had concealed his family there during the Reign of Terror. Rommel was pleased. This was the perfect hiding place. He thanked the duke. They climbed down in silence.

As soon as Rochefauld was gone, Rommel brought Speigner to the ladder. It was painful but he hauled himself up rung by rung. They brushed away dust and spider webs. Speigner was still groggy, panting from exertion. He pointed at a statue. "Is that Joan d' Arc?"

Was the American hallucinating? Rommel told him to stay there and remain very still. "Don't touch anything. I am going to let the Gestapo search the building. I will come back when they are gone."

Leaving Speigner, he returned to the study. Lange reported that the Gestapo was back with an SS escort. Rommel sent Lange to tell them that they would be allowed one hour to search the premises. Within minutes the black shirts were fanning through the chateau. Edel and several SS men entered the field marshal's office. Rommel stood aside.

Dog handlers brought German shepherds straining at the leash. Rommel whispered to Lange, "Bring Elbo to me. Be quick!" It took all his willpower to look bored as the dogs sniffed at the hidden panel. Lange returned with the dachshund puppy and turned it loose. Elbo shot across the room and began barking at the shepherds. The big dogs showed their fangs. The puppy retreated, then continued to bark. Rommel smiled. *Sic the Gestapo*!

The SS dog-handler was at a loss. One could not shoot a field marshal's puppy. Edel strenuously objected. After a few moments Rommel scooped Elbo up and pretended to scold him. The trained dogs had become too agitated to do their job. The handler took them away. Lange quietly removed the puppy. Rommel went to his desk and pretended to sign papers. He kept an eye on his wristwatch. When the hour was up, he ordered the Gestapo to leave. Edel threatened to report him. "Do as you like," he said. "Now, *get out*!"

As soon as the agents had left, he went to the passageway and called out. The trapdoor opened. Rommel waved at the American. "I am sending up a blanket and some food. You are going to have to stay here overnight. Don't make any noise."

A short while later, Lange climbed the ladder with a bedroll, candle and matches, some food and a chamber pot. He reached in his pocket and took out a book. "The field marshal sent you some reading material. He has no more use for this book. It was somewhat popular but is now *passé*."

Lange climbed back down the ladder. Max did not get the joke until he lit the candle and stuck it in an empty bottle. The book was *Mein Kampf.* There was an inscription in the front, a florid scrawl difficult to decipher.

für Oberst Erwin Rommel, mit besten Empfehlungen,

Adolf Hitler
Potsdam 1937

XXV

With every passing hour he considered a second landing at Calais most unlikely. The enemy bridgeheads in Normandy were expanding so fast his cartographers could barely keep up. The shifting battle lines were Hitler's worst nightmare. The 35,000 troops on the Channel Islands had surrendered without a fight, sacrificed for no purpose. He had advised the Führer to move them to defensive positions along the Normandy coast. These battalions alone might have turned the tide.

The fighting was fierce south of Bayeux, where General Fritz Bayerlein, who had served under him in Africa, commanded Panzer Lehr Division. The center of the German lines depended upon Panzer Lehr, which had been assembled and equipped for anti-invasion purposes. "The situation is terrible," Bayerlein reported by radiophone. "My men are calling the road from Vire to Beny-Bocage a fighter-bomber racecourse. Today I lost forty petrol wagons and ninety other vehicles. Five of my tanks were knocked out."

In the background Rommel heard firing. He imagined panzer crews at work, sighting enemy targets, pulling lanyards. Over the radio he heard an explosion. "*Was ist das!*"

"One of our ammunition trucks took a hit," Bayerlein said.

The terrain favored ground troops. In hedgerow country panzers fought at close range, easy targets for paratrooper bazookas. Rommel's radio operator picked up an emergency call from a single panzer. Surrounded and cut off from his squadron, the tank commander reported that he was out of ammunition. One of his caterpillar treads had been blown off. The tank was going in circles.

Rommel forced himself to think objectively. They had to win a battle. The peace process depended on it. Somewhere, somehow, they had to fight the enemy to a standstill. He wished Bayerlein *Viel Glück* and told the operator to connect him to Western Panzer Group.

It was time to move the primary reserve force commanded by General Baron Geyr von Schweppenburg. In addition, he placed some units of Army Group B under Geyr's command. "Throw the enemy off the mainland!" he told Geyr with a show of confidence. Neither mentioned their contretemps about where to position panzer reserves. He felt no satisfaction in having predicted that enemy aircraft would decimate Geyr's panzers before they reached the coast. The problem was that Geyr, given the failure of 1 SS Panzer Corps, was taking too long to launch his counterattack.

In the event that Geyr failed, it was imperative that divisions guarding the Mediterranean coast be moved north immediately. He was pressing OKW to approve the transfer. The LVIII Panzer Corps, with its four panzer divisions, was idle in the south of France. It could be moved up under cover of darkness. He would throw out a screen in front of the bridgehead, slow down the enemy advance and give the Wehrmacht time to dig in. Up to now neither Rundstedt or Jodl, however, had approved this suggestion. Jodl had gone so far as to warn Rommel not to meddle in strategic planning, adding, "Such matters are beyond your authority. Mind your own sector."

"They want to keep me under wraps," he told Speidel.

"Well, Hitler is afraid of you," the chief of staff replied. "He would never give you greater authority than you now have."

"Do you think he ordered the Gestapo to hound us?"

Speidel gestured impatiently as if this were to be taken for granted. "He would rather expose a commander's insubordination than win a major battle."

Even as they spoke, the Gestapo, backed now by a company of SS, was checking every vehicle that came in and out. If the American was at the chateau they were making sure he did not escape. It was clear that the American could not remain much longer. There was the problem of getting extra food and emptying his slop jar. The orderlies were beginning to take notice. Lange did not complain, but Rommel knew he did not like this nursemaid duty.

That evening the captain climbed the ladder with a fresh candle, food and a canteen. Rommel had sent Max a pair of old trousers to replace the torn ones. Lange watched the lieutenant try them on. The trousers were a couple of inches too short. When told that they were Rommel's pants, however, he did not complain. "They're fine." He sneezed.

"Catching a cold?" Lange said.

"Dust."

The kitchen staff was beginning to wonder why Lange had ordered them to double Rommel's portions. "The cooks asked why the general field marshal is eating so much."

"Does anyone suspect I'm hiding up here?"

"They are not fools but of course they will say nothing."

Lange reported that the Gestapo had demanded to search the premises again. Speigner had to leave as soon as possible. What they needed was a diversion such as an air raid. In the meantime they had to rely on bluff and guile.

They sat cross-legged on the floor. The light of a single candle cast their shadows on the ceiling. Speigner asked how the war was going. Lange drew lines in the dust. "The British have established a bridgehead near Caen. Our forces have been broken up by your air force. We have thrown up a screen of tanks to slow the enemy advance. It is too soon to predict the outcome." He stopped short of revealing Geyr's major counter-attack. The American gave him a curious glance. Lange changed the subject. "Well, we are going to get you out soon!" He started to leave. Speigner glanced pointedly at the chamber pot.

Again?

I'm afraid so.

What do you think I am, your chambermaid?

You should have thrown me out of that airplane.

Lange noticed the copy of *Mein Kampf.* "What do you think of the Führer's fantasy?"

Speigner waved his palm this way and that. "The starving artist never got over being rejected."

"He was a terrible painter."

"After he is dead, his paintings will be worth a fortune."

"May their value soon increase!" Holding the chamber pot at arm's length, Lange climbed down the ladder. Speigner held the candle so he could see.

XXVI

The Horch staff car passed every vehicle on the road from Paris to Rouen, commandeering the left lane and forcing approaching cars onto the shoulder. Rommel ordered, *Drive faster*! He and Speidel rode hatless in the rear seat, the wind whipping their hair. Ruge was in the front passenger seat.

They were returning to La Roche-Guyon after a meeting with Field Marshal von Rundstedt in Paris. The French capitol had been eerily quiet, sidewalk cafes deserted, the Champs d'Elysees empty except for motorcycle couriers who turned the grand boulevard into a speedway. Shops were closed and shuttered. Rommel noticed a sign in a window which read: *Ouvrir après la guerre.*

Von Rundstedt had greeted his visitors cautiously. He knew what they wanted. Rommel lumped him with all the *vons* propelled to the top ranks by social position. Like Speidel he was more of a desk soldier than field commander. He and Rommel had clashed over holding back reserves. Now that his theories had gone up in smoke it was time to face the music. Eager to make amends, Rundstedt agreed to draft a memo to Hitler warning of dire consequences if the enemy broke out of his bridgehead. If they were unable to stabilize the front in the next 24 hours, he wrote, the situation might "force fundamental decisions."

Rommel wanted stronger language, but Rundstedt would not change the report. He agreed to telegram Field Marshal Keitel, chief of the High Command, and relay Rommel's suggestions. "The enemy has total superiority in the air," Rommel dictated while von Rundstedt took notes. "Reserves cannot be brought up without paralyzing delays. The SS panzer corps is bogged down in defensive struggles. Heeresgruppe must be content with building up a connected front between the Orne and the Vire." It occurred to him that Keitel might be persuaded to present the telegram to Hitler.

Rundstedt put down his pen. "The Führer is no fool. He knows things are going badly. We must anticipate what he will do if the invasion succeeds–which it has. He'll put a good face on it and pretend there's a silver lining. He simply won't face reality."

After they left Rundstedt's office, they called upon his chief of staff, General Blumentritt. Speidel told him of the secret circle, led by Strölin, Beck and Goerdeler, organizing cells to prepare for surrender. Blumentritt seemed cautiously impressed. This was the first he had heard of the conspiracy. He asked what they would do if Hitler rejected the ceasefire proposal. Speidel shrugged as if this presented no serious impediment. Ruge spoke up. "If necessary we will *force* him to agree."

As the Horch roared back to La Roche-Guyon at 120 kph, Rommel turned to Speidel and said, "If the subject of assassination had come up, what do you think Blumentritt would have said?"

Speidel shouted to be heard. "He knows we mean business. I told him I had been to Wurttemburg to meet with Karl Strölin in your behalf." Rommel stared at the forested hills flashing by. Speidel was still spinning his web. If enough people were convinced that he was part of the conspiracy, it must be so.

Speigner sat on the blanket and flipped through *Mein Kampf*. As a researcher at the War Department, he had obtained a first edition of Hitler's autobiography. Now, upon second reading, his impressions remained unchanged. Hitler's fanatical loathing of Jews ran deep. He infused a hollow existence with hatred, inflated the Nazi balloon with bigotry.

"In strong contrast to the Aryan is the Jew. Scarcely any people on earth has its instinct for self-preservation so well developed as the so-called 'chosen people.' The Jew has never had a Kultur of his own; he has always borrowed from others and has developed his intellect from contact with the intellect of other peoples. Unlike the Aryan, the Jew's desire for self-preservation does not go beyond the individual."

He had never given his ethnic background much thought. If asked, he would have said that he was an American. His father was an atheist. His mother, whose maiden name was Rosen, was a non-practicing Jew. In rural Indiana where he grew up, religion was left to the individual. Freedom of choice was his parents' gift to him. Whether they had done him a favor was yet to be discovered. It had been enough to get through high school, to finish a chemistry experiment, impress the cheerleader sitting next to him, drag race on country roads with his friends. The summer before his senior year he attended a Christian Bible school. He was bored. In the fall he escorted a girlfriend to

Temple. He enjoyed the rabbi's jokes. His mother was thrilled that he'd attended a service but did not push him. She honored the "old ways" and wanted him to respect Judaism as a code of conduct.

Now, alone in an attic with the vitriolic narrative of *Mein Kampf*, his freedom repressed by Gestapo and SS, he felt his Jewish half rising. His mother had put away a Menorah and candles for him. As a child he would take them out and play with them. Why were there seven candles? What magic did they possess? He could have read the *Torah* and found out. One day his mother casually remarked that if he wanted to convert, she would go with him. "*You first*!" she said. He could hear her laughing. "You can be my rabbi and teach me what you have learned."

As he turned the pages Hitler's ravings seemed directed at him personally. *How could anyone believe this bullshit?* If the Brown Shirts had not swallowed it hook, line and sinker, the world would never have heard of Adolf Hitler.

"The black-haired Jewish youth waits for hours, with satanic joy in his eyes, for the unsuspecting girls, whom he shames with his blood and thereby robs the nation."

How a civilized, educated people could give credence to such raving lunacy much less–? Was that a scratching noise? He resumed reading.

"It was the Jews who brought the Negro to the Rhine, always with the same thought and clear aim in the back of their heads¾to destroy the hated white races through 'bastardization,' to tumble them from their cultural and political heights and to raise themselves to the vacant place–"

Hinges creaked. He pinched out the candle. During his time in the garret, he had memorized every sound. He knew when birds were making nests, when they were fighting or mating or tending to their young. He could tell if the wind was blowing from the north or the west. Now he concentrated on the alien noises. He imagined dust piling up under the door as someone pushed it open. He felt the flashlight beam before he saw it. Tentacles of light crawled over the antiques.

Lange had told him that Rommel had gone to a meeting. What he didn't say was when he would return. The field marshal seldom arrived anywhere on time. He liked to go his own way, stop and examine something that caught his attention, go on side treks.

"What are you stopping for?" Rommel said impatiently.

Daniel had pulled off in a grove of trees. "Enemy aircraft, *Herr Generalfeldmarschall.*" Rommel ordered him to keep going. Speed was their ally. How many times did he have to tell him? Daniel drove back to the highway and pressed the accelerator. Rommel stopped watching the speedometer after it passed ninety kph. The fighter was no longer in sight. Speidel took up where he left off describing Hitler's *Endlosüng.* "There is a camp at Dachau, near Munich, and also Auschwitz and Treblinka in Poland…"

"Those camps were established," Rommel interrupted, "for 'preventative custody' or for 'resettlement.' That is what we were told."

The camps were killing fields, Speidel went on. Just as Keitel and Jodl had to face the fact that the war was lost, Rommel and Ruge and Lange, even Daniel–everyone on Rommel's staff–had to look at what was happening. Jews were being killed by the tens of thousands!

"How is that possible!" Rommel muttered to himself. Korporal Daniel looked uncomfortable. He told the driver to keep his eyes on the road.

Yes, it could be done, and was being done at that very moment, Speidel went on. The camps were efficient at killing. Gas chambers. Ovens for disposing of the bodies. The stench of burning flesh like a pall over the countryside.

"Shut up, Hans. Enough!" He indicated Daniel, who had gone pale.

"Would you close your eyes and cover your ears? Our government is committing crimes against humanity. It is we, the Wehrmacht, who keep the Führer in power."

Rommel tried arguing, "We are professional soldiers. We are not to blame for what *they* did." Yet inn his heart he knew.

Lucie had taken him to an open house celebration in Ulm, a rare social outing. People made a fuss and congratulated him on past victories. Nobody mentioned Heinrich and Himmler and the camps. Even to reflect on government-sanctioned crimes against humanity was to incriminate oneself. Better to pretend nothing was wrong. *This was Hitler's secret weapon.* Nobody wanted to admit having stood by silently as he arrested Jews,

Catholics, gypsies and homosexuals by the thousands and sent them away God knows where, never to return. Their silence made them complicit. Thus, on this festive occasion, the good folk of Ulm fell all over themselves complimenting the *Herr Generalfeldmarschall*, their hero, a soldier of unblemished reputation. As long as there was an Erwin Rommel, the center was holding. Even his enemies had praised him for abiding by the Geneva Convention. He remembered what Lt. Speigner had said in Libya, hours before he was shipped off to a German prisoner of war camp. "You are a hero to the Eighth Army, did you know that? They have an expression for chivalry in battle. They call it 'doing a Rommel.' Your fairness is what makes you dangerous. Both sides respect you. You make war honorable so that all the rest-Hitler's persecution of Jews and Free French and Poles, the camps where civilians are interned-all of that can go on."

The Horch straddled the center of the highway. Daniel was gripping the steering wheel with both hands, forcing oncoming vehicles onto the shoulder. Rommel reached over and tugged at the wheel to bring the car back into line. He had been ill-used by Hitler but he had been a willing accomplice.

He crouched on all fours, ducking the shafts of light. Between him and the searcher were rows of dusty furniture-statues, urns, plates, boxes of things tied with string. There were no footprints in the dust, hence no reason for the searcher to suppose that he was in the far corner of the attic. Things crashed to the floor. A cloud of dust rose to the rafters. Inside the cloud flashlight beams were like flashes of lightning. To keep from sneezing he squeezed his nose so hard it brought tears to his eyes.

The Horch twisted and turned through the narrow streets of La Roche-Guyon. Arriving at the chateau entrance Rommel saluted the guards. The Gestapo agents were nowhere to be seen. As they pulled into the parking area, Ruge complained that the ride had made him stiff. Rommel suggested they go for a walk in the garden.

His furnishings, sparse as they were, seemed to have multiplied: blanket, candle, mess kit, canteen, book, chamber pot. He thought of pulling a tarp over his corner and hiding under it.

Chairs squeaked as they were shoved aside. A bed frame was toppled. A statue fell over with a crash. Why hadn't someone heard what was going on? Why hadn't someone come to investigate? Lange or the desk sergeant. Hadn't the field marshal left instructions that the Gestapo were not to enter the building!

He thought of his chamber pot. Did it smell? Was there a residual odor of candle wax? To keep down smoke he always pinched the flame instead of blowing it out, but any smell of human habitation would stand out against the blank scent of dust.

They walked the garden path, side by side, hands behind their backs. "What can we do?" Rommel used Ruge as a sounding board which he often did.

The admiral glanced up with a look of determination. "End the war as soon as possible. Let the western powers put the Führer on trial!"

Surrender was the only solution. Yet Rommel wondered if Eisenhower would come to the table if Hitler was not present. "Put yourself in Eisenhower's place. Would *he* call for a ceasefire if Churchill and Roosevelt were opposed to it? Would *we* believe Eisenhower personally spoke for all the Brits, Canadians, Russians and Poles and Free French? Is it not the height of naiveté to think Eisenhower would take me at my word?"

There was a second agent. He was sure of it. If he tried to escape someone would be waiting. One cat flushed the mouse while the other watched the hole. The screeching noise continued as more piles of junk were shoved aside.

He wanted to believe Eisenhower would listen. All the profiles he had read described the allied commander-in-chief as thoroughly professional. They continued through the garden, lush from a recent shower. How did Eisenhower feel about the Russians? Wouldn't he understand-wouldn't any sensible man-that the Germans preferred the west over the communists?

He piled his possessions in the middle of the blanket and tied them in a bundle, then opened the trap door. He took an old tarpaulin thick with dust and pulled the stiff canvas over the door as he closed it. He climbed down the ladder. Pain shot through his thigh. The wound had almost healed but the muscles were weak.

With his free hand he gripped a rung, holding the bundle in the other. He smelled urine. The chamber pot had spilled inside the blanket. He balanced on one leg while boxes thudded overhead. The scraping of things being moved continued, vibrations, squeaks and then–nothing.

Ruge believed that the distrust between the Anglo-Americans and the Russians was the reason Churchill wanted to meet with him. Patton had been quoted as saying that the Americans and British would take Berlin before the Russians.

He had dreamed of teaming with Patton. The two of them going after the Russians. Never before had he mentioned this to anyone, not even to Lucie.

He hung on with one hand. His fingers were cramping. He propped the bundle between him and the ladder and waited for the tarp to be swept aside, the trap door to be yanked open.

There were quick steps on the gravel path. Lange ran up and reported that the Gestapo was searching the chateau.

This was the last straw. The Gestapo had invaded his quarters while he was gone. He sprinted after his aide. "Remember the ceasefire," Ruge called. "You must not take a chance of being investigated."

Noises came from the field marshal's study, a familiar voice barking commands. It sounded like Rommel. Angry words were exchanged the stairs on the other side of the attic.

"Get out! Out, out!"

It was Rommel. He was sure of it. The floor creaked above him. The searcher was still there. Rommel was shouting across the attic, demanding the Gestapo leave at once. The floor creaked. There was a mumble of conversation. The agent was demanding to be allowed to complete his search. He was certain someone was hiding in the attic.

Another man interceded in halting German. Speigner had heard the voice before. The man told of a servant who had disappeared. This unfortunate incident had occurred recently. The man had hidden in the attic, which would account for any sign of habitation. Speigner recognized the speaker as the Duke de la Rochefauld. The Gestapo agent continued to complain, his voice receding down the stairs. Moments later the trap door opened. It was Rommel who peered sternly into the shadows.

XXVII

All of the staff knew that he had an American in his quarters. The Gestapo were stopping everyone. Military couriers were detained for hours. The duke's chef was handcuffed while SS troopers tore through his shopping cart.

To lift his men's spirits he started a rumor that the American had gone over the fence. Speidel and Lange were to inform the immediate staff that the man "who was not there" was not there. If the Gestapo had spies inside the chateau–as he assumed they did–the word would get out. That evening, instead of sending food to the attic by Lange, Rommel took it himself, along with a bottle of wine and two glasses.

Speigner was surprised to see him. "What's the occasion?"

Rommel sneezed. "Your imminent departure."

Speigner lit a candle and stuck it in a bottle. His hands shook with excitement. Rommel pulled the cork. "You leave in the morning. It will be dangerous." He filled the glasses with vintage Bordeaux from the duke's cellars. "*Salut.*" The plan was for Daniel to go over the fence and attract the Gestapo's attention. While the guards were distracted, the field marshal and Speigner would ride out the gate as if nothing was wrong.

Won't they search the car?

Yes, but they will not find an American.

"You are Daniel's replacement. Your name is Dietzel. We are preparing the necessary papers."

In North Africa he had tracked Rommel at a distance, making informed guesses, trying to anticipate his next move. Now he guessed the Desert Fox's formula for success: *Do whatever is necessary to win.* Rommel drained his glass and set it upside down. Here was the message Speigner would take to the *Amis*. He wanted Montgomery and Eisenhower to know that he had talked the SS into accepting a ceasefire. "One of the first things the British and Americans will want to know is whether the SS generals in my sector have agreed to follow my orders. The answer is yes."

Speigner asked the day and time of the proposed ceasefire. "As soon as Eisenhower and Montgomery respond in the affirmative and my wife and son are safely out of Germany. I will order my area commanders to tell their units to cease firing, then give myself up to the *Amis* and go on the radio to explain to the German army what is going on."

A gust of wind assaulted the eaves, almost extinguishing the candle. The moaning of the wind subsided. The flame flickered back to life. "Tell the Herr Minister Churchill something for me. Tell him that we did not know what Hitler was." Rommel spoke so quietly that Max had to lean closer. "Those of us in the regular army believed we were fighting for our country. The bad thing about war is that you become accustomed to it. Pretty soon you do not notice bodies lying about. Tell Minister Churchill '*Wir sind sehr betrübt.*' We are sorry." His shadow rose ahead of him as he stood. "I will come for you at dawn. Try to get some sleep." He opened the trapdoor.

Speigner asked if he might spend his last night downstairs. Perhaps in a closet. Rommel shook his head. "Remain here. I told my officers you were gone. I would hate for them to think their commander is a liar." He promised Speigner a shave. "No one on my staff is allowed to grow a beard," he added, referring to the American's week-long growth. Max stood up, leaning over to avoid bumping his head against the slanted ceiling. Rommel saw that the pants were too short.

"My trousers do not fit you very well."

"They're fine. Thank you."

He held the candle so Rommel could see as he descended the ladder. It occurred to him why the field marshal had brought the wine. He had come to say goodbye.

XXVIII

Oberfeldwebel Daniel was to go over the garden wall at 0600. He had been issued a weekend pass. If caught, he was to say he was having an affair with a married woman. Her husband was "watching the gate." This romantic angle was Daniel's invention. Rommel would have never thought of it. Lange, wearing Daniel's cap, was to drive the car to the front of the chateau. He would then come inside, give the chauffeur's cap to Speigner, who was to drive Rommel out the gate.

Max inspected his reflection in a mirror. He was dressed in the uniform of a Wehrmacht corporal. He was fresh-shaved and rosy-cheeked. Rommel said, "My God, you look a little like Daniel! *Sprechen Sie nur Deutsch, ja?*"

"*Jawohl, Herr Generalfeldmarschall*!"

They went into the foyer. The military receptionist glanced at Speigner and quickly found something else to do. Rommel checked his watch. The time was 0601. A car door slammed. Seconds later Lange entered. He gave Daniel's cap to Speigner, who gave them a thumbs up, went outside and held the car door for Rommel. After the field marshal was in the front passenger seat, Max went around to the driver's side and got in.

"*Anlasser*?" The dashboard appointments confused him. He did not know how to start the engine.

"*Da*!" Rommel turned the ignition key on, then pointed to the starter button. Speigner started to push it without disengaging the clutch. Rommel warned, "Ah, ah, ah." He had assumed the lieutenant could drive. Daniel was over the wall, the Gestapo in hot pursuit, and here they sat. Speigner disengaged the clutch and started the engine. He had trouble finding first gear. Rommel snorted as if to say, What now?

"*Schalthebel*?"

Rommel reached over, grabbed the gearshift knob and thrust it into first.

"*Danke, mein–*"

"*Sich beeilung*!" Hurry up!

The luxury car lurched forward in first gear. Speigner's instructions were to stop at the gate and let Rommel do the talking.

"Halt!" an SS guard shouted. "Where are you going?"

"That is no business of yours!" Rommel was relieved to see that the Gestapo agents were not there. They were presumably chasing Daniel.

"I must search the luggage compartment," said the guard. He opened the trunk, then closed it and came back to the driver's side. "This is not your regular driver," he said.

Rommel rolled down the window. "I have more than one driver. This is Dietzel. He is replacing *Oberfeldwebel* Daniel."

"Let him speak for himself," the guard said.

"I am in a hurry!" Rommel said.

"I must see his papers!"

Max submitted the identification papers that had been prepared. He was Korporal Rudolf Dietzel, permanent residence: *Lindenstrasse 505*; hometown: *Frankfurt*; province: *Taunus*. The papers were authentic-looking with the forged signature of a personnel officer. His present assignment was chauffeur at *Heeresgruppe B*. The guard looked at the papers and then at Speigner.

"State your serial number."

Speigner started to rattle it off, then gave the number hesitantly as if he rarely was required to do so.

Where is your permanent home, Korporal?

Frankfurt.

Ah, then, you have attended the Wagner festival?

This was a simple trick. He pointed out that the Wagner festival was held in Bayreuth, not Frankfurt. The guard handed him the papers. "Wait here."

Rommel glanced over his shoulder. The guard had probably been told that someone had gone over the wall. The Gestapo had triumphed. Their diligence had paid off. By now, however, Herr Edel had no doubt questioned Daniel, guessed that something was odd and was on his way back. "Drive on," he said. Speigner did not need to be told twice.

Holding his machinepistol at the ready, the guard jogged alongside. "*Halt*!"

"I have a war to fight!" Rommel called. Speigner found second with a screech of grinding gears. "*Nach links*!" Rommel said. Speigner turned left at the next intersection, glancing in the rear view mirror. The guard had returned to his post. They proceeded through the village of row houses and white-roofed cottages. People stopped to stare at the staff car.

When they reached the open road, Rommel told him to pass every slow vehicle and to drive in the left lane. The field marshal's flags mounted on the bumpers caused drivers of transport trucks and armored half-tracks to swerve out of the way. Rommel relaxed, took his hat off and talked about how the war was going. He omitted the fact that Geyr von Schweppenburg's headquarters had been bombed before he could get his panzers moving. Geyr had survived, though virtually all his staff had been killed or wounded. The counterattack had bogged down. The best they could do was plug gaps. "I should invite the Führer to come to the front," he joked, "so he can see for himself what is happening."

"Would he come!"

"No, of course not. He rarely ventures outside his bunkers. Someone might take it in his head to shoot him."

Speigner was curious. What was Hitler like ?

There was no denying his ability to influence people, Rommel said. To be with him was like being under a sun lamp. One went away glowing with false confidence. Yet out of his presence, once the lamp was turned off, reality set in. "There is no telling what he thinks after his generals leave him. Perhaps he congratulates himself on having put one over on them. His greatest *coup*, however, is fooling himself into believing what he says."

Bullets kicked up dust. An RAF fighter was attacking the car. Speigner looked for a place to pull over. "Do not stop. Keep going!" Rommel was calm as if this happened every day.

He was not about to try to outrun a Spitfire. He disobeyed Rommel and pulled off at the first house he came to. The Horch fish-tailed into a barnyard and skidded to a stop. Chickens flew everywhere. A rooster landed on the hood. The Spitfire roared overhead. Fortunately the pilot did not see them. He backed the car up, sensing Rommel staring at him.

Would you like to drive?

No, you are doing very well.

Rommel estimated it was twenty miles to the front. They headed west. The traffic picked up. Most of the vehicles were returning from the battle: transport trucks, ambulances, armored cars and motorcycles. A *Kübelwagen* bounced past with six officers packed in it. At a checkpoint, Speigner spoke flawless

German to an MP who questioned him. The MP waved them through.

Abandoned trucks littered the muddy roadway. There was a stench of cordite. The ditches were strewn with helmets, packs, ammunition belts, weapons. A tank pushed an armored car off the road. Retreating German soldiers looked defeated, their faces blackened, the wounded hanging onto anyone who would assist them. Oblivious to the battle raging a few miles away, burial details arranged bodies in rows. Out of respect for the dead they communicated with hand signals. Rommel put his hand on the door handle. He wished he could pay homage.

What do you want to do?

Keep going.

Over the next rise they encountered a German soldier shooting another soldier with his pistol. The dying man fell in plain sight of other soldiers. Rommel explained that *Feldgendarmerie*, military police, had orders to execute deserters. "I regret to say this has become necessary. If the soldiers thought they could get away with desertion, there would be mass hysteria." Speigner wondered if the U.S. Army shot deserters, as well.

A tank battalion was dug in on a hill. Rommel admired the positioning of men and machines. He had Speigner pull over and went to speak to the commander. This was part of Panzer Lehr Division supporting the Caen defense line. The colonel, whose head was bandaged, was obviously flattered that the field marshal had stopped to talk. They had taken casualties, he told Rommel, but the line was holding. "We are up against British Seventh Armored. They know we are not going anywhere. The best thing we have going for us is this country." He gestured at the hedgerows. Then he added, "Are we to receive reinforcements?"

Rommel promised to see what could be done. They fell silent. Both of them knew there were not enough reserves. After a moment, Rommel asked where the closest British position was. The colonel pointed to a ridge two miles away. An incoming round exploded in the distance. The colonel warned that the nearest bridge had been knocked out. If the *Herr Generalfeldmarschall* wished to observe, he would send a security detail. Rommel said there was no need. The colonel persisted, "Please, take care." A man with his head bandaged worried about his comrades. Rommel had seen this many times.

"Danke, Herr Oberst," he said.

The colonel advised him to keep off the roads. The Tommie artillery spotters could see everything. They were on the ridge to the southwest. Rommel got in the car and ordered Max to drive on. A half-mile down the road they came to the final checkpoint. Panzergrenadiers manned a machinegun nest surrounded by sandbags. Unseen in the green hills ahead was the enemy. Speigner searched the ridge, looking for movement. He realized with a start that he had just thought of the British as "the enemy."

"Bitte, Durchgang ist verboten!" A grenadier lieutenant told them they were within range of enemy machineguns. With all due respect, he said, the *Herr Feldmarschall* should turn around and go back.

"Is there another road into the valley?" Rommel said.

The junior officer cast about as if this were a hypothetical question. "Perhaps, a cow trail?"

"Danke schön." Rommel waved Speigner on. "Let's get as close as we can." They bounced along the cow trail. British artillery had plowed up the pasture. Speigner found a gap in a hedgerow and drove across a rocky streambed, water splashing on the windshield. The track ended on the side of a hill. He turned the car around so that it was pointed in the direction they had come. They got out. "The *Amis* are there." Rommel pointed at the ridge. "Less than a kilometer away."

His leg felt strong enough, though walking was the least of his problems. If they didn't shoot him, he could walk all day. Rommel got out Max's original tunic and a captured U.S. Army cap hidden under the rear seat. Cows suddenly appeared among the trees, grazing on the thin grass. Max took off Daniel's coat and put on the tunic. He clipped his lieutenant's silver bar to the cap. Rommel squatted on the ridge, at home in no man's land. He took a handkerchief out of his pocket and told the lieutenant to wave it as he approached the other side. At that moment, a burst of machinegun fire stuttered on the ridge, followed by small arms fire. The thump of a mortar joined in. From above the clouds came the monotonous drone of airplanes.

"They are advancing," Rommel observed. "Infantry behind armor. You better get going." He remembered the card. He had decided it was necessary to reply to Churchill in writing. "I have not had a card printed after I came to France, but here is one from when I was living in Wiener Neustadt. It has my previous address." Max read what was written.

> *Herr Minister Churchill,*
> *I am at your disposal.*
> *Erwin Rommel*
> *Kommando Heeresgruppe B*

The firing stopped. "Go now," Rommel said. He picked up a dry branch and tied the handkerchief to it. He did not notice a change in Speigner. The American tensed his muscles, spread his feet and balanced his weight.

"Why don't you go with me?" Max said.

Was the *Herr Leutnant* thinking of overpowering him? Surely not. His leg was barely healed. "I admire your spirit. You will need it if we are to succeed." He reminded Speigner why he had to stay with his army. He not only had to get his family out, but he had to give the ceasefire order in person.

Speigner felt let down. They were so close. This might be his only chance to get the field marshal across the front lines.

Rommel was careful to keep his distance. "You have my telegraph call number. I will be watching for your reply. Either 'Proceed to point A,' for the Americans, or 'Point B,' for the British. Very well, good luck!"

He returned to the car. The moment Speigner was out of sight, Rommel went to the crest of the hill to observe. He spotted a camouflaged machinegun emplacement halfway up the opposite ridge. A sniper was perched in a tree, greenery covering his helmet. It was a reconnaissance squad. This was a good place to cross. How easy it would have been for him to go with the *Herr Leutnant*.

XXIX

He crossed the wooden bridge. A fast-flowing creek swirled below. All his senses were focused on hidden firepower in the woods. He raised the stick with the handkerchief. His footsteps drummed hollowly on the boards. As he reached the other side, a machinegun fired a burst over his head. He waved his handkerchief and shouted, "*I'm American!*" The handkerchief wrapped itself around the stick. He was trying to straighten it when a voice said, "Step forward."

The cow track continued on the other side of the bridge. He followed it toward a copse of trees. The firing had come from there. A bush, *shrubbus cocknius*, said, "I've got you, mate. Come on!" The articulate shrub sprouted from a camouflaged helmet. Under it a brown and green face sighted down a leafy sniper's rifle.

He dropped the handkerchief and raised his hands. Hearing English spoken was like crossing an international dateline. The sniper said, "Keep your hands where I can see 'em. There's a good chap."

"*What's the password!*" said another voice.

The sniper waved his rifle. "Right, then, what's the bloomin' password?"

He glanced down at the discarded handkerchief. "Could the password be *peace*?" Laughter spilled out of a hedgerow. He found himself looking into the barrel of a .50 caliber machinegun. Soldiers in camouflaged fatigues swarmed around him. "I'm an American!" He pointed to the silver lieutenant's bar.

"Only half American," one of the soldiers said, pointing at his ill-fitting, grayish-green, Wehrmacht trousers. They hustled him into a jeep. It was a Willys, he noticed, manufactured in the states. A soldier sat on either side of him. They passed Sherman tanks with red and white Union Jacks painted on the turrets. The only British-made vehicle he saw was a Rolls Royce armored car like the ones he had seen in Egypt.

He was escorted to a communications battalion. Inside the

HQ tent, an operator in fatigues manned a compact switchboard. The soldiers took him to a captain at a field desk. He held up his hand while he spoke into a radio receiver. The soldiers waited, picking at their camouflage, rearranging leaves. Speigner glanced at the machineguns cradled in their arms, grenades clipped to their tunics. He was grateful to be alive. The captain dismissed the troopers. He rapped his knuckles on the desk. "Empty your pockets."

He took out Rommel's business card. He hated to show it to a junior officer but hoped it would give him credibility. The captain glanced at it without apparent interest. The next item was the Rudolph Dietzel identification papers. This got the captain's attention. "*Was bedeutet dies!*" He repeated the question, adding, "*Konnen Sie mir das sagen?*"

"Yes, I speak German."

The Captain seemed determined that he reply in German. Reluctantly he did so. "*Ja, Ich verstehe...es ist nicht wichtig.*"

"Sit on the ground and put your hands on your head. Do it *now*."

The captain awkwardly waved a pistol as if unaccustomed to handling it. Speigner obeyed. He sat with legs crossed, hands clamped on his head. He realized that the intelligence officer suspected him of being a double agent. He could not believe he had not thrown away the Dietzel papers. He asked to be taken to Field Marshal Montgomery. The captain turned the card over and read the note. "You're saying you have seen Rommel?"

He seized the opportunity. "Field Marshal Rommel sent a personal message to the prime minister. It's a reply to Churchill's message, which I delivered to him. You can check with Special Branch. They sent me into France with an escort, two commandos, Dan and Eric..." The captain lowered his pistol. Speigner cautiously stood, keeping his hands on his head. "What about my lieutenant's bar?"

"You could have gotten that off a dead soldier."

"All right, my pants then. Rommel gave them to me. They were his. They're too short, see?"

The captain looked at him, then at the identification papers. Was he Korporal Dietzel, Lieutenant Speigner, a double agent, or certifiable? "Stand at ease," said the captain and put a call through, turning away to speak privately. After a minute he rang off. "I've arranged for you to see Field Marshal Montgomery."

"Thank you," he sighed.

Montgomery's headquarters were located in a chateau surrounded by parks and lakes. There were bomb craters around the building. A guard escorted Speigner inside. In the foyer were statues of French heroes. The guard sat him down on a bench, set his rifle down and lit a cigarette, cupping his fingers around the match.

"What are you doing?"

"Put a cork in it, mate."

Max heard a receptionist tell a caller that Viscount Montgomery was not accepting calls at the moment, no exceptions. *Viscount*? The operator exclaimed to the desk sergeant, "That was the P.M.!" Max got up and went to the reception desk. His guard dropped the cigarette and hurried after him, groping in his pocket for handcuffs. "May I speak to the Prime Minister?"

The receptionist was taken aback. The guard was about to put on the handcuffs. Speigner returned to the bench. After a while, the receptionist left her station and brought him a cookie–a "biscuit," she called it–clucking over him as if he were suffering from battle fatigue.

An aide appeared and escorted him and the guard to Montgomery's office. Like Rommel's, it was in the chateau library, with bookshelves on every wall. Montgomery was seated behind a desk signing papers which another aide pushed in front of him. Speigner started to sit in a straight-backed chair. Without looking up from what he was doing Montgomery frowned. The guard nudged Max. He stood at attention. He had been at Eighth Army Headquarters in Libya when General Auchinleck's staff received word that "Monty" was coming to replace their commander. They had not been thrilled at the news.

He tried to organize his thoughts. How to begin? Salutations from *Herr Generalfeldmarschall* Rommel?

Finally the Viscount said, "Be seated." He sat down, the guard standing behind him. "What's this about?" Montgomery rubbed his hands as if he expected a good tale. Max began by conveying Rommel's personal greetings. It was a mistake. The field marshal, compact in stature, quick in gesture, stared incredulously. A mere lieutenant presuming to speak for a field marshal! Max hastily started again. He described Rommel's releasing him from POW camp to carry a peace offer to England. When he mentioned Churchill's positive reaction to Rommel's offer, Montgomery snapped, "Why was I not informed?"

Viscount Montgomery launched into a psychological profile of Rommel. "Highly overrated, in my opinion. Had things going his way in North Africa until we caught onto his game. Hiding his tanks behind a screen of anti-tank guns–those damned Eighty-Eights–picking off our tanks one by one. Made him look like a genius! We got onto him and turned things round!" He stopped short and fiddled with his fountain pen. What did the lieutenant say his name was?

Speigner, sir.

German.

Yes, sir.

"I hear you have whole battalions of Japanese, Negroes and Navajos. Wasn't aware there was a *German* battalion." He chuckled at his own joke, twisting in his swivel chair. Speigner repeated his message. Rommel was waiting for a reply. Montgomery than asked about Rommel's whereabouts. Max hesitated. He explained that he had been hidden in an attic.

"Rommel had a Yank in his belfrey, eh!" Again swiveling in the chair, glancing at his aide.

Speigner presented Rommel's card. Montgomery held it between thumb and forefinger. "I delivered the Prime Minister's card to Field Marshal Rommel. This is his response. He wishes to meet and arrange a ceasefire! He will order the German army to surrender. The SS generals have agreed to obey his orders."

Montgomery inspected the card as if it were a forgery. "Where is Wiener Neustadt?" Was it not preposterous to think that the prime minister would fail to inform him, the commander of British Expeditionary Forces, of a secret correspondence with Rommel? Nothing like that could go on without his knowing about it! He returned the card as if it no longer interested him. "This ceasefire business is neither here nor there. Rommel's whipped and he knows it. I'm not surprised he's crawling to us." The Germans were showing signs of collapse. This could be a device to gain time to re-arm and bring up reserves.

"Sir, he gave me this card himself!"

"It's very possible you are quite sincere in believing what you have been told, but I can tell you this. If Rommel himself came to me hat in hand, I'd tell him the same thing. We've come too far to stop now."

"Sir, it's a matter of saving lives."

"Saving *face*, more like! Well, Leftenant, that will be all." His pen squeaked as he resumed signing orders. His aide turned the pages for him. Speigner did not move. He could not believe this was it–and all because of an imagined slight by Churchill. The guard tapped him on the shoulder. Montgomery did not look up as they left.

At the reception desk, the clerk who had given him a biscuit advised him that he was being transferred to Counter-Intelligence. This was standard procedure when an agent came over. He protested that he was not an agent. He had to get through to the prime minister. His guard said mildly, "Easy does it, sir. This will get sorted out and you'll be on your way." The clerk spoke into an intercom requesting a military police escort.

XXX

Security was tight around *Wolfsschlucht Zwei*, Hitler's hermetically sealed bunker at Margival, north of Soissons. The Führer's SS Escort Commandos stopped Rommel's car and asked for identification. Rommel asked if the Führer had arrived.

"I am not at liberty to say." The guard stepped back and saluted. Daniel drove inside the compound. Rommel glanced at General Speidel. "You would think I had asked about miracle weapons."

Wolf's Lair-Two was located in a wooded area near a railroad tunnel in which a train could be hidden. There were camouflaged bunkers for meeting rooms and a mess hall with a view of the Soissons Cathedral. This was the first time Hitler had used the secluded retreat.

They went into the mess hall and were greeted by von Rundstedt and his chief of staff, General Blumentritt. Even though Rundstedt was the ranking officer, Rommel was to serve as their spokesman. They exchanged a nod of acknowledgment. History was riding on this meeting. Field Marshal Jodl and Hitler had already arrived. They had been flown from Berchtesgaden to Metz, then taken by automobile to Margival.

Hitler liked to keep his generals waiting. They took this opportunity to compare notes. Enemy air superiority was eroding German defenses. The logical strategy was to pull back beyond the Seine and make a stand. Hitler had ordered the army to hold at the Orne near Caen. Men were being sacrificed for nothing. An especially grievous mistake was trying to hang on at Cherbourg. Rommel was prepared to say that this was a hopeless cause. The generals agreed that they should cut their losses, regroup and counterpunch, keeping the enemy off balance. Then with the army still intact they would inform Eisenhower that Germany was ready to negotiate.

"Perhaps a putsch can be avoided if Hitler will meet us halfway. That would prove he is capable of reason," he said. Speidel disagreed, adding that the Führer's insanity was a given.

"Try not to say anything to set him off," Rundstedt cautioned. "His tantrums are getting worse."

Hitler, flanked by Jodl and the chief adjutant, General Schmundt, received them in his inner sanctum. The conference room was in the center of the bunker. There were no windows. Lighting was indirect. A military map was laid out on a table. A map of France stood on a tripod stand. The field marshals put their hats under their arms and saluted. Hitler sat brooding on a stool. Behind him two SS officers stood guard. He did not bother to greet the field marshals. He looked at no one and yet was aware of every glance. Two army stenographers came in and set up portable typing machines.

Jodl had long functioned as an extension of the Führer's authority. Hitler hid behind him and let it appear that it was Jodl, not he, who rejected their proposals. Rommel and von Rundstedt and their chiefs of staff waited in silence. Everyone knew what was coming.

Hitler's appearance was startling. He was grey and frail. He tapped the map with a pencil like a beggar thumping his drum. He fiddled with his glasses, taking them off, putting them back on. "*Willkommen, meine Herren,*" he said without looking at anyone.

He raised his voice. "I must tell you how disappointed I am that you allowed the enemy landings to take place. We prepared long and hard, yet you have let me down. No, no, do not apologize. It is too late for that!" He waved airily though none of them had responded. "The enemy has landed. That is a fact. Now, it is your duty to hold the fortress of Cherbourg at all costs. Do you hear? *At all costs.*"

He called for reports, then slouched on his stool and resumed tapping his pencil–*tap, tap, tap*–like an elocution teacher marking time. Rundstedt started by summing up the dwindling options. They had to make the most of their remaining resources. Then he turned the meeting over to Rommel, who as commander of the invasion front was in charge of strategy. The stenographers hesitated, fingers poised over machines. The only sound was the tapping of Hitler's pencil.

"The enemy is superior on land, sea and in the air," Rommel began. "There is not enough protection from enemy air attack. Inadequate advance information led to the success of the invasion. The Luftwaffe and Naval reconnaissance are to blame." The rebel generals nodded encouragingly. They were of one mind, Rommel their voice.

"As he did in Africa, Montgomery employs saturation bombardment followed by armored assault. He is relying on mass formations to break through. By the way, it is *not true*–" he hesitated for emphasis. "That my coastal forces were 'caught napping,' as was reported in an intercepted enemy communiqué. OKW should not have jumped at this report as if it were fact. The coastal divisions fought hard and slowed the enemy advance, causing many casualties, until their weakly fortified positions were overrun. I myself know, from firsthand inspections of the front lines–" He glanced at Hitler. "That the division commanders fought heroically to their last ounce of endurance. Panzers, especially the Tigers, have been effective in individual counterattacks, but armor alone cannot hold the invasion back. Air superiority is wearing down the reserves, along with naval bombardment, battering them to pieces before they reach the front. They dare not venture within range of battleship guns!"

Hitler drew circles on a notepad. He did not glance up even when Rommel whacked the map with a wooden pointer. The battle came down to a mathematical equation. Enemy forces outnumbered Germans two to one. "Cherbourg," he said as planned, all of them aware that this was a pivotal issue, "will be overrun in less than two weeks."

This test was a crucial part of the script. He paused so that Rundstedt could ask permission to withdraw troops from the Cotentin peninsula. There was no point in sacrificing crack units in a doomed cause.

Hitler replied in a calm manner meant to impress. "I accept that the Cotentin will be cut in two, but Cherbourg, because of its deep harbor, must be defended to the death. The best and most experienced field commander must be given command of the garrison. They must hold out for another month to give the navy time to place more mines in the harbor. That will keep Normandy from being supplied by sea. Thus denied the deep port of Cherbourg, the enemy supply line will fail. Without supplies, he cannot succeed!" He glanced around, daring anyone to contradict him.

"Our troops at Cherbourg must not be sacrificed," Rommel said flatly. "The old idea of 'holding the fort' is backward thinking." They waited to see how Hitler took this. When he did not reply, Rommel went on, "We must adjust our thinking and shift forces where they can be more effective. Flexibility is our only hope."

Still, Hitler said nothing. Rommel pressed the issue, observing that all fortresses were meant to be bypassed. The allies would isolate Cherbourg and push on to Paris. Cherbourg, Dunkirk, Dieppe, Pas de Calais, Cap Gris Nez, Le Havre–these fortifications were tying up 200,000 men and equipment while the enemy went around them. "Have we learned *nothing* from our mistakes in Stalingrad, Tunis and the Crimea?"

Jodl, the mouthpiece, began to argue in favor of the fortresses. The Führer nodded to himself, agreeing with this voice of reason. Rommel was not ready to relinquish the floor. He had never forgiven Jodl for refusing him supplies at Alamein. Jodl would have destroyed his career if Hitler had not ordered him to take over the defense of France. He began listing the options open to the enemy.

"*One*, if we let them break out at Caen and Bayeux, the way will be open to Paris. Politically and psychologically, that is very significant. *Two*, they also must cover their flank, which means sealing off our forces in the south and west. In that case, they will thrust past Avranches–*here*–to cut off our intact divisions positioned here and here, in Brittany. The choice is very simple.

Which is more important, Paris or Brittany?" *Tap-tap-tap* went Hitler's pencil.

Eisenhower could be expected to play it safe and not head for Paris before sewing up the Cotentin peninsula. In the meantime, Montgomery's Second British Army would do what it did best: hammer away methodically. "They have time and resources on their side," he said. "Between twenty-two and twenty-five divisions are in place, with two or three more arriving every week." How long could the German army keep going, outmanned and outgunned?

He looked directly at Hitler. "The enemy breakout is only a matter of time." The rebel generals murmured agreement. The pencil tapped in metronomic precision. "We have no 'Seine defense line,'" Rommel added preemptively. "Or any other defense line! It is the height of delusion to keep referring to a fictitious *line*."

Hitler sat drawn in on himself. He waited for Jodl to speak but, for once, the High Command had nothing to contribute.

"I must ask for two things," Rommel went on. "*One*, the authority to respond rapidly, with the nearest divisions, before the enemy can consolidate his gains; and *two*, a plan to deal with the capture of the Contentin peninsula by the Americans and the withdrawal of German forces behind the Orne at Caen."

Rundstedt seconded the motion. All eyes were on Hitler. Like a corpse coming to life, he rose from his stool, unwrapping his arms. "I cannot agree with the assessment of the *Herr Feldmarschall*!" He appraised the generals with their hats tucked under their arms. "Who came up with that estimate of enemy troop strength? *Patton*?" On cue, Jodl and Schmundt chuckled. Then there were the bloated casualty figures. Well, not to worry. Correct estimates would shortly be available.

Jodl made notes as if reminding himself to "adjust" the casualty figures. Hypnotic, swaying, pounding an imagined podium, Hitler began to speak of the heralded V-weapon. "It passed its initial test with flying colors! *One thousand* fired at England yesterday for the first time." Rommel's look of surprise delighted him. "You did not know that, did you! *Think of it.* A thousand V-bombs, each delivering a ton of explosives. England reeling in chaos, so many fires to put out, a groundswell of protest, citizens clamoring to end the war. I tell you, the V-bombs will prove decisive in Germany's *great victory* over Britain." He glanced about in triumph. Before anyone could contradict him, he called for his press secretary and began dictating a press release about the V-bombs.

Rommel glanced at Rundstedt and Speidel. The Führer was staging one of his celebrated flanking movements. With these "miracle weapons" there was no possibility of defeat. Therefore, no surrender. After a moment Rommel inquired if the V-bombs might not be better employed against the Allied staging areas in southern England or even at the bridgeheads in Normandy.

"*No, no, no*!" Hitler cried, spittle flying. "They are not accurate! We cannot let the enemy know we cannot hit what we are aiming at." He summoned the general in charge of V-weapons, who happened to be waiting in the next room. This general confirmed that at several hundred miles range, the V-bombs could stray up to ten miles from their targets.

Hitler dismissed him and continued, "You see, it is impossible to launch guided missiles at enemy positions on French soil. This would endanger German troops in the bridgehead areas. Likewise, it is pointless to aim them at the ports in the south of England. No, let us hit London again and again and the British will come crawling."

Rundstedt brought up the failure of the Luftwaffe. Where was air support? One by one the marshals tacked on complaints. Everybody, including Jodl, loathed Hermann Göring. Even Hitler had to agree. Yes, the Luftwaffe had been derelict in its commitment. Yes, he had been deceived by the commander of the Luftwaffe and his technical advisers. Too many types of aircraft, he said profoundly, had been developed simultaneously. They should have emphasized fighter manufacture. He pounded the imaginary podium. "*I guarantee delivery of one thousand jet fighters in two weeks. They will turn the tide.*"

"Two weeks will be too late," Rommel said quietly. A thousand such planes could not turn the tide. The Allies had twenty-seven thousand fighters.

Hitler turned on him. It was the moment they had been waiting for. "You are wrong, *Herr Feldmarschall* Rommel, to speak of enemy airpower as if it were a mythical force which we cannot overcome." Like a genie trapped in a bottle, he squinted at the impudent generals. "If this were so, I would have heard about it from the Luftwaffe or Naval Intelligence. Such estimates are *ridiculous*!"

Rommel said, "I would like to see someone from OKW, the Luftwaffe or Navy Intelligence visit the front lines and witness the bombing and strafing. They hit us night and day. With no end to it. Conflicting orders based on false information keep coming from the 'Green Table' in Berlin." He glanced at Jodl. "My assessment is based on first-hand observations at the front!"

Hitler waved in dismissal. This was facile nonsense.

Rommel burst out, "You demand our confidence but you do not trust us yourself!" This was tantamount to insubordination. Hitler sat on his stool, avoiding eye contact, and waited for his pet to save him. On cue Jodl presented a plan: If 9 and 10 SS panzer divisions were brought in from the Russian front, they could turn the tide.

"Yes, that's a good idea!" Hitler said thoughtfully as if this were the first he had heard of it.

Rommel was silent. There was no way that reinforcements could reach the front in time. Then Jodl brought up the possibility of mass-producing jet fighters. Hitler leapt off the stool. "Yes, yes, it can be done. *Masses* of jets in *complete* command of the skies. The enemy fighters will not see them coming. We will blow them to *bits*! We will shatter the Allied air force. The combined use of V-bombs and jet aircraft, the stabilizing of the eastern front, will bring about the collapse of Britain's war effort! This is *unvermeidlich*!" he shrieked –*inevitable*!–and in the same breathless tone announced that lunch would be served *jetzt*, right now! Mess stewards awaiting their cue wheeled trays into place.

According to fastidious routine, Hitler sat at his own table. A plate was served for him, rice piled with vegetables. A taster made sure it was not poisoned. Though they hated to watch, it was impossible not to stare at the taster, an enlisted man not happy with his job. When he did not die, Hitler leaned over his plate and gobbled the food. Arranged on his table were vials and liqueur glasses containing pills and medicines. He morosely consumed the medications. The SS guards stood implacably behind his chair.

In the middle of lunch the air raid siren went off. The station commander of *Wolfsschlucht Zwei* reported enemy aircraft. The conference was moved to the Führer's private air-raid shelter. There was room only for Hitler, his bodyguards, Rundstedt and Rommel, their chiefs of staff and Hitler's adjutant, Gen. Schmundt. Field Marshal Jodl remained in the conference room. Inside the bomb shelter, liberated from the stenographers' inhibiting presence, Rommel seized the opportunity to speak frankly. "There is *no way* to stop the Allies in Normandy," he declared. "Once they break out, the way is clear to Germany. Rome is lost, Italy will soon follow and we cannot hold the Russian front forever."

Hitler listened in growing anger. "Our home guard will be rushed to the eastern front. They can hold the Russians until our manufacturers produce more jet aircraft–"

Rommel raised his voice. "Our worst problem is Germany's isolation from the rest of the world. There is no help, no ally we can count on. It is my duty to advise the Herr Führer that we must consider ways of bringing the war to an end. I have some suggestions if you will hear me out."

Hitler shouted, "I have never learned the word *surrender*!" The thick walls muffled the explosions of bombs outside the bunker. Lights flickered off and on. Rundstedt and Speidel glanced at Rommel, subtly encouraging.

"Politics must come into play." He chose his words carefully. "Otherwise the situation in the west will deteriorate to the point that we will soon be overrun."

Hitler said coldly, "Leave politics to me!"

"But surely you must see–"

"You are *not* to concern yourself with the future course of the war," Hitler hurried on. "You are limited to your own sector of authority in Normandy."

He was on the verge of telling the Führer exactly what he thought of him when Rundstedt interrupted. "Under the circumstances, we feel that it will be necessary to treat France differently, with diplomacy and tact, and to limit the activities and authority of the Secret Police."

"I shall thank you to speak no further of such matters," Hitler said. "Has the bombing ended? Open the door."

They emerged from the shelter. The meeting resumed. Jodl, according to his instructions, played devil's advocate. At 1600 hours Rommel had had enough. Like a puppeteer Hitler was only interested in pulling strings until the final curtain. Rommel bowed curtly to Jodl, putting OKW on notice, then left the bunker without taking his leave of Hitler. Everyone noticed this.

Later, outside the complex, he compared notes with Rundstedt and Speidel. "I do not think we can trust the Führer to make a rational decision, do you?" he said. Rundstedt agreed though with his usual caution. It was *unfortunate* that the Führer could not see the need for a plan of surrender.

"Catastrophe is a better word," Rommel said.

For Speidel, the meeting had not been a total loss. He had spoken with Hitler's adjutant, Gen. Schmundt, who was so impressed with Rommel's warnings that he intended to send a general to observe at first-hand how the battle was going. "I suggested that he bring Hitler to La Roche-Guyon," Speidel went on waggishly, "and offered to entertain the Führer myself."

He began fantasizing about poisoned caviar and champagne. Across the parking lot SS guards were watching. Von Rundstedt took the hint and left. Moments later his staff car passed through the iron gates.

"Well, with any luck the Führer will not be physically able to visit La Roche-Guyon," Speidel said. Rommel did a slow double-take. "Von Stulpnagel has entrusted Colonel Klaus von Stauffenburg with the task of killing him."

Speidel insisted that he look at a memorandum from Stauffenburg appealing to him to "take independent action at once to end the war." He scanned the memo. A blustery wind rattled the paper. "I am not in favor of assassination. How many times do I have to say it?"

He looked at his chief of staff as if to say *There must be another way.* Could they not contact the corps commanders, instead? Have each of them compile a report on the crisis in Normandy predicting the complete collapse of German forces in Normandy? Get all the generals in compliance and present it to Hitler along with an ultimatum? Speidel merely shrugged and got into the car.

XXXI

Military Intelligence was housed in the town of Cruelly. Armored cars, tanks and trucks crowded the streets. Soldiers played soccer with children. The jeep in which Speigner was riding had stopped for a convoy of tanks. A colonel wearing a tanker's helmet directed traffic, thrashing his arms and yelling, "*Come on, you bloody idiot!*" The drivers of the Matildas roundly cursed each other.

MPs marched him into City Hall. The Mayor's office was full of division clerks filing papers and answering telephones. His Honor, *le maire*, was passing out flowers, celebrating liberation from *les boche*. A small girl with ribbons in her hair sat kicking her heels. "*Regardez, Papa*!" she called to the mayor, showing off a wreath she had plaited. The British paid court to her as if she were a princess. Speigner was charmed. This little girl was France's future. Just then a British general entered the office and asked the mayor to preside at an awards ceremony. When was this to take place? Right away, said the general. The recipients were waiting outside. "Heroes cannot be made to stand and wait!" said the mayor. He took his daughter's hand.

Speigner thought it was folly to hand out medals in broad daylight. What about the Luftwaffe? Just thinking about this exhausted him. On his last night in the attic he had slept fitfully, falling asleep at dawn. The birds had made a racket in the eaves. Yet without that time, alone with the birds and Hitler, he might never have rediscovered a part of himself that had been missing. Someday he'd know why there were seven Menorah candles.

"*Korporal Dietzel*!" a company clerk shouted.

He went to the counter and signed in. The clerk mocked him with a Nazi salute. Had no one informed M.I. that he was an *American*? The town mayor gave him a baleful glance and held his daughter to protect her from the war criminal. He informed the clerk he was a lieutenant in the United States Army assigned to Special Services Branch. "*Gehen Sie, Korporal-Leutnant*!" The clerk directed him to the mayor's private office, which was being used for interrogations.

The door closed behind him. He had a sinking feeling

that he was back where he started. The British in refusing to acknowledge his identity had created a myth: *Who is Rudolf Dietzel?* Someone was playing "God Save the Queen" on a victrola. He went to the window. French civilians had gathered outside the church for the awards ceremony. The mayor, his daughter holding his hand, appeared beside the general on the steps of the little cathedral. The soldiers waiting to be decorated came to attention. The townspeople waved miniature flags, Union Jack, Stars and Stripes and Tri-Color of France. The clouds parted. Brilliant sunlight streamed through. The general had barely begun to make his remarks when the crowd looked up. Speigner thought they were staring at him: Rudolf Dietzel, Nazi criminal. Then he heard the whine of a *Stuka*. The first time he'd heard this sound was in a documentary film of the Spanish civil war. *Run*! he thought. The general ordered the honorees to remain at attention.

A few of the civilians applauded. *Régardez le brave général anglais*! They would show the English, *n'est-ce pas*? They, too, could ignore the *Stuka*. They, too, could laugh at death. Bullets raked the square. They came to their senses and scrambled for cover. Everybody, including the general, ran. The little girl fell. Her father picked her up. There was a huge explosion in front of the church. Smoke and debris flew everywhere. Speigner ducked. The window miraculously remained intact. When he looked out, the *Stuka* was rising above the clouds. The anti-aircraft guns futilely plugged away. The square was a shambles. There was screaming and panic. Speigner searched for the little girl. A small, still figure lay in the rubble.

The mayor carried his daughter back to city hall. A medical station was hastily set up. While the town burned, the general ordered the medal-winners back into line and handed out Victoria Crosses and Hero of the Realm ribbons, the bright medals and colored bits of cloth visible from the second floor window. Speigner felt a twinge of guilt as if he had led the *Stuka* to Creully.

Finding the door unlocked, he opened it a few inches and saw medics attending to the unconscious girl. She had been wounded in the head. The soldier behind the counter noticed him and yelled, "*Gehen Sie zurück, Korporal*!" Distraught and disheveled, the mayor went for the "*Boche*," tackling Speigner and punching him. The company clerk and another soldier pulled the mayor off. He continued to curse and spit. The clerk hustled Max into the interrogation room. Half an hour later he still had not gotten over the ugly scene.

An officer introduced himself as Major Leland. He explained that he would handle the "debriefing." He noticed that Speigner kept looking at smoke rising from the burning square. There was a wail of sirens. Fire engines came to put out the fires. Ambulances were trying to leave the square. Another traffic jam. The little town was in agony. Leland closed the blinds. Bombings might come and go but interrogations went on forever. He stood over Speigner and said, "Let's hear it."

He was Lt. Max Speigner of U.S. Army Intelligence. He was not Rudolf Dietzel. The German identity papers were forged. He gave his serial number and suggested that Leland have it checked out. He requested immediate assistance in contacting Churchill on a top priority matter. Before Leland could respond, another officer entered the room. At first Speigner did not pay him any attention. Then their eyes met.

It had been two and a half years since he and the former Oxford don had hitched a ride to an oasis in an ammunition truck. John Bright-Ashton might have just strolled back to their armored half-track with two cups of tea. He smoked what appeared to be the same briarwood pipe. He took the pipe out of his mouth and said, "Still up to your neck?"

Leland reminded Major Bright-Ashton who was in charge of the debriefing.

"I can vouch for this man," Bright-Ashton countered. "We worked together in Cairo. He's a Rommel expert. Knew the field marshal when he was a colonel of infantry. The last time he asked me for a favor he was promptly captured by the Germans. Some things never change." He relit the pipe. "Wondered what happened to you, old boy. Glad you made it back."

Leland pointed out that Bright-Ashton's presence was unnecessary. When this didn't work, he told him to leave. Speigner asked if either of them could get through to the prime minister.

"He was here only yesterday," Bright-Ashton remarked. "Visiting Monty's Tac-HQ, getting in everyone's way. A destroyer took him away so we could get back to work." Bright-Ashton had not lost his infuriating self-assurance. Max tried to stand up. Leland pushed him back in his chair. "When Field Marshal

Montgomery spoke with me, he had just *seen* Churchill? He never mentioned it!"

"Why should he?" said Leland.

Bright-Ashton observed, "Monty and the P.M. don't always see eye to eye."

"Would you please stop chatting up my prisoner?" Leland said.

Bright-Ashton acted as if intrigued. How *did* one get a message from Rommel to Churchill? Don't tell John something could not be done. He would find a way. Leland demanded that the intelligence expert get out. Bright-Ashton ignored him and addressed Max confidentially. "Would you like me to ring Number Ten Downing Street?"

"Yes, please. The prime minister should remember assigning me to Special Branch. I was parachuted into France, did anyone tell you? He's expecting to hear from me." He produced Rommel's card. Bright-Ashton started to examine it. Leland snatched it away. The prisoner's documents were forged. Why not this card as well? Bright-Ashton promised to see what he could find out. In the meantime, how about something to eat? A change of clothing?

"I'd like to keep the pants."

"Why, they don't fit very well!"

"They were Rommel's."

Bright-Ashton left the room whistling. Leland resumed the interrogation.

Rudolf Dietzel of Frankfurt.

Speigner of Indiana.

Bright-Ashton stuck his head in the door. "Really, Leland, I do know this man."

"Go away."

He wanted to think Bright-Ashton would check out his story. The ceasefire could happen overnight. They could all go home. The mayor's daughter would recover. Leland was asking about Rommel's headquarters. The question caught him unawares. When he hesitated, Leland called Bright-Ashton back in. He had been hovering outside the door, which made Max's heart sink. "Your friend knows where Rommel is," Leland said.

John cleared his throat and asked if Speigner would mind stating the precise location. Then they would contact the prime minister. He replied with heavy patience, "I was under guard the whole time. I rowed up the Seine at night. The villages all looked the same."

John began to fuss with his pipe. It was always going out. Bright-Ashton was playing him. They were not going to get another word until he heard from Churchill. Regardless of what they thought he was not there as Rommel's protector. He was the prime minister's envoy. Why wouldn't they at least check this out?

Leland continued to press for information. Max was just as adamant in his silence. Bright-Ashton said this was no way to treat an ally. It was absurd to think Speigner was working for the Germans. Leland smiled ironically. "Well, he'll soon be able to speak German to his heart's content."

Bright-Ashton accompanied him in the truck. John took his pipe out, then stuffed it into his coat pocket. The absent-minded gesture seemed genuine. The truck jerked along. They sat on a bench side by side.

"I brought back the deal of the century," Speigner complained. "Rommel wants to surrender. Montgomery won't listen. All he cares about is winning."

John agreed that Montgomery was bent on taking Caen. It didn't surprise him that the field marshal wasn't interested in a peace offer, genuine or not. Not that he doubted his friend's story. Still, there had to be a quid pro quo. It was up to Speigner. Before Max could reply, the truck turned into a field. He got out of the truck and saw where they were taking him–a POW holding area encircled by barbed wire. Inside were hundreds of German prisoners.

"You're putting me with *them*? You said I would be released into your custody."

It looked like the POW camp in Bavaria except that in place of starving, itching Yanks and Tommies, these prisoners were blond, Nordic and well fed. He smelled the sweet smoke of American cigarettes. A prisoner dug Spam out of a can with his fingers. He thought he recognized a *Jugend* uniform and hoped he was mistaken. The MPs signed him in. He passed through the gate. Three times a prisoner. Four if one counted La Roche-Guyon. Bright-Ashton called through the barbed wire, "You can set it right. One word from you and you're out. Understand?" A military policeman slammed the bolt home. The Germans hovered around him, exclaiming over his lieutenant's bar. It was like being surrounded by Doberman pinschers.

"*Haben Sie eine Zigarette*?" a soldier demanded.

He sidestepped along the fence after Bright-Ashton, snagging a finger on a barb. Was it a coincidence that the only man at Montgomery's HQ who knew him showed up at his interrogation?

"*Zigarette?*" the soldier persisted.

In Libya, the Italians had put up a fence on the Egyptian border. "The Wire" was a roll of barbed wire ten feet high and a hundred miles long. In a sand-storm, he and Bright-Ashton had followed it back to camp. Antelope carcasses were strung on it like *papier-mâché*. "Don't leave me hanging!" he called.

Bright-Ashton came back to the fence. "Here's the straight of it. Special Branch doesn't want to make peace with Rommel. They want to kill him."

XXXII

"*Hallo, wer ist da*?" she said. He waited for a click that meant someone was listening. All long distance calls were monitored by political officers. "*Hallo, hallo?*" There was fear in her voice.

"It is I, Erwin."

Mayor Strölin had arranged for her to use a private line in Ulm. Their home telephone was being tapped. No names were to be used.

"I was wondering, how is your health?" The formal tone warned her to be careful.

"Very well, thank you," she said.

"And the young man's?"

"He cannot get a pass, not even for a weekend. I was hoping there was something you could do." She would not leave without Manfred. With spies listening he could not say more.

She asked how the battle was going. The news was not good.

General Dollmann was dead of an apparent heart attack. General Marcks had been strafed in his jeep. "Marcks was wounded in the first attack," he told her, "but he could have gotten out before the enemy aircraft returned. His aide tried to get him to leave but he stayed in his car and waited for the fighter plane to make a second run. He told the aide, 'It is better this way.'"

"*Bitte*, be careful, my dearest!"

Using code names he related news from the front. The Great Raccoon (Hitler) had sacked the Statesman (von Rundstedt), replacing him with the Weasel (Field Marshal von Kluge), a longtime adversary of Rommel. Wholesale changes had been made in division commands, starting with the Bürgermeister (Baron General Geyr von Schweppenburg), whom Hitler blamed for the failed counterattack. Notifying Rommel by phone that he was officially out of favor and better watch his step, the Weasel had told him, "The first thing is, you must get accustomed to obeying orders like the rest." Rommel had responded, "You seem to forget you are speaking with a field marshal." Later he sent a memo inquiring why the Weasel had addressed him in such a manner, though he knew who demanded obedience.

He could not tell her over the phone that he had revised the Great Raccoon's order to the Cherbourg garrison, substituting "fighting to the last *bullet*" instead of "...the last man." Looking back he regretted not having disobeyed Hitler's victory-or-death order at Alamein.

"Can you win a battle?" she said cautiously. She knew that he needed a major victory to negotiate with Eisenhower.

Intercepted radio transmissions indicated Montgomery was moving up armored divisions. When OKW refused to give Rommel the intelligence he needed, he drove to the front lines and gathered information the old-fashioned way, from commanders in the field. The ever-cautious Montgomery relied on numbers, mass attack, superiority of force. Rommel would try to slow the armored advance, using mine fields and the accuracy of his 88s, the anti-aircraft cannon which could hit a moving tank at two miles. At Caen, he anticipated a heavy bombardment, followed by a British assault with hundreds of tanks.

This would be his last chance to stop Montgomery. Instead of a single, massive defense line, he was redeploying his forces in five groups, utilizing natural barriers. The 16th Luftwaffe and 272 Infantry divisions were dug in at Caen. Backing them up were

88s which he positioned on the ridges along with Tiger tanks, far superior to the slower, less thickly armored British tanks. In addition there were 194 field guns and 272 Nebelwerfer six-barreled rocket launchers. By massing formations, Montgomery made himself vulnerable to concentrated artillery fire. The third line was SS infantry, which held the villages along the roads. Farther back were forty-five Panzer Vs, backed up by remnants of *Hitler Jugend* division, in two battle groups with forty tanks each.

At Alamein he had stood on the dunes and watched Monty's forces advance. There was nothing he could do about it. At the end the enemy had six hundred tanks to his eighty. He had waited a long time for another chance. Every battle was a gamble, but with 88s on high ground he was content with the odds.

He could not tell her how the coup was proceeding, that Speidel was pressing generals to sign a Hitler ultimatum. Or that the war was lost. Or that they could not afford to lose the peace. Or that every hour he checked the telegraph for news from the American. He was waiting for Montgomery to break out of Caen. If his American friend contacted him before the battle, he would honor his commitment. Meanwhile, one fought where he stood.

"*Have you thought about our vacation*?" He had thought of a way into Switzerland. There was a trail that crossed the Swiss border in a forested area. They had hiked the path several times. She responded on cue, "Yes, we must go to that quiet place that we liked so much."

He knew how difficult this was for her. While he rallied his troops and contacted generals about a *coup d'etat*, she guarded the home front, her task more formidable because she did it alone–slept alone, ate alone, cleaned house, wrote letters, did whatever she had to until the family was together again. He could not tell her how much this meant to him. "Yes, the place where I tried to yodel."

She would never forget it, she said. The forest had echoed with his yodeling. Even the birds stopped singing. Her voice became heavy. "I do not think the young man will be given leave. His battalion has been placed on alert."

"Well, in the meantime, why don't you proceed directly to our summer retreat and he will join you when he can?" She was silent. Subterfuge was unworthy of him. She could not be talked into leaving without their son. This phone call could be their last.

He had to make the most of it. “When you and the boy arrive, contact the authorities–just as a courtesy–so that they can let me know.”

She was to contact the Swiss government and have them call the British consul. Then he would give the ceasefire order. “All will be done as you wish, my dear. When can I expect to see you?”

I will come as soon as I can.

My dearest, please be careful.

The thirsty camel drinks when it can.

She responded with a throaty chuckle. A thousand nights were in that laugh. She could smile, his woman, she could laugh while the Gestapo listened.

XXXIII

It had rained the night before. His clothes reeked. How long had he been in the POW holding area? Two weeks…three? He kept his blanket around his shoulders. He had a full beard. He was known as “the Old Man.” Sitting in the same place. Getting up only for chow or to relieve himself. He was often seen stamping his feet and complaining to anyone who would listen. His energy level was at an all-time low. He sat under his blanket and listened to bombers rumble past. A major battle had begun. The roads were jammed with French refugees leaving Caen and cursing the British who had bombed the city. They made obscene gestures at the planes.

His fellow prisoners were *Wehrmacht* with a sprinkling of Russian and Polish conscripts. The turnover was constant. He was jealous of the newcomers. Most were happy to have been captured, jovial, talking, making friends. They received a delousing, two meals a day and a blanket made in New Zealand. All they could think of was being reunited with their families. They traded food and cigarettes for a newspaper, interested not in war news but in the classifieds.

The prisoners were held for a few days, processed and transferred, usually to Scotland or Northamptonshire. The first day they walked the perimeter. Every one of them did it, all four sides of the fence, getting used to their limitations. Next they focused on each other, questioned prisoners who had been there a while. What was it like? How were they treated? They introduced themselves and asked about their fellow POWs. Who was that man? Where was he from? They embraced members of their own divisions.

There were major differences between this camp and the stalag where he had lived for one and a half years. The allied prisoners hated their captors and talked continually of escape. They would have rioted over a newspaper. Here, with food, blankets, Red Cross packets once a week-and no pilferage-the Germans were in POW heaven. They trusted their captors. Many were hoping to be sent to the U. S. "I always want to see New York," a prisoner told Speigner, trying out his English. "A fantastic city, eh?"

The word got out about him. He was a famous person. A friend of Rommel. A double agent. *There, that's him, huddled under his blanket. He never speaks to anyone.* Sociable types, undeterred, asked questions. One had a cousin in Detroit. How far was that from New York? How long did it take to get there by train?

A heavy set, muscular artilleryman captured in the battle of Caen came over and squatted next to Max. His name was Nikki. He claimed to be from Bavaria. He spoke perfect English with a slight German accent. What set him apart was that he knew that Max had been picked up by Rommel.

"How do you know that?"

"A motorcycle courier. He said he brought an American captive to Rommel's headquarters. The field marshal himself took charge of the prisoner. Was that you?"

He was noncommittal at first. The German accent sounded phony to him. He tried to get Nikki to speak German. Having been in a POW camp in Bavaria he knew the regional patois. Nikki however was interested only in Rommel.

Where were Rommel's headquarters?

What was his daily schedule?

Where did he go?

What did his car look like?

He gave vague answers in German. Nikki insisted they use English so he could practice speaking it. "How's my English? Is it getting better? Can you understand me?" Max said something in German, then asked if Nikki knew what was meant. "*Wissen Sie was das bedeutet*?"

Nikki saw what was going on. "*Ja, ich verstehe. Es ist kein Problem.*"

His German was school-taught, Speigner thought, without a regional accent. He asked where in Bavaria was Nikki from. "Little village, you wouldn't have heard of it. What you would call a 'hole in the road,' *ja*?"

"Nikki, I've got news for you. I know Bavarians. You learned German as a second language…*ja*?"

"My parents sent me to private school. That must be it." Complaining of diarrhea Nikki went to the latrine.

Two boys walked by, skinny, young for soldiers. There was something familiar about them. They kept to themselves and didn't talk to the others. They had torn the insignia off their uniforms. One of them had a hole in the front of his cap. There had been an "SS" on the cap the last time he saw it. Cherub and Mustache, the *Jugend* who had captured him, were no longer boasting about being in the SS. Not among these Wehrmacht regulars. He put the blanket over his head. When he looked, they were standing by the fence. Someone was pointing him out to them. *Practice your English, yes? There he is. The American! Go on, he won't mind.*

In a few minutes, they were back. He pulled the blanket over him like a hood. A face appeared in the circle. "*Das ist er!*" Cherub cried. "The dirty Jew American."

"You've made a mistake," he said from inside the blanket.

"Is not your name Speigner? Are you not the same one?"

Mustache said, "Are you a Jew or not? Tell the truth."

All the feelings he had felt in the attic came back. Hitler's rantings had stirred his pride. He was ready to fight at the first slur, the first insult, the first insinuation that he was not as good as anyone else. He stood up. The *Jugend* took a step back, ready to fight. He threw off the blanket. "Yes, I am a Jew."

They tackled him at the same time. He didn't care if he got hit as long as he got in his own licks. He landed a hard right to the belly of Cherub, who caved in, the wind knocked out of him.

For all his bluster, Mustache, too, was a lightweight. Cherub revived, however, and succeeded in pinning his arms behind his back. Mustache began taking roundhouse swings, with long, slow windups. He managed to avoid a direct blow to the face. The wild punches glanced off his cheekbones.

Someone grabbed the *Jugend*, pulled them off. Nikki tossed them to the ground like toys. "No fighting, mates. That's the rule. Go on, now, or you'll be sorry. Go on or I'll take it out of your hide." Nikki helped him to his feet. "How are you."

"Okay." He felt his jaw. A tooth was loose. He picked up his blanket and wrapped it around his shoulders. "I thought you were at the latrine."

Nikki said that he was on his way back and saw what was happening and came to help.

Vielen Dank.

Gern geschehen.

Nikki hesitated. Did Churchill send Speigner back to France? Was it true that when Rommel picked him up, the Gestapo surrounded his headquarters? Was it true that Speigner hid in the attic?

"How did you know that?"

"A little bird told me."

With the *Jugend* around it wouldn't hurt to have an ally. He reluctantly confirmed the Gestapo story, the attic, the secret passageway, the ladder he clung to while they searched.

"So Rommel's headquarters are located in the chateau of the Marquis de La Rochfoucauld?"

He covered his head with his blanket. After a while Nikki went away. He did not see the *Jugend* until they were standing over him. They had found a couple of toughs to back them up, probably Waffen SS, their patches and insignia also torn off. Cherub took off his shoe and slid the heel to one side, revealing a sliver of steel, a thin razor to be used in case of capture.

He jumped up and started to run. His leg, though healed, refused to cooperate. They caught him easily and herded him to the fence. The British guards were fifty meters away at the main gate. Nikki was nowhere to be seen. The *Jugend* were arguing in German. He could hear them over his shoulder as they shoved him along the fence.

I saw him first, remember?

I was in charge of the patrol. I outrank you.

Only because you joined a week before I did.

It's my razor.

"Ow!" The older boy cut his finger trying to take the razor away. "You did that on purpose!"

"No, I didn't."

Cherub and Mustache began to fight. Max tried to get away. The SS thugs tackled him. He lowered his head and charged, but it was no contest. They pinned him to the ground and told the *Jugend* to hurry up before the guards came. Cherub and Mustache remained locked together. Each was cut and bleeding. Each was determined to make the other pay. The guards came running, firing their weapons in the air. Speigner raised his hands. The SS soldiers disappeared among the stampeding prisoners. The *Jugend* thrashed and punched, making animal noises. The guards watched for a moment, then hit them with gun butts and made them lie spread-eagled. They turned their faces sideways and cursed each other, furious but strangely satisfied.

XXXIV

Speidel asked him to consider a different vehicle. The Horch was too recognizable. "Take one less likely to be identified as yours, a half-track, something armored."

"I like the Horch," he said. "If we are attacked, Daniel is very good at speeding away."

As a compromise he assigned an air sentry, *Obergefreiter* Holke, to travel with them. Also in attendance were Captain Lange, and a staff officer, Major Neuhaus. A group of ordnance officers followed in a *Kübelwagen*. Rommel was going to see Sepp Dietrich. Dietrich had a network of trusted colleagues who could contact SS commanders based in Germany.

French refugees crowded the roads, their household goods piled on horse-drawn carts. White sheets were marked with fleurs-de-lis so the RAF fighter-bombers would not attack them. They recognized Rommel and doffed their caps, waving and yelling, as they always did, "*C'est Rommel, c'est Rommel!*"

"Look at that," he observed. "They are being bombed out of their homes by the Tommies and Americans. They hate them worse than they hate us."

"Perhaps we should cover our car with a fleurs-de-lis," Lange remarked.

Rommel ordered Daniel up to cruising speed. They soon arrived at 1 SS Panzer Headquarters near the village of Frenouville, about five miles southeast of Caen. He and General Dietrich went for a walk.

First they discussed the coming battle. 1 SS Panzer had suffered heavy losses in Montgomery's attack of June 29. Rommel picked up a stick and drew in the dirt. He made an X for Caen, then semi-circles south of the city representing his defensive positions. He expected Montgomery to lay down a massive barrage and attack with a phalanx of tanks. "As far as I am concerned," he said, "this will be the last significant battle of the war." Just saying this got his juices stirring. "We let the enemy establish a foothold," he said, throwing away the stick. "But now we have a chance to show Montgomery a thing or two."

As to the ceasefire, things were falling into place. Dietrich was in contact with all the Waffen SS. "You are the boss," he assured the field marshal.

Dietrich noticed the heavy staff car and asked if it was the one that got stuck in the mud. "You should take a *Kübelwagen*. They are more maneuverable in case of fighter attack. The RAF is covering this sector like a rug." Rommel said he had not seen much evidence of strafing along the main road. Dietrich pressed the point. "Bayerlein had six cars attacked. *Six*! I have no idea how he survived. May *Dame Glück* ride in your lap, *mein Herr Feldmarschall*."

On the way back Rommel sat in the front seat, map spread on his knees. Neuhaus and Lange were in the rear seat with Air Sentry Holke. He told Daniel to take road N-179 to Livarot. More than once, they detoured onto secondary roads. Hulks of burned out vehicles littered the roads and ditches. Approaching Livarot they saw Luftwaffe Jagdbombers circling over the town.

"Those Jabos might hit us by mistake," he said. "Bypass the town. There is a dirt road that cuts through to the main highway between Livarot and Vimoutiers." Daniel warned that a dust trail might attract enemy fighters. Rommel calmly studied the map.

Obergefreiter Holke counted eight Jabos attacking ground targets in the distance. "*Herr Feldmarschall,*" Lange said, leaning over his shoulder, "we could be hit by one of our own!" He relented and told Daniel to park under a grove of trees. "Do you think we were spotted?" Lange was trying to see through the canopy of leaves.

Rommel searched the sky. "Holke, do you see anything?"

"*Nein, Herr Generalfeldmarschall, kein feindliches Flugzeug.*" No enemy aircraft.

"Let's go, Daniel," he said. The car approached the top of a shallow rise. There was a crossroads. Rommel studied the map. One road went to Lisores, and the other was the Usine Laniel access road.

In a steady voice, as if it were nothing to be alarmed about, Holke said, "Two enemy aircraft, behind us...turning, turning... they *see* us."

Rommel yelled, "Go, Daniel! Take the lane to the right." The Horch roared up the highway as Daniel accelerated to 110 kilometers per hour.

"First plane is diving!" Holke reported. "Leveling off now, range five hundred meters."

"Take the next right and hide behind those trees!" Rommel glanced over his shoulder. The enemy plane was starting to make its run. He clutched the door handle, ready to jump. Twenty millimeter rounds slammed into the roadbed behind them. Daniel braked sharply to turn into the lane–50 meters, 25 meters–then high explosive shells struck the staff car.

The windshield exploded. Daniel slumped over the wheel. The car plunged across a ditch, then bounced back onto the road. As the Horch spun around, Rommel was thrown out. Lange and Holke sought cover in a ditch. A second plane came in to strafe them. He lay in the road, semi-paralyzed, one eye cavity filled with blood. A Spitfire filled his narrow circle of vision, cannons flashing. He remembered General Marcks. *Leave me here. It is better this way.*

Lange and Neuhaus watched as bullets kicked up dust. Their commander did not move. As soon as the Spitfire was gone they ran to Rommel. Amazingly he had not been hit by bullets, though his wounds from the crash were quite severe. Daniel's left arm was all but blown off. Lange and Holke, both of whom escaped injury, dragged the driver out of the burning car. Bleeding where a shell had struck his holster, Neuhaus limped across the road. "I think my pelvic bone is broken. What happened to the field marshal?"

Rommel was lying where he fell. He was unconscious but his pulse was steady. Lange tried to mop the blood out of his eye cavity. They carried the field marshal to a gatekeeper's lodge in the Usine Laniel forest. A Frenchman who had been repairing a fence before the attack offered assistance.

"*Où est la ville la plus proche?*"

"Vimoutiers, *deux* kilometers." The man held up two fingers.

"Is there a hospital...*l'hopital?*"

"*Non, monsieur. Cependant, voilà un hopital d'armee dans Bernay.*"

"How far is that...*combien de kilometres*?"

"*Quarante, monsieur.*"

Forty kilometers. Lange glanced up and down the road. The Horch was on fire, leather seats crackling, dashboard curling up as it melted. Neuhaus said, "Where the devil is the rest of the convoy?"

Lange examined Rommel more closely. His left temple had been smashed. He would die unless the bleeding was stopped. "There is Lescene's Pharmacy in Vimoutiers," the Frenchman suggested. "We go to Monsieur Lescene for our ailments. It is the closest thing we have to a surgery." Lange caught only two words, *pharmacie* and *Vimoutiers.*

The first vehicle in the trailing convoy approached from the rear. Lange flagged it down. "We're going to Vimoutiers!" he yelled. "What took you so long?" The driver explained that the others cars had gone through Livarot and were trapped by air attack. "We were going at a snail's pace, I can tell you, and the *Herr Feldmarschall* goes so fast...besides, you took a different road."

"Never mind the excuses, help us get him in your car," Lange ordered. They carried Rommel to the car and laid him in the back seat next to Daniel, then drove to Vimoutiers. During the five-minute trip Rommel came to, and began groaning. To Lange this was a good sign. Rommel was aware only that his head was in someone's lap. He started to ask about Daniel but before he could say a word he passed out.

In Vimoutiers, they stopped in front of the pharmacy and blew the horn. Marcel Lescene, the pharmacist, rushed out and examined Rommel, finding steel splinters in his back, glass fragments in face and head. He also was suffering from a concussion. Then the chemist looked at Daniel, declaring it unlikely he would survive. The pharmacy had little medicine for gunshot wounds other than sulphur and morphine. He produced a stretcher and told them to bring the field marshal inside.

Rommel was aware of being lifted onto a stretcher. He felt no pain, only numbness. It bothered him that he could not see out of his left eye. They set the stretcher down on the floor of the pharmacy. Lescene's wife fetched medicine. The chemist knelt beside Rommel and gave him two injections of etherated camphor.

"This is rather old-fashioned," he told Lange and Neuhaus, "but it will stimulate his heart and keep him alive for a few hours until you get him to the hospital at Bernay."

Lange used the phone to call Army Group B and report the strafing. Speidel took the call. He was alarmed but calm, as if he had been expecting this to happen. Rommel was notorious for riding the roads in the equally notorious Horch. The chief of staff asked to be kept informed. He suggested that they should not wait for an ambulance but take Rommel directly to the Luftwaffe hospital at Bernay. In the meantime, Speidel would have Major Behr of Rommel's staff and Dr. Schuenig, resident physician at Heeresgruppe B headquarters, meet them at Bernay. After Lange hung up, Lescene, curious about Rommel's uniform, asked the identity of the patient.

"He is Field Marshal Rommel."

The chemist said, "I recognized him from his picture."

"He doesn't look like himself," Lange said.

He woke up in the operating room at Bernay's *Luftwaffenortlazarett*, the military hospital. While he was being X-rayed, he asked about Daniel and was told not to worry. Doctors discussed the diagnosis: "A severe skull fracture, smashed temple and cheekbone, left eye severed, concussion." Rommel heard a familiar voice, Daniel's, saying, "My field marshal, my car...don't cut my tunic. You'll cut the money in my pocket."

He passed out. When he awoke, he was in a second-floor room of the hospital. He looked around wildly. His head was swathed in bandages. He was unable to see out of his left eye.

Lange sat by the bed. "An RAF plane attacked us." Lange explained about taking him to the pharmacy in Vimoutiers, how Monsieur Marcel Lescene had saved his life with an injection.

"Daniel...?"

Despite massive blood transfusions the corporal had drifted into a coma and died during the night.

Poor Daniel! So many dead. A lifetime would not be long enough to grieve. He tried to sit up and demanded to be returned to Heeresgruppe B Headquarters. He almost blacked out from the effort. Lange said getting out of bed was not an option, though Dr. Schuenig was conferring with the Luftwaffe surgeons about transferring the field marshal to Le Vesinet, east of St. Germain, to be placed under the care of Dr. Esch. "The doctors say you must rest for at least a week. *Sehen Sie*, here is Major Behr!"

Behr stuck his head in the door and asked permission to come in. Rommel was shocked to find that he was unable to raise his hand. "Has Montgomery commenced his attack?" He fought to stay awake. It was maddening to think of his men going into battle without him. For this to happen when he was poised to surrender and stop the fighting was the worst thing he could imagine.

"The British hit us with a massive bombardment but I can report that our lines are holding," Behr said.

His spirits rose. Lange and the doctors were too cautious. He did not need more than one eye to beat Montgomery. The British would not be able to penetrate all five defense lines. One night's rest and he would be up and going. If necessary, he would direct the battle from bed. They could set up a map on a tripod. He tried to sit up, struggling against the bedclothes. Searing pain rocked his head. Behr and Lange exchanged an uneasy glance.

He squinted at them with his good eye, panting for breath. "They missed me, *ja*?"

XXXV

They locked him in a room with a view. An orderly brought three hot meals a day. *Does the Leftenant take coffee or tea?* He had his own shower and head. He was given clean clothes. As his mind resisted, his body settled in. He began to look forward to meals. He lay in bed and listened to telephones ring somewhere. At night he heard footsteps outside his door. Special Air Service was at its busiest after dark.

He requested a newspaper and was given the June 7 issue of *The London Times*, whose headlines trumpeted successful landings in Normandy. Also the latest issue of *Punch*, whose political commentary and satire he once would have found entertaining. He stared out the window for hours on end, imagining himself stealing among the trees, returning to La Roche-Guyon–but to what purpose?

A week went by before they brought him to interrogation. There were several officers present, including a brigadier general. At first he thought it was a court martial hearing. He was almost relieved when the questioning began.

Major Leland picked up where he'd left off. Where was Rommel's office? The chateau library? On the north side of the building? How well it was guarded? What time of day did Rommel make inspection tours? How many officers rode with him? Were there armored cars or half-tracks in the convoy?

The regimental commander, Brigadier McCloud, reminded him that he was in a theatre of war. Unless he cooperated fully, Special Air Service had little choice but to treat him as a counter-espionage agent.

"I *am* cooperating," he shot back. "No one is cooperating with *me*." In a theatre of war, peace was a non sequitur. He was reminded of Rommel's passing comment on his "Asparagus," the anti-glider obstacles: *I did not put them in the right place.* War, like the earth, kept on turning.

"I'd like to apologize for something," he said.

McCloud looked startled. "Eh, what's that?"

He felt responsible for what had happened to Dan and Eric. Because of him they had been placed in harm's way. The brigadier glanced at the major. They obviously had no idea whom he was talking about. There were thousands just like Dan and Eric coming off the assembly line, brand new, rust-free and ready for service.

"About that attic," Leland persisted, "is it possible that four men could get inside it and have access to Rommel's quarters? I mean, in terms of space. Could they fit in the passageway behind the hidden panel?"

Who? A commando team sent to kill Rommel? McCloud became conciliatory, smiled briefly, leaned forward in his chair. "We need you to lead us in." He felt his skin crawl. "We need someone who knows how to enter and leave, how to get past the guards." He wanted to throw his chair at them.

"I was wondering," Leland prompted, "where Rommel walks his dog."

"Elbo?" He spoke before he thought.

"Good, that's good," Leland said encouragingly.

If the puppy barked, the assassins could call its name. They were aware that Rommel exercised in the park above the chateau. What time of day did he walk? Had the Lieutenant accompanied him? He interrupted the questioning, saying that if his peace mission had been called off, as they seemed to indicate, he would like to be told by the prime minister himself. After that, he would be glad to tell them anything they wished.

McCloud called for a recess. As Speigner was taken away he noticed the brigadier congratulating Major Leland. What had he said? Confined in a windowless room, he paced back and forth, trying to remember. He wished he were back in the POW compound where the worst it could do was rain.

That night he tossed and turned, dreaming of Rommel, Admiral Ruge and Speidel strolling along the Seine, a sniper lining them up in his crosshairs. At daylight, there was a knock at the door. Lying in bed fully clothed, he did not respond. The door opened. John Bright-Ashton came in with a breakfast tray which he set on a small table. "Hello again. Thanks to you, I'm on loan to the parachute chaps."

"I'm sick of your games," he said. In Egypt they had been friends. That seemed like a different war. Bright-Ashton sat in a folding chair.

"I told them you wouldn't crack," John said. "Stuck my neck out for you. Rather stupid of me. Drink your coffee before it cools." He had rung a friend at Whitechapel and left word that Speigner was back in British hands. That was the best he could do. He had not, however, mentioned that Montgomery was keeping the Lieutenant under wraps. Despite everything, SAS was prepared to set up a meet between Rommel and Brigadier McCloud.

His instincts, and Bright-Ashton's poker faced expression, told him that the British were having trouble at Caen. Had Rommel's panzers stopped Montgomery? "How is the battle going?" he said.

"We've reached the outskirts of Caen." Bright-Ashton appeared frank and cordial. *Damn the British! Every one a Shakespearean.* "It's no secret that Monty is behind schedule. The Americans are on the move and that makes him nervous. They've captured Cherbourg and here we sit on our bloody beachhead. Sure you don't want the coffee? Waste not, want not."

Afraid to ask the obvious, Max asked anyway: *Had anything happened to Rommel?* Bright-Ashton sipped coffee and made a small production of setting the cup in the center of the saucer. "They want you to look at some film."

Something had happened. Time, plodding along up until now, sailed off and left him flatfooted. He went to the window. The sun was shining. The lake shimmered. He asked for clearance to telegraph Rommel. John shrugged. Max thought he was going to say, *You'd ask for the moon*! Instead, he replied, "I'll have to grease the wheels," and left immediately.

He returned in an hour to report that the SAS commander had given his approval. Max tucked in his shirt. Although he was getting what he wanted, he felt uneasy as he followed Bright-Ashton to the communications department. A telegraph operator took his dictation and tapped out a message in International Morse Code:

TO: FIELD MARSHAL ROMMEL
COMMANDER, ARMY GROUP B
FROM: VIOLET
PROCEED TO POINT B.

They waited fifteen minutes. Thirty. The Germans did not acknowledge. The operator remarked, "Contacting the enemy is highly irregular."

An orderly came to the communications department. The brigadier wished to see Lt. Speigner. He and Bright-Ashton were taken to a screening room with a motion picture projector. He had a feeling that this, too, was scripted, along with Bright-Ashton's call to Whitechapel. Had the telegraph really been sent? Brigadier McCloud entered with a flourish, tossing his hat on a peg. He gave Speigner a glance of appraisal.

"We've started the ball rolling," he said. "It's up to you." A commando placed a chair for Speigner in the center of the room. Bright-Ashton stood behind the projector. McCloud sat off to one side where he could observe.

The film began. A wing-camera tracked a German staff car racing down a rural road. A dust trail marked its path as the car approached a side road lined with trees. On either side were cultivated fields. He recognized the Horch and willed it to get away. Bursts of silent machinegun fire ripped the road. The car veered crazily from one side to the other, spun around and stopped. There was a downed figure, perhaps an officer. The film ended with staccato flapping of loose film through the projector. The sounds tore at him like bullets.

Did you recognize the fallen man?

I couldn't tell.

Well, the film is very short. Let's take another look, shall we?

McCloud had the projectionist rewind the film and run it slowly, unreeling it frame by frame. He could feel their eyes on him. The car, stricken, doomed, burning. Bullets striking the ground in slow motion, kicking up dust. They had made slides from the wing camera film and showed it in various clever ways, enlarging the image, adding contrast. The downed officer's features remained blurred. His face looked shot to pieces.

"I don't know," he lied.

Commandos were trained to focus intently on one object. In this case, he was the object. Every man in the room watched his face as McCloud observed that this was the only staff car the RAF strafed that day. Of all the sorties, this one stood out. Would the Lieutenant happen to know if Rommel made inspections in the area? The car had been strafed near the town of Livarot. The RAF was fairly certain that they had killed a general officer. The question was which one.

Come off it, Leftenant, hands across the sea! Everyone knows that you are familiar with this car, and that you have, in fact, driven it!

It's a Horch.

Now we are getting some bloody where! Was that his car in the film?

Hard to say.

McCloud ordered the projectionist to run film. Speigner did not have to look at it again, having memorized the figure sitting straight and erect in the front seat, a short man stretching for every inch of height. Once he had spotted Rommel while flying over the Sahara in an RAF reconnaissance plane. The field marshal had a habit of leaning forward and holding onto the windshield to steady himself. In Libya, he often stood on the passenger seat of his armored van, his head protruding through an opening in the roof. With this added height he could see for miles. Such a commanding presence was unmistakable even photographed a plane going 300 mph, slightly out of focus, the image shifting, dots on a screen. There was but one Desert Fox.

He looked away, not wanting to see it a fourth time, and saw a familiar face. The man immediately exited. It was the POW who'd protected him from the *Jugend.* Nikki, a commando? Perhaps everything, including this film, had been staged.

"I'll make you a deal," he said.

There was no way to tell if the officer they had strafed was Rommel. However, if they would release him on his own recognizance, he would go to La Roche-Guyon and find out if the field marshal was alive. What he asked in return was a guarantee that any assassination mission would be put on hold. As much as SAS relished the opportunity of knocking off the Wehrmacht's greatest general, not from the air but up close and personal, Knight takes Rook, *checkmate*–

"Look here!" McCloud protested.

–As much as they quarreled over who would have the honor of killing Rommel, it would be unthinkable to risk commandos on a suicide mission if Rommel was already dead. He could save them the embarrassment.

The brigadier grudgingly gave in, or seemed to give in. "If the field marshal is alive, I will be happy to meet and talk about a ceasefire. If you can verify that he has been killed, we shall deal with his successor–Rundstedt, Kluge, whomever."

Bright-Ashton adjusted the projector, his face half-hidden in shadow. McCloud was studying the back of his hand. "All right, you may go, but any guarantees will end tomorrow. Rendezvous at the Dives River, south of Frenouville."

He heard himself saying, "Does SAS have my false identification papers, the ones that got me into trouble?"

"The forged documents? For Corporal...Dietzel, if I'm not mistaken?"

"Do you have a German motorcycle and a uniform?"

McCloud said eagerly, "We have more captured enemy equipment than we know what to do with. We'll give you a BMW with a sidecar. Bring Rommel back with you!"

XXXVI

Pain rocked his temples. He tried to switch it off mentally. All his life he had believed in mind over matter. To fight pain, it helped to be angry. He imagined Montgomery gloating, "We got Rommel, did we? Damned fine shooting!" Well, they had not gotten him yet. He refused to give Monty the satisfaction–even though he would gladly surrender his baton to the son of a bitch.

He had been wounded before, though not this severely. He could accept pain and nausea, loss of vision in one eye, deafness in one ear. What he could not accept was being confined. The doctors would not even allow him to go to the toilet. He would show them. He opened his right eye to see if the nurse had left. To see above the bandaging covering half his face, he had to turn his head like periscope. She was gone. He swung his legs over the side of the bed and waited for the nausea to pass.

In Africa an artillery round had blown up his car. The officer riding next to him was killed. He had been untouched. Another time, an exploding shell blew off the heel of his boot. A steel fragment lodged in his belt, leaving his belly green and blue while the skin remained unbroken. During the 1940 blitzkrieg in France, a shell fragment struck him in the face. Now, his luck had run out. He was a broken down Horch being towed to the garage. Still, he might have one run left.

The door opened. He lay down, anticipating a scolding. The visitor was Hauptmann Lange. "*Bitte, Herr Generalfeldmarschall*, may I come in?" He welcomed his aide, turning his good ear toward him. It lifted his spirits to see that Lange had escaped injury. This was like being given a second pair of hands. He sat up to give the impression that he was better. He wanted word to spread: *Rommel is back!*

"Something has happened," Lange said.

"*Ja*, I believe a Spitfire attacked my car." He smiled and almost blacked out. "Is it about Caen? Did Montgomery break out?" He knew a battle had taken place. The din of refugee caravans on the highway had awakened him. The entire population of Manche seemed to be on the move. One eye and one ear were enough to tell him that.

"We have contained the breakout."

His heart was pounding. He kept his right ear turned toward Lange. The captain summed up the battle thus far. Montgomery had thrown waves of bombers at Caen, reducing the outskirts of the city to rubble. Then a massive armored assault of hundreds of British tanks overran the front lines–the 16th Luftwaffe and 272nd Infantry divisions–just as Rommel had predicted. Montgomery's sally then bogged down under the massed fire of the 88s on the ridges south of Caen. Tiger tanks counterattacked and smashed the British vanguard, destroying some 120 enemy tanks. The British had retreated to the River Orne while German units moved up to reclaim their positions.

He grinned until his face cracked. To hell with the pain. This victory had been a long time coming. Until now the Allies had had everything their way. Now he had leverage. It was imperative that a ceasefire be arranged immediately. Lange shook his head. "What's the matter?" he croaked. "We *won*...didn't we?"

"There is something else," Lange said.

Hitler's bunker at Rastenburg, in East Prussia, had been blown up. The bomb was in a suitcase under the conference table. Several officers, including General Schmundt, had been killed. Hitler escaped with only minor injuries. "I didn't want that," Rommel said softly.

"*Verzeihung*?" Lange leaned forward as if he, too, had a

problem hearing.

He did not think it would happen so *soon*. The plotters should have waited for the army to back them up. How could they have acted without the consent of all the generals? The headstrong fools. No field marshal would have authorized such a gangster-like act. Rundstedt? Kluge? Impossible. A doctor stuck his head in the doorway and saw Rommel sitting up.

"The *Herr Feldmarschall* is advised to lie on his back!" He came and stood over Rommel. It was for the patient's own good. Rommel sank back on the pillows. On the way out, the doctor cautioned Lange not to stay too long.

He envisioned a room filled with smoke, the dead and wounded covered with rubble while Hitler stumbled out, unscathed. Fate protected madmen while it destroyed the innocent. The Führer was dangerously unstable, a menace–all that went without saying–but as the elected head of state he was not outside the law, he *was* the law. In March, the field marshals had presented him with a manifesto declaring their loyalty. Rommel had signed it along with the rest.

There would be a purge to end all purges. How close to the *Putsch* had Speidel been, or Ruge, or Stulpnagel? Within his circle, Stulpnagel and Speidel had been the only officers who pressed for an assassination. Without Speidel, how would he coordinate the ceasefire? Who else knew which generals to trust? He felt a need to talk to his wife and asked Lange to bring him a telephone. His injuries gave him a perfect excuse. "Lucie must be notified about the strafing. I do not want her to worry unnecessarily."

It took the better part of an hour to get clearance. The hospital operator refused to put a call through until the political officers monitoring the switchboards authorized it. Rommel himself got on the line three times to demand to be connected. Finally the call went through. He was hoping beyond hope that Lucie and Manfred were in Switzerland. When she answered, he sank back, depressed. "Hello, my dear," he said.

She was thrilled. How was he? Speidel had sent her a telegram saying he had been shot! Where was he hurt? He lied, saying that it was not as bad as it might have been and that he was feeling better every minute. He did not tell her that his doctors had given him up for dead.

"I may have to wear an eye patch but other than that I should recover fully. The doctors say the concussion will take a month to heal. The bad part is I have to lie still."

"*Bitte*, do what they tell you! Hans said you had a concussion and your cornea was severed."

"It will heal, they tell me."

He asked about the Rastenburg bombing, what news she had heard. Lowering her voice, she said that she only knew what was in the newspapers, adding that when it happened, she did not know what to think. Both were aware that at every telephone exchange between Bernay and Herrlingen, silent listeners, Nazi men and women, were monitoring them.

"It was *mad* to harm the Führer," he prompted. "I don't know anyone who wanted that!"

His expression of shock was genuine. He believed in chain of command as other men believed in God. At the same time, he opposed the High Command and chafed under their control. All this Lucie knew well. After a pause, she said cautiously, "Violence only leads to violence."

"*Ja, das ist richtig*!"

She changed the subject, saying in a conversational vein, "Well, our vacation will have to wait."

Across France and Germany, he felt ears being pressed closer against receivers. The professional eavesdroppers would have noted Lucie's change in tone. He tried to sound casual. "Don't put off the vacation. Take the young man with you."

"I have not spoken to him for several days. It's quite busy here. We have officials dropping by."

Gestapo. Did they suspect that he had participated in the assassination attempt? The Herr Korporal distrusted his generals. All field marshals periodically came under investigation. Only Jodl and Keitel, perennial yes-men, were exempt, along with Nazi ministers like Goebbels and Himmler.

"Do what the doctors tell you. I wish they would let me come see you."

"That is not possible. I will write to you."

Ich liebe dich sehr.

Ja, ich auch.

He handed the receiver to Lange. He did not allow himself to wonder if this would be their last conversation. It was going to be difficult, perhaps impossible, to get them out of the country or for him to surrender to the *Amis*. His only option was to get the generals to sign Speidel's ultimatum and have Kluge present it to Hitler as a *fait accompli.*

He passed out again. When he awoke, Speidel and Ruge were sitting in the room. The moment he opened his good eye they came to the bed. His mouth was so dry he could not speak. Speidel gave him a glass of water. He could barely raise his head to drink.

"About the coup," Speidel said.

"*Ja*, tell me."

Count Stauffenberg, a veteran of 10 Panzer Division in Africa, had placed the bomb under the conference table. Unfortunately, the heavy table deflected the blast and saved Hitler. "There is talk of a purge." Speidel dropped his voice as footsteps passed in the corridor. Officers by the score were being arrested, tortured and shot. The Führer was on a rampage.

As early as 1939 when Poland fell, Hitler had suspected some of his generals of disloyalty, though he had never doubted Rommel, commander of the Presidential Guards. It made him sick to remember how he marched his battalion up the *Kurfürstendamm*, the Führer's guardian angel, the roar of the adoring crowds ringing in his ears. *Sieg Heil...Sieg Heil!*

There was more bad news. General von Stulpnagel had attempted suicide. He had blinded himself with a pistol shot. During an operation, under anesthesia he had called out the name Rommel. The Gestapo reported this to Hitler. Speidel had gotten hold of a memorandum ordering the summary arrest and execution of the plotters and their families.

Why their families!

"Hitler is calling for 'the extermination, root and branch, of all those even remotely inculpated in the Putsch. They and their families are to be liquidated; to perish as though they had never been born, and their children after them.'"

"As if they had never been born," he echoed.

"I may be arrested," Speidel said. "I do not think I will be implicated, but no one is above suspicion." Rommel felt a wave of nausea. In the heat of battle he never gave death a second thought, but this was like being hunted by a mob with knives. "Anything from the American?" he said. Speidel's reply surprised him.

"There was a dispatch over the wire addressed '*To Field Marshal Rommel, from Violet.*' We did not know what to make of it. Political officers snapped it up. I feigned ignorance. What else could I do?"

Speidel had made a copy. He opened his briefcase and took out a paper hidden in the lining. Rommel could not believe his chief of staff had not reported the dispatch. What was more important, now, Hitler's purge or a ceasefire? Heart pounding, he listened. "Proceed to Point B." Speidel read out loud. "What is Point B?"

The British were for it! They were so *close*. "We could meet at Frenouville," he said, thinking out loud.

"What?" Speidel said.

"Did you confirm receipt of the telegram?"

"How could I?"

"Then the *Leutnant* may believe I have given up, or changed my mind...or perhaps he now thinks I am not sincere."

"The RAF may be aware that your car was strafed," Ruge said. "Perhaps they assume you are *kaputt*."

"*Ja*, but I am not!" Defiance was pain. Followed by nausea. Ruge had met with Sepp Dietrich to discuss the failed coup attempt.

"He said to tell you the SS is backing the Führer," the admiral said. "There is no longer a chance that any of them, including Dietrich, would obey a surrender order from anyone but the crazy corporal. He told me, quote-unquote, 'I fight at the pleasure of the Führer.'"

So much for Dietrich. Without the SS, how could he control the German army? There was one alternative. If a surrender demand were to come from the *West*, something in writing that he could take to OKW, then he would not have to give the order to cease firing. Perhaps Wehrmacht units could surrender individually along the front. The western powers knew that Germans were ready to lay down their arms. They knew that Germany feared the Red Army. "The Russians," he burst out, "are a menace to western civilization!"

Ruge and Speidel glanced at each other uneasily. Speidel went for the doctor, who came and checked Rommel's pulse. He scolded him for entertaining visitors. "You want to see what your skull looks like? *Einen Augenblick, bitte*." He ducked out of the room. Rommel was muttering about a future Germany loosely attached to England as a commonwealth, like Canada. Just then the surgeon came into the room holding a skull and a hammer. "Look here!" he cried, beating the skull's temple flat with repeated blows. "That's what your skull looks like. Now do you believe me? Lie down, *Herr Feldmarschall*, or I shall not be responsible for the consequences."

Rommel settled back, muttering, "That is what it feels like, a hammering when I sit up."

"It could cause an aneurism," the doctor warned. After he left, Speidel said, "Kluge is coming to take over."

Rommel was horrified. "Can't you handle things until I am back on my feet?" Speidel shrugged. It was out of his hands. "Then ask Kluge to give me a few weeks."

"The war cannot wait, my friend," Ruge said.

They started to leave. Again Rommel stopped them. "Am I under suspicion?"

Ruge found it impossible that Hitler would suspect *him*, of all people. Speidel took exception. The Führer suspected *everyone*. At that point the doctor came back to make sure they left.

Alone, Rommel settled into the pain as if lowering himself in boiling water. He had won a great victory at Caen. Now he was paying for it. Having taken Cherbourg the Americans were free to attack St. Lo. Patton would race Montgomery to Paris. In the meantime, Hitler was purging his generals while he was flat on his back. Unable to save his family. Unable to cross over to the *Amis*. The RAF had done its job.

XXXVII

On either side of the highway were fields of wheat. French farmers maneuvered their plows around burned out tanks. Revving the motorbike, Speigner stopped at a Y in the road. Posing as a Wehrmacht courier he wore a leather coat, helmet and goggles. A Luger automatic was holstered outside the coat. Secreted in his boot heel was McCloud's memorandum guaranteeing Rommel safe passage. He estimated that he was an hour from La Roche-Guyon. He took the road to the east, leaning over the handlebars and molding himself to the machine.

Above the noise of the motor, he heard another engine. He looked in his rearview mirror but the noise was coming from overhead. A Spitfire made a low pass, then banked in a wide circle. Would bombs start dropping on the chateau as soon as he led the RAF to its target? He thought of the film of the Horch crashing, 20 mm rounds tearing up the road, a motionless figure lying on his back.

With his attention on the aircraft, he failed to notice the checkpoint until too late. A German soldier flagged him down. He came to a stop. A captain of *Feldgendarmerie* ordered him to shut off his engine. He handed over his Rudolf Dietzel papers. The military police kept their machinepistols trained on him.

"*Militärische Anweisung*!" The captain wanted to see his orders.

"Special assignment, sir." Using a Bavarian accent he added,"Verbal orders only." Even in the document-obsessed Wehrmacht it was routine for combat units to operate without written orders. This practice allowed frontline units to improvise and redeploy.

"Remove your goggles," the captain said. "Who sent you?"

"*Herr Feldmarschall Rommel.*" He removed his goggles. A small truck cautiously approached the checkpoint. Inside was a French family, their possessions piled in the rear, a mattress tied over the cab. The soldiers made the civilians stop.

The captain drew his pistol and disarmed Max, tossing the Luger away. He tried not to panic. The captain accused him in an almost bored manner of being a deserter. "*Absolut nicht!*" he protested. He was a courier. Were not couriers given freedom of movement? *Nein*, a spy in a German uniform, said the captain. They were popping up all over the provinces.

"*Bitte*, if you will contact Heeresgruppe B, Field Marshal Rommel can verify who I am."

"*Rommel ist kaputt*! Turn around and face the ditch."

Rommel was what? Face the ditch? What for? Was he going to be shot? He heard something going on behind him, a woman speaking French. "If you are attached to Army Group B, you would be aware what has happened to Rommel." The captain cocked his pistol.

His Luger was lying on the ground. How many rounds could the captain get off before he reached it? Facing in the opposite direction he said, "You could radio Heeresgruppe B. The chief of staff, General Speidel, will vouch for me." Thoughts tumbled through his head–excuses, lies, half-truths. Rommel was expecting him within the hour. If he didn't get through there would be repercussions. He was to be turned over to General Speidel. There was to be a ceasefire. The war would be over. They would all go home. Would the captain shoot the personal courier of a field marshal? These fragmented thoughts spun like confetti in a descending vortex. *They cannot shoot me*!

There was a deafening report. He dove to the ground. Bullets kicked dirt in his face. The clay around him was stained red. He checked himself for wounds. The blood was that of the captain, who lay dead, hands at his side as if volunteering for an important assignment. The military policemen had all been killed in a matter of seconds. The passengers of the truck, a man and a woman, were holding submachine-guns. The children sat calmly in the rear seat as though shooting Germans was a family tradition. French resistance fighters. The *Maquis* did not accidentally shoot Germans. McCloud must have sent them.

"*Attendez...que s'est-il passé?*" he said.

"*Allez, allez*!" The woman gestured towards the east. The man picked up Schmeissers and Lugers and threw them in the truck, then jumped on the running board. *Bonne chance, mes amis*, he tried to tell them. The woman stuck her head out the window. "*Allez, allez*!" He kick-started the motorbike and took off in the opposite direction.

He passed a FLAK battery in the woods nearby. The gunners were standing in a chow line. If they had noticed small arms fire, a deserter's death was *Nichts* to them. The only life that was important was one's own. High above the Spitfire banked leisurely, out of range. The gunners did not look up. An enemy plane could not be allowed to interrupt *Mittagessen*.

In less than an hour, he stopped at the main gate of Rommel's chateau. The SS guard recognized him. "*Du bist der Chauffeur! Der Frankfurter, ja?*"

He touched his saddle bag. "*Depesche für den Herrn Generalfeldmarschall.*"

The guard inquired why *Herr Feldmarschall* Kluge would

receive a message addressed to his predecessor. Speigner shrugged as if the affairs of field marshals were a mystery. The guard waved him through. He raced the engine–as if in love with his machine–and drove around the circular driveway. The courtyard was deserted. He parked and entered the building, leather pouch under his arm. *Tocka-tocka* sounds reverberated from the stone fireplace. It was like coming home. When he took off his helmet and goggles, the desk sergeant recognized him.

"*Depesche für Herrn…*" The sergeant clapped his hands, then spoke into the intercom paging Hauptmann Lange. Speigner remembered the *Feldgendarmerie* captain saying *Rommel ist kaputt.* Lange hurried down the spiral staircase, told the desk sergeant to call Herr General Speidel, and took Speigner into Rommel's study. Packing boxes were everywhere.

Lange kept glancing at the windows. "You *would* come today, of all days."

"The field marshal…?"

"Has been wounded." Lange switched to English. "One of yours, an RAF fighter-bomber, attacked his car. He is in hospital." He gestured at the empty office. "As you can see, we are packing his things and expecting at any moment the arrival of the new commander."

"Marshal Kluge?"

"How did you know?"

"The SS at the gate thought my dispatch was for Kluge."

Lange said, as if thinking out loud, "I myself expect to be transferred. General Speidel as well." Rommel had been wounded and relieved of command. He was on convalescent leave. Any hope of a ceasefire had been dealt a harsh blow. If only the RAF had left him alone!

"*Ja, Herr Hauptmann*, if only they had."

Speidel came in and asked to see what the American had brought. Max pulled off his boot and extracted McCloud's memorandum, which was folded into a tiny square. Speidel scanned it. "A brigadier, why not Marshal Montgomery?"

"He was not forthcoming."

Speidel lowered his spectacles. Max explained about being put in detention and Field Marshal Montgomery taking him for a double agent. Although Montgomery was not interested in a ceasefire, Churchill had expressed a willingness to meet with Rommel. Something might yet be salvaged. Brigadier McCloud had promised safe passage, he added, though these words left a bitter taste in his mouth.

Speidel replied, "The *Herr Generalfeldmarschall* is in no condition to travel. Nor is he able to arrange a ceasefire. He asks that the Allied High Command make the first move. That is how it must be."

Shouts rang out in the foyer. A motorcade had arrived. Lange said, "*Kluge ist hier.*" Max imagined officers buttoning tunics and grabbing caps. Speidel told Lange to greet the field marshal's party and present them to the Duke and Duchess. He turned to the American. "Your motorcycle has a sidecar, *ja*?"

"*Jawohl, Herr General.*"

Kluge and his entourage had entered the chateau. At any moment they might appear in the study. Speidel told the desk sergeant to bring the American's motorcycle around to the rear. They went outside and waited until they heard the motorcycle coming. Speigner put on his helmet.

The sergeant brought the bike. Speidel got into the sidecar. Max took control and drove around to the front of the chateau. He was prepared to accelerate as he approached the gate, but the SS guards did not stop him. It must have looked to them as if Korporal Dietzel had orders to pick up the chief of staff. They proceeded through the village until they came to the main road. Speigner heard the droning of an aircraft. Was it the same Spitfire? In his rearview mirror, he noticed a black Citroen staying with him. He wondered if he should he tell the general that they were being followed. Perhaps he was imagining it. He asked Speidel how Rommel was responding to treatment, shouting to be heard over the engine noise. The reply surprised him.

"He is finished."

"He's going to die?"

"Oh, he will recover from his wounds," Speidel said.

XXXVIII

The black Citroen turned off and was replaced by a motorbike ridden by a man and a female passenger. When he stopped at an intersection to let an army convoy pass, the motorbike pulled off and waited. He turned west on the Bernay highway. As he passed through a village the motorbike fell back. A beat-up red Renault took its place. At a military checkpoint at the Bernay hospital, the MPs recognized Speidel and waved him through. From the skies came the drone of a fighter plane. Max could hear it above the rumble of the bike engine.

Were RAF pilots matching shillings to see who would bomb the hospital? *Hate to do it, old chap, but war is war.*

He followed Rommel's chief of staff into the building. Smiling doctors and nurses bowed to the general. Max took off the helmet but kept the goggles on. Weighed down by secrets he followed Speidel up a flight of stairs. They came to a private ward. Speidel hesitated at the door. "You will be shocked at his appearance. Let me see if he is awake."

They could all be soft rubble, human bits and pieces, at any moment. A doctor passing in the corridor gave him a professional frown. He removed the goggles. Speidel motioned to him. Rommel was propped up in bed, pillows behind his head. Half of his face was covered by bandages. He looked shrunken and pale. Max was shocked. Small talk-sorry this happened, how are you feeling, hope you will get better-seemed pointless.

Rommel in the Bernay hospital...Repeat: Luftwaffe hospital... Bernay. Dispatch by French Resistance received by British Intelligence. Decoded. Transcribed. Rushed to command and control.

The lieutenant's shocked expression irritated Rommel. People expected him to be invulnerable. "I had given you up for dead. Of course, I am the one who should be dead." He managed a brief smile, remembering what his personal physician, Dr. Albrecht, had said after examining him. "I have always taught my medical students that a man with such injuries could not survive." To which he had replied, "It only shows what kind of a

Swabian fool I am."

Max unconsciously stood at attention as he rattled off a report. Montgomery was not inclined to honor a ceasefire. He had no way of knowing if his message had gotten through to Churchill.

Speidel added, "And yet the commando gangsters are hoping the *Herr Leutnant* will take you to them in a sidecar."

"Do you think I would get there alive?" Rommel said. Pain leaked through him like acid.

How would they do it? Would it be a neat bombing run, a squadron of B-17s unloading incendiary bombs at two thousand feet?

Max wanted to tell about the Spitfire and the beat up, red Renault, but what came out was a garbled account of how he tried to contact Prime Minister Churchill. A message had been sent to Whitechapel, or so he had been told. Had Rommel received his telegram saying to proceed to Point B?

"By then I had been wounded." Rommel shrugged, even this slight movement causing pain. "They won't let me out of bed. Is it possible that a ceasefire order could come from the *Amis*? It is too late for me to do anything more."

Bombing was haphazard. Maquis would shoot their way into the hospital, spraying machinegun fire, killing doctors and nurses along with their main target.

Rommel fought another bout of dizziness. He recovered and focused on his visitor. "It is impossible, you see, because I am not able coordinate the ceasefire. It is very difficult under these circumstances. Did Montgomery send you to see Churchill?"

"He put me in a POW camp with German prisoners."

Rommel stared over the lump of bandaging. "They locked you up you with *Germans*!"

"Yes, because of my false papers. You know, 'Korporal Dietzel.' The forgery used to get me past the Gestapo." He glanced at Speidel, who had arranged for the false documents.

"You should have destroyed them," Speidel remarked.

"There was no time, *Herr General*."

The door burst open. Max started, expecting a fusillade of bullets. A doctor had come to check on Rommel. "You should not be sitting up!" he said. Rommel weakly tugged at the blanket. He thought the American looked nervous. Why did he keep glancing at the door? "Well, *Herr Leutnant*, as you can see, I have no means of contacting our generals. All I can do is to try to get you out safely."

Rommel was concerned about *his* safety! He dropped the helmet and held out his hands, begging them to believe he had nothing to do with it. *With what*? Speidel said. Brigadier McCloud had him under surveillance. A car and motorcycle had followed him, the *Maquis*. Speidel was furious. The American had tricked him to gain access. He was about to call the guards when Rommel stopped him.

"As to the strafing of your car," Max hurried on, "I was shown an RAF film. I did not tell them the car belonged to you, although I recognized it."

Rommel observed that the RAF had been strafing Germans since planes were invented. The Luftwaffe would do the same if they could. "Tell Monty he has not killed me yet!" he said.

But what about the *Maquis*? It was dangerous for the field marshal to remain there. "Frankly," Rommel replied, "it hurts to think about getting onto a stretcher." He wasn't worried about the Maquis. They were hell on telephone lines but left combat troops alone.

The lieutenant's suggestion had given Speidel an idea. He asked Max to wait until he returned, then went out, closing the door behind him. Max was astonished. *They trusted him.* Trust was civilization. Trust was détente. The tragedy for Rommel as a soldier was that he had fought for *eine verlorene Sache*, a lost cause, under a commander-in-chief who trumped up excuses to wage war, who refused to listen to his closest advisers, who could never admit to a mistake. All that was left was the dream. That Rommel could have met with Churchill in Switzerland–the Prime Minister of England and the future minister-president of Germany. That he could have dictated a ceasefire order over the radio. That they, he and Max, might have met in Normandy after the war.

Isn't this where your artillery turned back Montgomery?

Yes, I stationed eighty-eights on that ridge. Our Tigers made a stand in this valley. They were outnumbered but they made their presence felt.

It might be said, Herr Feldmarschall, that you won your greatest victory when you agreed to lay down your weapons. Do you find that ironic?

I could see peace happening between the armies as if watching from an open turret. I could see soldiers from both sides, former enemies, putting their rifles on the ground and exchanging cigarettes.

You led from the front. By setting an example you gave others the courage to resist Hitler.

I cannot take credit. I never was much good at following orders.

Speidel returned to the room. It was time for the American to go. A diversion had been arranged. Rommel spoke up, his voice tremulous with mischief. If the SS stopped the *Herr Leutnant*, he was to tell them he was General Bayerlein's nephew! *Yes, why not!* He raised a hand in farewell and wished the lieutenant a long life. He hoped the victors would prove magnanimous. "*Bitte*, my thanks to Minister Churchill for having faith in the German people. We hope someday to prove worthy."

Max put his heels together and bowed.

XXXIX

In the emergency room, orderlies were dressing a dead man in what appeared to be Rommel's tunic, wrapping gauze around his head. At first Max did not make the connection. "*Hier ist Ihr Freiwilliger*...your volunteer," said General Speidel. Army doctors and nurses went on treating the wounded as if it was none of their business if a general wanted to dress up an enemy corpse. Max couldn't stop staring at the dead man.

Speidel said, "Let me introduce you to Airman O'Reilly. His bomber was shot down near Bernay. You would be doing the Royal Air Force a service by returning his remains. If he is mistaken by the French Resistance for a field marshal, *c'est la guerre*, eh?"

He was to create a diversion. This was a court martial offense assuming he made it back. The dead airman with his sandy hair and sharp features did resemble a young Rommel. He thought of the field marshal lying helpless in bed. "My orders are to rendezvous with Special Air Service at the Dives River."

Speidel had a plan. "Field Marshal O'Reilly" would be placed in the sidecar and given a hero's farewell. A surgeon in the operating room, hearing English spoken, looked up. "*Was sagen Sie?*"

"*Nichts, Herr Doktor.*"

Speidel ordered sentries to form an honor guard on either side of the stretcher. Two orderlies carried the corpse while the rest fanned out around Speigner's motorbike. An escort of four military police motorcyclists waited at the curb. The orderlies placed the body dressed in an officer's tunic and hat into the sidecar. "Where are the *Maquis*?" Speidel whispered.

Red car with the hood…the bonnet raised. Pretending to work on the engine.

Ja, ich verstehe.

The orderlies strapped the body in place. The airman's head lolled forward. Speidel pushed the corpse upright and jammed the officer's hat on its head. Max put on his motorcycle helmet and held out his hand. Speidel saluted. "We do not shake hands. You are a Korporal, remember? *Achtung*!" He called the honor guard to attention. Max mounted his machine and kick-started the engine.

They rode in formation, the BMW and sidecar in the center surrounded by the escorting motorbikes. This motorcade turned west and gunned past the red Renault. The Frenchman slammed the hood and jumped into the car. Max shifted gears. The corpse's hat flew off. By the time the Renault had turned around, the cyclists had a half-mile lead. Pedestrians turned and stared as they roared past. A road sign read "Lisieux 30 km." He kept an eye on the rear view mirror in case the *Maquis* took it in their heads to shoot. The Spitfire made a pass over the highway. The Renault dropped back. On the outskirts of Liseux they came to a checkpoint. An MP sergeant approached them.

Dieser Mann ist tot!

Ja.

Was zum Teufel! What did the Korporal think he was doing!

Max calmly handed over his Dietzel papers. "I picked this man up at the Luftwaffe Hospital in Bernay. General Speidel can verify the orders." The sergeant examined his identification, then gave it back. Where were they taking the body? "*This is General Bayerlein's nephew*!" It was as if Rommel was speaking through him, down to the Bavarian accent. The dead man was a hero of the Reich to be buried with honors! The sergeant glanced respectfully at the privileged corpse. He came to attention and offered directions to Panzer Lehr Division, near Argentan.

"*Danke*." He had no idea that General Bayerlein commanded Panzer Lehr.

"When you come to town centre," the sergeant pointed at the church steeple, "Argentan Road will be on your left."

The convoy took off. At the intersection they did not turn left but continued on towards Frenouville. Near the front lines the highway was virtually deserted. In a field dotted with fresh craters, a German anti-tank battalion was dug in. The gunners showed little interest in the motorcade. The MPs came to a stop. The lead rider waved at Max. All four turned around and took off in the opposite direction. He was on his own.

The Renault was no longer in view. Perhaps the *Maquis* had relayed his whereabouts to spotters in the hills. The Spitfire continued circling. The straps around the corpse had loosened. "General Bayerlein's nephew" slid down in the sidecar, head lolling. It did not matter. They had almost reached no man's land. He resumed driving west. The war zone was being reclaimed by nature, grass sprouting in half-buried helmets, flowers blooming beside burned out vehicles, speckled cattle grazing in scarred pastureland. A raven perched on the butt of a rifle, its bayonet jammed into the ground. He blew his horn. The raven flew away.

They would order him to write a confession. He was good at writing reports. He would write that Rommel's failed ceasefire was no one's fault, and everyone's. He would write that he had been foolish to think he could make the British listen–as they had listened in North Africa–or that they would delay the invasion. He would write that at the pivotal moment, when Rommel escorted him to the front lines, he should have dragged him to the foot bridge and called for help. He wished he had done this even if Rommel refused to cooperate until his family was safe. He would write that he had been trained to observe the enemy, to predict tendencies, to offer strategies, to serve his country as an intelligence officer, but that he had no training in diplomacy. He would write that he considered his actions, even though he had failed, to have been his paramount duty to his country. He would spend the rest of his life wondering what he could have done to affect the outcome.

He came to a bridge. A sign read *Fleuve Dives.* The river was swollen by rain. At a British checkpoint on the opposite side, Brigadier McCloud stood in the road waving him on. Bright-Ashton, Leland and other officers were congratulating each other. McCloud pumped his fist. History was about to be made, Marshal Rommel in bag and SAS credited with his capture. He did not blame them. They were just doing their jobs.

In their brief encounter before the war, Rommel had been an infantry colonel traveling with a group of *Wehrmacht* officers. They explored Civil War battlefields and discussed cavalry tactics. War was theory, a subject for classroom discussion. Yet as they walked the battlefields at Brice's Crossroads and Shiloh, both knew better. In North Africa, he had fought a priest of desert warfare who had learned better than anyone to respect the Sahara and to get the most out of men and machines. Now he had encountered a very different Rommel. Though commanding thousands of soldiers and machines of war, this field marshal could not control the outcome. Though armed and dangerous–*Tell Monty he has not killed me yet!*–he was eager to give up his weapons. Of the three Rommels, the one with bandages covering half his face, blind in one eye, Gestapo at the gate, was the one he would remember.

The idling of the bike's engine echoed off the bridge. The sun was warm in his face. There was little doubt that he was facing a court martial for disobeying orders, creating a diversion, using a corpse to impersonate a field marshal, aiding and abetting the enemy. Still, he had brought a soldier home. In a world gone crazy, that made as much sense as anything.

XL

By Aug. 8, 1944, Rommel's fever was gone. His pulse and blood pressure had improved. The bruises and swelling around his injured eye had disappeared. Without waiting for orders from Berlin, he signed himself out of the hospital and went home.

His house in Herrlingen was being watched by Gestapo agents. Switzerland was a tantalizing sixty-two miles away but might as well have been the far side of the moon. He phoned Heeresgruppe B headquarters only to learn that Speidel had been arrested. Setting his pride aside, he wrote to Hitler in behalf of his chief of staff. His letter concluded, "You, mein Führer, know how I have exerted my whole strength and capacity, be it in the Western campaign 1940 or in Afrika 1941-43 or in Italy 1943 or again in the west 1944. One thought only possesses me constantly, to fight and win for your new Germany. *Heil, mein Führer*, E. Rommel."

Hitler did not reply. He was hanging confessed conspirators from meat hooks. Even the detached and politically correct Field Marshal Kluge was caught up in the purge and committed suicide. When Rommel went on walks, he carried a pistol and advised his son to do the same. He received a phone call from General Burgdorf, summoning him to Berlin. Suspecting foul play, he refused, citing his doctor's advice not to travel.

Vice-Admiral Friedrich Ruge came to visit. Lucie prepared a festive meal as if all was well. During dinner they labored to make small talk. Rommel joked that on Oct. 15 he would officially be retired and no longer entitled to a staff car or guards. Later, he and Ruge went into the study and talked until midnight. He told Ruge, "I shall not go to Berlin. I would never get there alive."

They discussed how long it would be before the Wehrmacht collapsed. The army had been forced to retreat all the way to the Rhone valley, while the British army had linked up with Patton's armored columns near Dijon. Paris had been liberated. The papers were full of General de Gaulle's triumphant stroll down the Champs Elysees.

On October 14, Manfred, 16, joined his parents at Herrlingen, arriving early in the morning. He wore a private's uniform of an anti-aircraft unit. He and his father had breakfast and went for a walk under the watchful eye of the Gestapo. Rommel had donned his favorite uniform, the plain brown tunic of the Afrika Korps. He took his son into the garden and explained that he had something pass on. He wanted to open up the world of higher mathematics to him. To Manfred's surprise, his father began to lay out the basic principles of calculus. They stood in the garden, eye to eye, Rommel lecturing, Manfred doing his best to understand. At last, Rommel gave up and embraced his son.

A meeting had been arranged with two generals, Maisel and Burgdorf, of the Army Personnel Branch. He suspected that the reason given–to "discuss further use of his services"–was a cover in order to do away with him. He held onto the possibility, however slim, that they might offer him a command in the east. When Manfred innocently asked if he would accept such a command, Rommel put his arm around his son's shoulder and said, "*Jawohl.*"

At noon the generals arrived in a green staff car with Berlin license plates. They went into the study with Rommel and gave him a written order. He read it, inquired if Hitler were aware of it, then asked for time to think. Burgdorf handed him two ampules of cyanide and said he had personal orders from Hitler to prevent Rommel from shooting himself. The cause of death was to be attributed to brain damage suffered in the strafing, an "honorable death" to preserve his reputation. Rommel asked what would happen to Lucie and Manfred if he refused. Burgdorf shrugged.

A few minutes later he emerged from the study and advised Lucie what was about to happen. Manfred found his father standing in the doorway, his face pale. Rommel said, "I shall be dead in a quarter of an hour." He embraced his wife and son and told them goodbye for the last time. Then he tucked the field marshal's baton under his arm and got into the staff car. As Manfred followed, he could not help noting his father's coolness and presence of mind. At the last second Rommel gave his house keys and his wallet to his son while Lucie watched from the doorway.

The car drove away with Rommel sitting in the back seat. A few hundred yards down the road, the car pulled over. Maisel and the driver got out, leaving Rommel alone with Burgdorf. When they returned, the soldier once praised by Churchill as "a very daring and skillful opponent…and may I say across the havoc of war, a great general," was dead.

Epilogue

Could the events in *Rommel's Peace* ever have come to pass? In any story portraying real people and drawing upon historical events, the reader is entitled to know how much is fiction and how much fact.

This much is true: As early as 1942, in a conference at Hitler's headquarters to discuss the military situation, Rommel had declared, "The most essential thing to understand is that we cannot win the war."

The people of Germany, too, were coming to realize that the tide had turned; the days of blitzkrieg and swift conquest were over. The belief in ultimate victory had faded. Now all that remained was a grim fight to the death.

The political branch of the German Resistance had made discreet inquiries with the British and American embassies in Lisbon and Rome, and also through the Vatican, asking unofficially whether the Allies would consider peace terms. Roosevelt, however, having made a stand at the Casablanca Conference demanding unconditional surrender, ignored such tentative probes and questioning which, in any event, did not come from Hitler but from his clandestine political opponents.

How close did Rommel come to pulling off his "separate peace"?

On July 9, 1944, nine days before his car was strafed, he was visited by Dr. Caesar von Hofacker, a cousin of Col. Stauffenburg (the man who would later deliver the explosives to Hitler's bunker), and Dr. Max Horst, another conspirator. They showed Rommel a secret memorandum outlining von Stulpnagel's views on the military and political situation, ending with an appeal to Rommel "to take independent action to end the war." Hofacker asked him how long the Wehrmacht could hold out in the West and Rommel replied, "At the most, fourteen days to three weeks."

On July 12, Field Marshal von Kluge also came to La Roche-Guyon and asked Rommel to issue a statement making it clear to Hitler exactly how long the invasion front could be held. Rommel promised to contact his division commanders and put the question to them. After touring the battlefield, he and Speidel drafted an ultimatum to Hitler which concluded: "The troops are everywhere fighting heroically, but the unequal struggle is approaching its end. It is urgently necessary for the proper conclusion to be drawn from this situation." Rommel signed the ultimatum on July 15 and sent it to Kluge to deliver to the Führer.

"I have given Hitler his last chance," Rommel told Speidel. "If he does not take it, we will act." On the following day, in a conversation with the chief operations officer of 17 Luftwaffe Field Division, Rommel remarked that if the Führer did not see reason, he was ready to surrender the western front to Montgomery. "Only one thing matters now," he said. "The British and Americans must get to Berlin before the Russians do!"

Rommel adamantly refused to join the plot to assassinate Hitler. "I always had the impression he never thought [the plotters] would really do anything," Manfred told me. "They talked theory, because they had no troops [to back up the assassination]. My father often talked about an attempt on Hitler's life but he was against it because thought a dead Hitler was more dangerous than a living one. So, if necessary, surrendering was by far the best thing to do, because although Hitler could influence the Germans he could not influence General Eisenhower after the [western] front was opened."

On July 18, Rommel returned to the battlefield to obtain SS General Sepp Dietrich's guarantee that he, along with the other SS commanders, would obey Rommel's order to surrender to Montgomery. On the way back to his headquarters he was strafed and wounded.

Had Roosevelt and Churchill not announced their "total and unconditional surrender" ultimatum, had the German people known that their nation would be revived by the Marshall Plan, had Roosevelt been less confident of his ability to outmaneuver Stalin, had Rommel not been wounded on the road to La Roche-Guyon, the course of history might have been quite different. Peace eluded Rommel but in accepting a higher responsibility he exchanged the role of Rommel, the Desert Fox, for one largely ignored by history, yet whose commitment, sacrifice and courage were of greater measure: Erwin Rommel, citizen.

Selective Bibliography

Carell, Paul. *Invasion–They're Coming!*, trans. by E. Osers (New York: E.P. Dutton, 1963).

Churchill, Sir Winston. *The Second World War* (Boston: Houghton Mifflin, 1950) Vols. 1-6.

Fraser, David. *Knight's Cross: A Life of Field Marshal Erwin Rommel* (New York: Harper Collins, 1993).

Hart, B.H. Liddell, ed. *The Rommel Papers* (New York: Harcourt, Brace & Co., 1953).

Irving, David. *The Trail of the Fox* (New York: Thomas Congdon/E.P. Dutton, 1977).

Law, Richard and Craig W. Luther. *Rommel: A Narrative and Pictorial History* (San Jose: Bender Publishing, 1980).

Lewin, Ronald. *Rommel As Military Commander* (New York: Ballantine Books/D. Van Nostrand Co., 1970).

Montgomery, Bernard Law. *The Memoirs of Field Marshal Montgomery* (Cleveland: The World Publishing Co., 1958).

Ryan, Cornelius. *The Longest Day* (New York: Simon and Schuster, 1959).

Speidel, Hans. *Invasion 1944* (Westport, Connecticut: Greenwood Press, 1971).

Young, Desmond. *Rommel, The Desert Fox* (New York: Harper & Row, 1950).